S0-ACQ-978

Also by Jon A. Jackson:

GROOTKA
HIT ON THE HOUSE
THE DIEHARD
DEADMAN

THE BLIND PIG

JON A. JACKSON

A DELL BOOK

Published by
Dell Publishing
a division of
Bantam Doubleday Dell Publishing Group, Inc.
1540 Broadway
New York, New York 10036

ISBN: 0-440-21714-8

Reprinted by arrangement with Dennis McMillan Publications

Printed in the United States of America

Published simultaneously in Canada

February 1995

10 9 8 7 6 5 4 3 2 1

RAD

For Fred and Sergeant Wonny

ONE

Patrolman Jimmy Marshall sat at the wheel of the squad car parked in a dark alley off Kercheval Avenue. A light October rain fell steadily and coldly. Marshall and his partner, Ray Stanos, watched a young black man across the avenue. The man could not see them. He wore a wool athletic jacket with leather sleeves and on his head was a dark knit watch cap. He paced up and down in the recessed doorway of an abandoned furniture store, hands in pockets and shoulders hunched against the cold.

Marshall and Stanos were beginning to get chilled themselves. The engine was not running, so there was no heater, and they had opened the windows slightly to prevent fogging.

"C'mon," Stanos breathed impatiently, as if speaking to the man across the street. "What's he doing? He buying or selling?"

"If it's dope, he's selling," Marshall said. "If it's guns, he's buying."

"Christ! Goddamn rugheads." Stanos quickly looked to his partner and muttered, "No offense."

Jimmy Marshall didn't say anything. He was used to the mental lapses of Stanos, who often seemed to forget that Jimmy was black.

"I'd give anything for a cigarette," Stanos said. The car was silent then, a silence broken by the rain and intermittent crackle of the radio.

After a while, a small black boy in a yellow rain slicker and wet tennis shoes came squishing along the alley. In the darkness he did not notice the two men in the squad car until he was nearly past them, then he stopped. He stood there, mouth hanging open absently, and stared at the officers. Jimmy Marshall rolled down his window, and without taking his eyes off the man across the avenue, he half whispered, "Go on home. It's late."

"What you-all doin'?" the kid asked.

Stanos leaned across the seat and snarled, "Beat it!"

The kid moved away slowly, looking back over his shoulder. He turned past the brick building at the corner of the alley and disappeared. Stanos sighed.

The radio whispered to them, "Nine-three, dispatch."

Stanos keyed the microphone: "Dispatch, nine-three."

"Man with a gun, nine-three," the dispatcher said, as calmly as if he were giving the time. "That's Collins Street. Number 3667, between Mack and Charlevoix. See the lady. Name is Fox."

Jimmy Marshall started the car and put it into

gear. They rolled out of the shadows to the mouth of the alley as Stanos jotted the information on the Activity Log clipboard and responded to the dispatcher: "Nine-three en route, ten-four."

The car wheeled right, displaying the words "Detroit Police" painted on the doors. The man who waited by the furniture store turned instantly and walked in the opposite direction.

Stanos craned back to watch and swore, "Shit. Blew a half-hour on that crud."

The squad car sizzled through wet intersections with flashing lights but no siren. Jimmy Marshall did not go to a "Man with a gun" call with sirens wailing. That could draw gunfire.

It was impossible to predict what a "Man with a gun" call would turn out to be. Perhaps a man walking down the street with a cardboard tube under his arm, or kids with broomsticks shouting "Bang, you're dead!" Once it had been a frustrated factory worker, drunk, firing his deer rifle out his apartment window. That one had put a .30-06 slug into the hood of the squad car. For that he was ultimately sentenced to three months of twice-a-week outpatient therapy at Lafayette Clinic.

It wasn't far to Collins Street, but the neighborhood changed radically from slummy multiple-family tenements to frame bungalows, owner-occupied homes built in the twenties and thirties to house automobile-factory workers. Marshall figured the neighborhood was 80 percent white. They had fences around tiny lawns and some had side driveways. Most had a garage in the rear, accessible from the alley, but it seemed that the garages must be full of something other than automobiles, for the street was lined with parked cars on both sides, leaving only a single lane for traffic.

Marshall cut the flasher as he turned onto Collins, but he did not cut his speed, despite the narrow traffic lane. He prayed that no one would suddenly open a car door or step out from between parked cars. He slowed to forty as Stanos counted down the addresses. A few houses short of 3667, he pulled into a parking spot.

"Flak jacket?" Stanos asked. Marshall thought it would be wise. They struggled into the bulletproof vests. They got out into the rain and locked the car.

A middle-aged white woman stepped from behind the storm door of 3667, wearing a quilted housecoat and slippers, her arms folded in front of her. She stood in the shelter of the porch as the officers approached, Stanos slightly to the rear and to one side, both of them with hands resting on the grips of their holstered service revolvers.

"Mrs. Fox?" Jimmy asked.

"I'm the one who called," the woman answered. She spoke in a hoarse whisper.

"What's the problem?" Marshall asked. He stepped onto the porch while Stanos stayed at the foot of the steps, in the rain, looking about him constantly and intently.

"It's Mr. Vanni's garage, next door," Mrs. Fox said. She pointed toward the rear of a white frame house ten feet from her own. "I saw a man go into the garage and he had a gun in his hand. And Mr. Vanni isn't home."

"You saw the gun clearly?" Jimmy asked.

"Oh yes," Mrs. Fox said. "It was in his hand. Maybe I'm just nosy, but I know it wasn't Mr. Vanni."

"Is the man still there?" Jimmy asked.

"I think so. You can see the garage from my kitchen window."

The two officers entered the house and followed Mrs. Fox through the lighted living room, where a television set talked quietly to itself. It was a very neat, pleasantly furnished home. The kitchen light was off and they did not turn it on. Mrs. Fox pointed to the large window over the sink.

"I came in here, about five minutes ago, to get a glass of water and I saw him. He was as bold as brass. Just walked up the little walk there from the alley and opened the side door of Mr. Vanni's garage and stepped inside. He didn't turn on the light."

There was no light shining through the window of the garage door.

"What did he look like?" Jimmy asked her.

"He was shorter than you," she said, "and he had on a dark windbreaker, but I didn't see his face clearly."

"Was he black?" Stanos asked.

"No, I don't think so," Mrs. Fox said.

"Are you alone here, Mrs. Fox?" Jimmy asked.

She nodded. "My husband works the night shift at Plymouth."

"All right," Marshall said, "I want you out of this room. Stay in the front of the house. We don't want anybody to get hurt."

She was docile and went into the front room, where the television set was. She sat down and looked at the set.

Marshall and Stanos went back to the car. The radio crackled: "Nine-three, dispatch."

"You forgot to give him a ten–ninety-seven,"

Jimmy said to Stanos. "Ten–ninety-seven" meant "Arrived on scene." On a "Man with a gun" call the dispatcher would periodically check with the dispatched unit. If there was no response, he would alert other units.

"Dispatch, nine-three," Stanos said into the microphone. "That's a ten–ninety-seven. Lady here says she saw an armed man enter her neighbor's garage, behind 3661 Collins. Neighbor is not home. We're leaving the vehicle now, gonna check out the garage. Ten-four."

All over the East Side and downtown, men in various bureaus and offices hearkened to this monitored broadcast from car 9-3. Detectives at Robbery —Breaking & Entering paid special attention, as did the duty officers at Precinct 9, the home of car 9-3.

Stanos turned to Marshall. "Let's arm up," he said.

In the trunk of the squad car was a wooden box known as the coffin. It contained two Remington 12-gauge automatic shotguns, with ammunition: double-ought magnum loads, each containing nine pellets of approximately .33 caliber. Also in the coffin were two SN Speediheat gas grenades for outdoor use, two EN blast dispersion gas grenades, or "soup cans," for indoor work, plus gas masks.

"I'll take a shotgun and cover the alley," Stanos suggested. "You go to the door. He won't be able to see you so easily."

"Gee, thanks," Marshall said.

Stanos missed the sarcasm. "All right, then, you take the alley and I'll go in. I don't care."

"It's all right," Jimmy said. "Let's go."

Stanos picked up the shotgun with relish and

loaded it with six shells. He walked down the street three houses, then cut through to the alley, holding the shotgun at port arms.

Jimmy Marshall carried a six-cell flashlight in his left hand and his .38-caliber Smith & Wesson revolver in his right. When he was sure that Stanos was in position, he walked slowly and quietly through the back yard of the Vanni residence until he came to the side door of the garage. The door was not completely shut. He stood to one side, then kicked the door open.

"Police! Come out!" he shouted.

There was immediate movement within. Someone ran to the alley door and began to slide it upwards on its tracks.

Marshall dropped to his knees and thrust his upper body into the side door opening. He flicked on the powerful flashlight. He saw a man, stooping to duck under the half-raised garage door.

"Hold it!" Jimmy shouted.

The man stretched an arm toward Marshall and there was a terrific blast of light and thunder from a pistol in his hand. The noise rang in the hollow spaces of the garage. The bullets sang off the concrete floor near Jimmy's head and whacked into the rear wall. Jimmy threw the flashlight away from him. It skittered under a vehicle parked in the other bay of the garage.

From the cold concrete floor, Jimmy saw the man perfectly silhouetted by the alley light. The man stooped under the door. Jimmy cocked the hammer on the .38, but he did not fire.

The man ducked outside and ran.

"Stop!" Stanos shouted.

A second later . . . *BA-WHONG!* the shotgun roared. The alley resounded. Then it was silent.

"Jimmy! Jimmy!" Stanos shouted.

Marshall lay on the concrete floor, listening. He could hear doors opening nearby and windows being raised. "I'm all right," he yelled to Stanos. He scrambled under the vehicle and retrieved his flashlight. Then he stood and turned on the garage lights. The vehicle was a bright-red Chevrolet sports van. The walls of the garage were hung with fishing poles, a ladder and snow tires. Jimmy hoisted the garage door the rest of the way and stepped outside.

A body sprawled face down in the alley, in the rain. Stanos stood casually over the body, the shotgun cradled in his left arm. He looked up at Jimmy. "You okay?"

"I'm okay," Marshall said. He stared at the body.

"I thought he got you," Stanos said. "He shot twice."

"He missed," Jimmy said, still staring at the body. Then he looked at Stanos. "You okay?"

Stanos looked surprised. "Me? I'm fine." Then he looked down at the body. "He ain't, though. I was only a couple feet away when I let go." He took a deep breath. "It was easy," he said.

Jimmy Marshall looked at him sharply. "What do you mean?"

"I thought it would be hard," Stanos said. "But it's easy." He was a young man, tall and broad-shouldered, but now his face looked hard and older. "Guess I got a vacation coming," he said. He referred to the department policy of an automatic three-day suspension (with pay) that came when an officer shot a citizen. It was for the protection of the officer. Sometimes the officer was transferred to another precinct.

Marshall wondered if he had seen the last of Ray Stanos. It depended on who the dead man was, he supposed.

"I'll go call in," Marshall said. He ran to the car. "Dispatch, nine-three. I need a wagon."

That would wake them up. The Detroit police operated its own ambulance. Immediately one rolled out of the 9th Precinct, lights flashing and siren climbing.

"In the alley, between Collins and Goethe, north of Charlevoix," Jimmy told the dispatcher. Then he added the phrase that would bring them all to the scene: "Possible fatal." It was clear to every listening official that someone was dead in the alley behind Collins Street. But that was not for a patrolman to determine.

Two detectives were on their way from Homicide, downtown. A man was en route from the Central Photo Bureau, another from the Wayne County medical examiner's office, and a whole van of them from the Scientific Bureau. The "blue" lieutenant from Precinct 9 responded, along with any loose detectives. Several blocks away, a large black Chrysler bearing four huge detectives—"The Big 4"— whipped a U-turn on Mack Avenue and came rocketing back toward Collins. Downtown, the man from Robbery—Breaking & Entering sat back in his chair: this sounded to him like a job for Homicide.

Within minutes the alley was full of flashing lights and sirens winding down. Neighbors looked out of upstairs windows or stood in the rain with coats held over their heads like tents. The police allowed no unofficial persons into the alley.

Jimmy Marshall squatted in the empty bay of the garage and made notes on a "Preliminary Crime Report." Ray Stanos walked aside with the "blue" lieutenant from the 9th. The ranking Homicide detective, Lt. "Laddy" McClain, stood in the open entry of the garage and watched the medical examiner and the photographer at work. The men from the Scientific Bureau carefully dug out the bullets embedded in the garage wall. Brilliant lights on stands had been set up to assist them.

The Big 4 was present. The boss of the crew, Dennis "the Menace" Noell, all six feet and seven inches of him, surveyed the scene placidly, hands in pockets. After a few minutes he said something to McClain, glanced again at the body and shooed his boys back into the Chrysler cruiser.

McClain looked at the body, which had been rolled onto its back now. "Don't look like a punk to me," he said to his partner, Joe Greene.

Joe Greene said, "A pain in the ass."

The two of them looked around for a precinct detective, somebody on whom they could palm off what was likely to be a difficult case to close if the dead man couldn't be identified. They both spotted their man at the same time.

Detective Sergeant Mulheisen, from the Chalmers Street Station—9th Precinct—picked his way slowly through the crowd of onlookers and police personnel. He was a six-foot-tall man, well built, nearing forty and thickening at the waist. He had sparse, sandy hair and wore no hat, despite the rain—he held a folded newspaper over his head and he smoked a long cigar. He had a mild, pleasant face, but what most people noticed was that his teeth were long. They weren't bucked, just slightly longer than average, and they had distinct spaces between them. Because of this he was known on the street as Sergeant Fang.

"Mul," McClain said affably, "come in out of the rain."

Mulheisen stopped and looked down at the body, then he stepped into the shelter of the garage.

"You got another cigar?" McClain asked.

Mulheisen fished out a leather cigar case and handed a large cigar to McClain. He offered one to Joe Greene, but Joe Greene shook his head. Mulheisen handed McClain a small, shiny Italian cigar cutter. McClain clipped off the end of the cigar and returned the clipper.

Mulheisen looked around the garage and noticed Jimmy Marshall, who nodded to him. Mulheisen nodded. At last he turned to McClain. "Looks like you got yourself a queer one, Lad," Mulheisen said.

"Nah, it's a grounder," McClain said. "A thief. He made a mistake and shot at one of your boys there." He gestured toward Marshall. "So your other boy"—he pointed a thumb at Stanos—"opens up with the duck gun and what you got is your limit."

Mulheisen smiled vaguely but said nothing. He watched the medical examiner turn the dead man back onto his stomach. The back of the windbreaker was torn and bloody.

"This'd be a good one for you to take, Mul," McClain said. "A grounder. Look good on your record."

"Hah!" Mulheisen shot back.

"I got a couple dozen murders on my back, Mul, no lie. Your boys did this, anyway. What are you doing these days?"

"Mutt and Jeff," Mulheisen replied, referring to a long string of armed robberies that had plagued the 9th Precinct for months.

"Mutt and Jeff! You shouldn't be doing crap like that, Mul! Look, I'll fix it with your lieutenant, what's his name, Johns. And I'll get you some slack from that jive-ass inspector of yours, Buchanan."

The tour doctor from the medical examiner's office was through with the body. He was willing to declare that "John Doe" was dead. Cause of death, apparent gunshot wound, pending autopsy and police investigation. The attendants loaded the body onto a wheeled stretcher. Mulheisen detained them so that he could take a closer look. The dead man was clean and well-shaven, white and apparently in his late twenties. Rain fell onto the unblinking eyes and into the open mouth. The man looked calm and intelligent. He wore neat, well-pressed slacks and a blue nylon windbreaker. On his feet were new athletic shoes.

"What did he have on him?" Mulheisen asked McClain.

"Nothing in his pockets but a dollar bill and a key. The key's probably to a hotel room, but it isn't stamped."

Mulheisen gazed at the face. "And a gun, too?"

"Right. Colt .38. Fired twice. Frank's got it." McClain nodded toward Frank Zeppanuk, of the Scientific Bureau.

Mulheisen stood up. McClain, some inches

taller, threw a heavy arm about Mulheisen's shoulders. "Hey, c'mon, okay? This is a grounder, Mul. As a favor. Please?"

Mulheisen grimaced, showing his teeth in what could have been a grin or a snarl. He punched McClain playfully in the stomach. "Okay, Lad. As a favor. You keep Johns and Buchanan off my ass."

McClain punched Mulheisen's shoulder. "You got it, pal." He and Joe Greene loafed off into the rain, McClain shielding his cigar with a cupped palm.

A patrolman approached Mulheisen with three civilians in tow. "Mul, these people tried to drive into the alley. This one claims he lives here." He pointed to a handsome young man in an expensive white raincoat.

The man stepped forward and held out his hand. "I'm Jerry Vanni, Officer," he said. He was tall and slender with a well-groomed black mustache and the rain was ruining his carefully shaped haircut. Vanni gestured to his companions, a young woman wearing a rain scarf and a belted trenchcoat and a stocky fellow with a heavy face that probably needed a shave every six hours. "These are my business associates and good friends, Miss Cecil and Leonard DenBoer."

Miss Cecil took a step toward the corpse, looking at it with interest. In the light Mulheisen could see that she was quite attractive, with a pale complexion and sharp features. Brilliant red hair glowed beyond the edges of her rain scarf.

"I told you she should have stayed in the car," DenBoer complained to Vanni. He wore a bulky car coat that looked damp and tight.

"I've seen dead men before," Miss Cecil said.

"Where was that, Miss Cecil?" Mulheisen asked.

"In Vietnam, Lieutenant. And the name is Mandy."

"The name is Mulheisen, Mandy, and it's Sergeant."

"Oh. I thought a homicide investigation would be conducted by a lieutenant," Mandy Cecil said.

"It's not a homicide case," Mulheisen said.

The young woman looked down at the corpse. "He just tripped and fell, I suppose?" she said innocently.

Vanni stepped forward. "I didn't know you'd been in 'Nam, Mandy," he said.

"I'm sorry, Jerry," she said, smiling at him. "I thought I had told you everything."

Vanni colored slightly.

"What were you doing in Vietnam?" Mulheisen asked. "Nurse?"

"Intelligence," Cecil answered. "I was in the Army."

"Hmmm. Well, you've seen dead men before, then. You ever see this one?"

The woman shook her head. Vanni looked at the corpse and he, too, shook his head. DenBoer seemed unable to take his eyes off the dead man, but he said that he had never seen the man before.

"Okay, get him out of here," Mulheisen said to the ambulance attendants. He turned back to Vanni. "This is your house?"

"That's right."

"You live here alone?"

Vanni smiled slightly. "Most of the time," he said. He glanced at Mandy Cecil but she did not react.

"How about you?" Mulheisen said to DenBoer.

"I live over on Canfield," DenBoer said, "just a couple blocks from here."

Mulheisen jotted down the address and took Mandy Cecil's as well. She lived in an apartment in St. Clair Shores, near Lake St. Clair.

"What brings you all together tonight?" Mulheisen asked.

Vanni replied, "It was business. We had dinner together and we were coming back here to discuss a new venture. Then we saw all the commotion and wondered what was going on. What *is* going on, Sergeant?"

Mulheisen didn't have a very clear idea himself, and he didn't like to expose his ignorance. He motioned the trio to one side and asked them to wait. Then he listened to Marshall and Stanos repeat their story for the fourth but not the last time. When he had it straight he returned to Vanni and his friends and gave them an abbreviated version.

"I don't get it," Vanni said. "What was the guy doing in the garage? Was he after the Chevy?"

"It doesn't look like it," Mulheisen said. "The door is unlocked and he had plenty of time to hot-wire the car if he'd wanted to. He doesn't seem to have disturbed anything at all. No, I'd say he was waiting."

"Waiting?" Cecil said. "Waiting for what?"

"Probably for Vanni," Mulheisen said. "What's your usual procedure when you come home, Vanni?"

Vanni shrugged. "Well, I drive up . . . I get out of the car . . . I lift the door. . . ." He made a bending and lifting movement and stopped with his hands over his head.

Mulheisen said, "And there's a man in the garage with a gun. And you're perfectly outlined against your headlights. You'd make a nice target, Vanni."

There was a brief silence, then Vanni burst out: "But that's absurd! Who would want to—" He stopped, unable to actually say the necessary words.

"That's what I'd like to know, Vanni. Any candidates?" Mulheisen asked.

Vanni shook his head. "Of course not. It's ridiculous."

"No enemies?" Mulheisen asked.

Vanni shrugged. "Oh, maybe an irate husband or two," he said in a jocular tone. Mulheisen did not respond to the joke and Vanni reddened. "Well, not really."

Mulheisen sighed. "All right. I'm not going to push it tonight. It's late. I'd like to see you folks tomorrow. Where can I get hold of you?"

"We'll all be at work," Vanni said. "I've got a trucking company on Eight Mile Road, near Gratiot. You can stop there. Mandy and Lenny are officers of the company."

Mulheisen took the address and the telephone number. He waved good-bye to Marshall and Stanos and walked off into the darkness, still holding a newspaper over his head to shed the rain. There were very few onlookers left, most of them departing when the body was removed.

When they were back in the squad car, Marshall said to Stanos, "I had that guy in my sights, you know."

"Why didn't you blast him?" Stanos said.

"I don't know. I never shot nobody," Marshall said.

"I never shot anybody, neither," Stanos said.

"But it was easy. I thought about it a lot. I thought it would be hard, but it's not. I mean, like the guy's there and, suddenly, you don't even think about it, you just ice him."

"Yeah, well, I don't know. I just didn't shoot."

"Don't worry about it," Stanos said. "Long as I'm around, nobody shoots my partner."

Jimmy looked at him in the darkness of the car. Stanos smiled calmly.

TWO

Every weekday morning, the precinct inspector reviews the important events of the preceding twenty-four hours and takes a report downtown to his meeting with the other precinct inspectors and the bureau chiefs, in the office of the chief of police.

Precinct inspector "Buck" Buchanan of the 9th was a small man for a policeman. He was slender and handsome, with silky black hair. He reminded Mulheisen of a seal. This morning Buchanan glanced through the report and said, "What's this about Dunkin slapping a woman?"

"A prostitute, sir," Ed Morgan, the "blue" lieutenant, said. "At first she claimed he raped her, but it's just bullshit. He picked her up in front of the Carib Club, across the street from the Uniroyal plant. He said she gave him a hard time and wouldn't get into the car. She was drunk and fighting with another hustler. I guess it was a sort of territorial dispute."

"My God," Buchanan said. "We can't have this. Can't Dunkin arrest a goddamn whore without a brutality charge?"

Buchanan had an absolute horror of brutality charges. The whole department was very sensitive on the issue, but Buchanan was nearly pathological about it. Especially disquieting to the officers of the 9th was the realization that Buchanan was not against brutality per se, he was just against brutality *charges.*

A case in point was that of Patrolman Henry Vaughan. While making an arrest of two men stopped in a car listed as stolen on the daily "hot sheet," one of the men turned unexpectedly violent. He knocked down Vaughan's partner, then leaped at Vaughan, who was busy shaking down the other suspect. Vaughan, pistol in hand, elected not to shoot but, instead, quickly transferred his pistol to his left hand, snatched out his regulation leather-wrapped sap and knocked his assailant silly with a fine backhand to the face.

Unfortunately for the man, and for Vaughan, the blow seriously mangled the man's mouth and chin. Out on bail, the car thief appeared on a popular television program called "Afro-American Angles." The show was a sensation, for the man could hardly speak. Patrolman Vaughan was accused of gratuitously beating a suspect while in custody. The officer was still on suspension and waiting for a hearing.

To the disgust of every officer in the 9th, Buchanan refused to comment to either the press or television reporters. Thus there was no one to tell the public the police side of the story. Privately, in fact, Buchanan was heard to say, "That Vaughan is shafting us. Why in hell didn't he drill that bastard instead of clubbing him?"

With this in mind, Lieutenant Morgan defended Patrolman Dunkin from the charge of having slapped a prostitute. "Dunkin's a good officer, sir. No previous problems. The woman was drunk and rowdy. I don't think she'll pursue the charge, and if she does, the Civilian Review Board will laugh at it."

"We can't take that chance," Buchanan snapped. "Investigate it thoroughly. Now, Darrow, what's the picture on this Collins alley thing?"

Lt. Darrow Johns was a portly man with dark-rimmed glasses. He was amiable and not stupid, but he looked like anything but a detective. He had the great virtue of absolute loyalty toward his superiors, a valuable factor when the superior had to choose between promoting two otherwise equally qualified candidates.

Johns fleshed out the bare bones of the Collins alley shooting that was contained in the inspector's report. He noted that Patrolman Stanos was automatically suspended for three days, but that he saw no reason to extend the suspension. He also said that McClain, of Homicide, had specifically asked that Mulheisen be assigned to the case.

"Mulheisen?" Buchanan frowned. "Why Mulheisen? Why not Maki, or even the kid, Ayeh? McClain says it's a grounder."

Buchanan did not like Mulheisen. He had a theory that Mulheisen had inherited a great fortune and was therefore just working the street for his own entertainment. He also believed that Mulheisen had secret connections with the very highest figures in police and political circles, not only in the city but in the state. It was true that Mulheisen's late father had been a union official and a tireless worker for the Democratic party. In later years Mulheisen *père* had held public positions that were political appointments. But the wealth and the influence were largely in Buchanan's mind.

Johns now explained to Buchanan that Maki was busy on Mutt and Jeff, and Ayeh would probably be assisting Mulheisen, anyway.

"Okay, okay," Buchanan said. He gathered his papers with a sigh and put them into his briefcase. He turned to an attractive blond woman with a figure that even a police uniform did nothing to diminish. She was Buchanan's driver and secretary. "Take me to my leader," he said. He said that every morning.

On the way out, Buchanan saw Mulheisen standing by the teletype machine, smoking a large cigar. He nodded slightly to Mulheisen and hurried by. Mulheisen did not acknowledge the faint greeting.

Mulheisen beckoned to Lieutenant Johns. Johns responded. One of Johns's virtues was that he was intelligent enough to know that neither Buchanan nor himself ran the detectives in the 9th. Mulheisen did. It was not stated—not by Mulheisen and not by Johns. Mulheisen was kind enough to pretend that it was otherwise.

"I've got to have Ayeh," Mulheisen said to Johns.

"I thought you would."

"And Jensen and Field, too."

Johns scratched his balding head for a moment. "Okay," he said. He started to walk away.

"Wait a minute," Mulheisen said. "What did Buck have to say about the shooting?"

"Nothing," Johns said.

"Nothing at all?" Mulheisen considered this, then said, "I guess I should have known. The man is dead, therefore no complainant."

On his way back to his office Mulheisen encountered Dennis the Menace. "What are you doing here this time of the morning?" Mulheisen asked. "I thought I saw you out on the Street about midnight."

"Can't keep away from the place," said the Big 4 boss. He followed Mulheisen into the little cubicle that was supposed to be an office. With Noell in the room there wasn't much space left for Mulheisen and the desk.

"Really?" Mulheisen said. "You don't have anything better to do?"

Noell shrugged. "I got divorced a couple months ago. Really, though, I enjoy it down here. Always something going on. What's biting you?" He perched his two hundred and forty pounds on the corner of the desk and Mulheisen inadvertently looked to make sure the desk wasn't crumbling.

Mulheisen dragged on his cigar. "It's nothing. I just had my analysis of Buchanan's character reinforced. He didn't even peep at that shooting last night."

"So? What's the big deal? The guy comes out shooting, so Stanos takes him off. Good riddance."

"He didn't have to blast him," Mulheisen said calmly. "Stanos was only a step or two away from the guy. What happened to the old nightstick routine? You bat the guy on the arm and he drops his gun. If he keeps up the funny business you spike him in the gut with the stick, or raise a knot on his head."

The Menace shook his head. "Old-fashioned,"

he said. "They still teach that crap at the Academy, but no one listens anymore. That's 'Steal an apple, Officer Flaherty' stuff. We don't have beat cops anymore, Mul. We got patrolmen. You know what they're up against out there?" Noell gestured vaguely toward the traffic outside Mulheisen's window, presumably to indicate a vast criminal population at large. "They got M-sixteens. They smuggled 'em home from 'Nam. What do we got? Popguns."

Mulheisen noticed Dennis's "popgun," prominently displayed on his hip. As the chief of the Big 4, it was not Noell's style to be subtle, hence the Colt "Python," .357 Magnum. Dennis claimed he needed the cannon for its knockdown power; precinct wags wondered how much consideration he had given to, say, a rock.

"Did Stanos shoot this bird with a popgun?" Mulheisen asked.

"For Christ's sake, the guy shot at his partner!" Dennis shouted. "What the hell's he supposed to do?" Noell went into a mock British accent: "Oh, I beg your pardon, sir, would you please deposit your firearm in the proper receptacle . . . It ain't like that, Mul. It's war out there. You gotta whack 'em."

Mulheisen had a pretty good idea what Noell meant by that. In the rear window of the Big 4 cruiser there was prominently displayed a Thompson .45-caliber submachinegun, the classic style with the drum magazine. The gun was meant to be seen, as the Big 4 themselves were meant to be seen. The Big 4's function as detectives was somewhat different from Mulheisen's. You don't put four huge monsters in a well-marked Chrysler and parade them around town during "prime time" for the purpose of detection. They are there to inhibit crime.

Besides the Thompson, Mulheisen knew that the Big 4 carried a Stoner rifle, a Sten gun, a full complement of Winchester Model 97 12-gauge pump shotguns, and a supply of ax handles. The Stoner Weapons System, to use the proper nomenclature, is a .223-caliber semi or fully automatic rifle that fires 12.5 bullets per second. The bullets have high velocity and low mass. As a consequence, they develop a phenomenon known as hydrostatic shock, which is simply a supersonic shock wave that arrives at the impact site immediately after the bullet does and causes widespread damage to animal tissue. The Big 4 customarily used a 30-shot banana clip. A 30-shot clip is exhausted in slightly more than two seconds, therefore two clips are taped end to end for quick reversal and resumption of fire.

The Sten gun was usually carried in a pocket behind the front seat. It is a 9-mm. automatic carbine that is very simple and hardy, an inexpensive, even crudely made weapon compared with the elegant Thompson. But it has a high rate of fire, it's compact and quite reliable, even if it is sometimes known as the Plumber's Delight, or the Woolworth Gun.

But the sight of the Big 4 walking into a barroom with ax handles dangling from their meaty paws was enough to quell most disturbances and banish thoughts of malefaction for hours at a time.

"You gotta whack 'em, Mul," Dennis said again. "You let up for a minute and they'll kill you."

"Kill you?" Mulheisen said. Somehow, it didn't seem likely.

Noell ignored him. "Now you take this creep I busted yesterday—"

Mulheisen winced, thinking that Noell gave new significance to the verb "busted" that went beyond the notion of mere arrest.

"—this Jackson. Calvin 'Speedball' Jackson. I been after this crud for years. You know how old he is? Eighteen. He's been stealing, dealing, trashing, since he was ten. But somehow, I remembered that Speedball turned eighteen this week. Don't ask me how I remembered; it's funny how things stick in your mind.

"So we're out cruising and everything's dead, so I says to Clay, 'Hey, it's Speedball's time. Let's go get him.' 'No warrant,' Clay says. 'We'll use the ol' Tennessee Search Warrant,' I says.

"Speedball's got him a nice little shack over on McClellan, the wages of smack. So I send Clay around to the back and I go up on the porch. Knock, knock, knock, real hard. No answer. Then Clay yells, 'C'mon in!' So I go in. Only the door is locked, so I had to open it with my shoe. Whaddaya think? The asshole's got his old lady sittin' right in front of the door and the door is all busted up on top of her! Ha, ha! What the hell was he thinking about? She supposed to be a decoy or something? I don't know.

"Anyway, this chick is all crying and everything, but I don't say shit to her. I go straight for the bathroom, but Speedball ain't there. I go into the bedroom and jerk the bed away and, sure as shit, Speedball is under the bed. He's shaking so bad I can't get him to stand still while I'm searching him, so I had to pacify him a little."

"You read him his rights, I suppose," Mulheisen said.

"Speedball knows his rights, don't worry about that," Dennis said.

"What did you find?"

"The guy's a walking pharmacy," Noell said. "You wouldn't believe it. I told him when I shut the door on him, 'This is it, Calvin. You ain't a juve no more. You're a keeper now.' "

Mulheisen wondered. If Calvin "Speedball" Jackson could afford a lawyer, or even if he got a public defender who wasn't hopelessly servile toward the court, the prosecutor wouldn't stand a chance. Illegal entry, no search warrant, violation of civil rights . . . Something seemed very wrong to Mulheisen. How was it that the department—to say nothing of Buchanan—could tolerate the Big 4 but threw up their hands in dismay on something like Patrolman Vaughan's alleged brutality? He supposed it was a matter of publicity and politics. For the benefit of the "bleeding hearts," the department would pillory Vaughan; for the "get tough with crime" crowd, they could proudly trot out the Big 4.

Mulheisen told Dennis that he didn't think that Speedball was a keeper yet.

The Menace shrugged. "He's in the system," he said. "The thing is, the courts won't put these bastards away, but if you beat on them enough, they hurt. You gotta whack 'em, Mul. Nothing else gets through their thick skulls."

"Dennis, Speedball will forget about you the minute his wounds heal. He's not a genius. What's he going to do, go to night school for a degree in pharmacy and join Rexall?"

"He'll get a nice vacation at Milan or Jackson before long," Noell said. "Maybe he'll learn a trade. Which reminds me: guess who I saw on the street yesterday? Good Ol' Earl."

"Good Ol' Earl?"

"You don't remember Ol' Earl? I sent him down six years ago. It was a gun deal. He was peddling some of that stuff they took in the Light Guard Armory raid."

Mulheisen shook his head. He was amazed by Noell's prodigious memory for the faces and records of criminals.

"He looked terrible," Dennis said. "All fat and squishy, like a slug. I chatted with him. He's staying at the Tuttle."

"Did you lean on him?" Mulheisen asked.

"Lean on Ol' Earl? I wouldn't lean on Earl. He's a hell of a good guy. Seemed awful glad to see me. Quite a gunsmith, Earl is. Not much chance to practice his trade for the last few years, though. But I guess he'll get back into it quick enough. Take him a while to catch up with the new stuff. I was telling him about this new cartridge Remington's got, the 'Accelerator.' It's a sabot."

"What the hell is a sabot?" Mulheisen was not well versed in guns and ballistics. He had never understood the tremendous attraction the subject seemed to have for some of his colleagues. He'd had a .22 rifle as a boy, plinking away at tin cans and muskrats along the St. Clair River. And now he carried a revolver, a .38 Smith & Wesson Chief's Special, with a shrouded hammer. He went to the firing range when required and he shot average scores.

"The sabot is a plastic vehicle, kind of like the

first stage of a rocket, that carries the bullet. It drops away a few inches beyond the barrel of the gun. The thing is, they can load a much more powerful charge that way. This mother starts out at over four thousand feet per second—it's really a .30-06 55 grain load, see? And flat? It drops less than—"

"What the hell's it good for?" Mulheisen asked. "Squirrels?"

"No, it'd go through a squirrel so fast the varmint wouldn't know he'd been hit," Dennis said. "It'd be a great assassination weapon. No ballistics! See, because of the sabot, the actual bullet doesn't touch the barrel."

"Oh, great! Just what we need: a better assassination weapon. Look, what is it about guns? What's the big attraction?"

Dennis thought about that for a minute. "They're nice," he said at last. "They really work, you know? Not like a lot of things, like a car that's supposed to be wonderful but it turns out just to be a gas hog. Except for the real trash on the market, the average gun is a really nice piece of work. They do what they're supposed to do, and they look like what they are. A gun doesn't look like a hair dryer."

"Some hair dryers look like guns," Mulheisen commented.

"That's what I mean," Noell said eagerly. "You realize that the basic form of the revolver hasn't changed in maybe a hundred years?" He hauled out his Colt Python. "Look at this. It's more powerful, it's stronger, but basically it's the same weapon that Wyatt Earp or General Custer used. About all we've done is improve minor mechanisms, improve the alloys, and beef up the firepower. It's pretty close to the absolute peak of its development." He caressed the blued steel lovingly. Mulheisen began to understand.

The Python, with its flared ventilated rib, was an elegant thing. It was ugly, too, but it had the immense attractiveness of any tool or artifact that is well designed and properly made. It was, as Noell had put it, one of those tools that has reached the peak of development.

"You and Ol' Earl are very close," Mulheisen said.

"Yeah."

"Ask him about this John Doe that Stanos shot last night."

"Sure," Dennis said. He got up from the corner of Mulheisen's desk. "You're wrong about Stanos, Mul. He's all right. He'll make the Big 4 one of these days. That's more than I can say for that rughead, what's his name, Marshall."

Mulheisen was puzzled. "Why is that?"

"No balls," Noell said. "Them spearchuckers'll all back down in the crunch."

Mulheisen was astounded. He knew that Noell's favorite bar was Lindell's AC, a bar where many of the Detroit Lions football players drank. Noell was no great football fan, but he enjoyed the company of men his own size—men who, as he put it, "can give a hurt and take a hurt." Among these athletes at Lindell's were many black men.

"What about your buddy Clothesline?" Mulheisen asked.

"Hey, Clothesline Harris is something else," Noell protested. "If all them jungle bunnies out there was like Clothesline, they'd blow us out. I'm telling you, Mul, it's war out there. I'd need more than a Python—maybe a bazooka."

Mulheisen couldn't take any more. He waved Noell out of the office, reminding him to ask Good Ol' Earl about the John Doe.

Jensen and Field appeared at the door. They were an inseparable team. Jensen was a square-faced man with a brush haircut that accented his brutal features. He was excellent at forcing admissions from suspects with his direct, challenging stare and blunt, almost mindless questions that thinly veiled a threatening violence. His very best friend, Bud Field, was a reticent but imaginative man. Together they made one quite good detective.

Mulheisen told them to check out the automobiles parked in the Collins alley neighborhood, on the chance that John Doe had driven to the scene. "Ask the neighbors to help you identify the cars," he said. "It'll save time."

He then called Firearms & Ballistics. They said that the .38 carried by John Doe #9-83 had been fired twice and the fragments of slugs recovered from the garage wall were of the same caliber. Having ricocheted off the concrete floor, they weren't in good enough shape for the Bureau to say positively that they had come from that particular gun, but it certainly seemed probable. The pistol itself was a Colt .38 Detective Special, with a snub-nosed barrel. Its serial number was not listed in the published numbers that Colt Arms provided the National Crime Computer System.

Mulheisen didn't like that. It suggested that the gun had been stolen from the factory, perhaps with several other guns, before the serial numbers were recorded. That suggested an organization, namely, the mob.

Mulheisen sat back and puffed on his cigar. He recollected the image of the dead man and mulled over it for a while. Then he called Identification and made sure that John Doe's fingerprints would be disseminated to the Royal Canadian Mounted Police as well as the FBI. Mulheisen felt that there was something vaguely foreign about John Doe. His clothes, for instance, were all brand new and they weren't worn in a truly casual way, although they were casual clothes. Rather, they were worn in a meticulous way, as if the wearer wasn't really accustomed to that kind of dress. If the man was an alien, he might have come across the Canadian border, which was just the Detroit River. It wasn't difficult to cross without being checked. Mulheisen had gone back and forth on the Ambassador Bridge and the Windsor-Detroit Tunnel many times without being asked anything other than "Where were you born?" For that matter, he had often sailed his little gaff-rigged catboat over to the Ontario side without any interference from authorities. If John Doe had crossed the border, he probably wouldn't have been noticed, but there was always a chance. He dispatched Ayeh, the young, hawk-nosed detective that everyone called Ahab, with a sheaf of post-mortem photographs to show to Bridge and Tunnel Border Patrol officials.

After that, he telephoned the Wayne County medical examiner's office. The autopsy on John Doe was done. The autopsist, Dr. Brennan, said he'd be glad to give Mulheisen a quick read-through of the report, although he hadn't finished it yet. There were some laboratory reports on request, but he doubted that they would be pertinent.

"Go ahead, Doc," Mulheisen said.

"We have a male Caucasian, five feet six inches in height, weighing a hundred and thirty-five pounds. Subject appears to have been in excellent health and physical condition at time of death. Well-nourished, well-muscled. External examination reveals nothing remarkable except for massive tissue destruction to upper left back and shoulder, with extensive scorching and tattooing and nine penetration wounds, consistent with shotgun-inflicted wound.

"Subject evidently a nonsmoker, judging from the pink and healthy-looking lungs. No evidence of heart disease, or circulatory disease—that's pretty unusual, Mulheisen, even for a thirty-year-old. Liver healthy, too. Stomach indicates a recent, light meal— some green vegetable substance that is evidently lettuce, and some soft white meal that suggests bread, possibly unleavened."

"Unleavened?" Mulheisen asked.

"Like Syrian bread, maybe," Dr. Brennan said. "Well, let's go on. Nine lead pellets recovered from the body. One pellet penetrated the heart and several penetrated the lungs. Bone fragments from the right distal portion of the—"

"Skip that," Mulheisen said. "We know he was blasted at close range by a 12-gauge. Is there anything unusual about this man, Doc? Anything out of the ordinary? Scars? Tattoos?"

"I was just coming to that, Mul. To tell the truth, I don't believe I've ever examined a body so free of abnormalities or distinguishing marks. No warts, no pimples, no moles, no freckles, no birthmarks, just a few calluses. Not a scar anywhere, including surgical scars and vaccination marks. I was relieved to see that he had a navel, else I'd have thought he was cloned, or hatched."

"No vaccination? You can't get a passport without a vaccination, can you?"

"I don't think so," Brennan said. "I'm not sure. Anyway, he couldn't have been in the Army without getting vaccinated."

"What do you make of it?" Mulheisen asked.

"I'd say he was a health nut, Mul. He was used to plenty of exercise, but not anything like tennis or weight lifting. Maybe a devoted swimmer. Not a runner, though. He didn't have the feet for it."

"That might help," Mulheisen said.

"He was bruised and scratched from the pavement when he fell. I checked his teeth. He has every one of his adult teeth, including the wisdom teeth and not a speck of decay, plaque or dental work."

"So he brushed regularly," Mulheisen said.

"His skin is tanned, except where he wore very brief trunks. That made me think he was from a southern climate and that he was a swimmer. His hair is dark and would be curly, except that it's cut very short. From his features and coloring, it is my opinion that he is of Mediterranean or Middle Eastern origin. But that's just a guess, Mul. Maybe his old man or his old lady was from Athens or Ankara."

"Or Cairo," Mulheisen said. "Okay, thanks a lot, Doc. Next time I'm down your way I'll stop for another look at him. Call me when the lab reports come in. In the meantime, of course, you'll hold the body."

"Sure," Brennan said, "but not forever. Let me know as soon as it's okay to release him."

Mulheisen rang his old friend Frank Zeppanuk, at the Scientific Bureau. They weren't well started on their tests yet, but Frank said that John Doe's clothing had no labels at all. The clothing was brand new and had never been laundered. "He had nothing on him," Frank said. "No rings, no medallions, no St. Christopher medal, not even an extra bullet. Seems like he wasn't very well prepared for an emergency."

"What about the dollar bill and the key?" Mulheisen asked.

"Oh, that. The key's a common one, no identifying marks. As for the dollar bill, if you can identify it, it's yours."

"Thanks, but what can you buy with a dollar these days?"

"A shot and a beer, some places," Frank said.

"Well, John Doe must have thought he needed it," Mulheisen said, "or he wouldn't have carried it."

He hung up and sat back, staring through the slats of the Venetian blinds on the cubicle's window. He puffed his cigar and watched the traffic rolling by on Chalmers Avenue. He smiled, or grimaced. For a grounder, the case was awfully interesting.

THREE

Before he left to interview Vanni, Mulheisen made one last telephone call to Andy Deane at the Racket Conspiracy Bureau. He gave Deane a full rundown on the man in the alley and asked, "What does it sound like to you, Andy?"

"Sounds like a mob hit man, all right," Deane said. "Kind of unusual for one of those guys to get caught like that. Could have been a fluke, though, being seen by the neighbor lady. Yeah, he could be a hit man—or was. Or he might have had another reason to be there."

"Like what?" Mulheisen asked.

"Maybe he was just delivering the gun," Deane said.

"To Vanni?"

"Why not? Maybe Vanni's a hit man. I never heard of him, but that doesn't mean he isn't."

Mulheisen found that an interesting notion. He

told Deane that he would send him a post-mortem photograph of the dead man to check against his files, and he asked Deane to run a check on Vanni for possible mob connections.

Jimmy Marshall stopped by just as Mulheisen was struggling into his coat. He asked Mulheisen if there was anything he could do to help on the investigation. "I'm off for a couple days," he explained. Mulheisen considered it. He could see that Marshall was young and eager, probably ambitious. It wasn't unusual for a young patrolman to volunteer for extra work. It wasn't exactly "brown nosing"; Mulheisen couldn't stand that. But he and Marshall both knew that if the younger man was going to rise in the force, he was going to need a "rabbi," an older man who would act as a sort of sponsor. This would be especially true for a black man. Mulheisen thought wryly that his sponsorship would not endear Marshall to Buchanan. But perhaps he could help the kid.

Mulheisen told Jimmy about the medical examiner's theory that the dead man had been an athlete, possibly a swimmer. He suggested that Marshall take one of the post-mortem photos and go to all the East Side gyms, YMCAs, athletic clubs—any place that had a swimming pool. Possibly, if John Doe had been in town for more than a day, he might have gone swimming.

Marshall practically ran out of the office.

Mulheisen got his four-year-old Checker out of the parking lot and drove out to Eight Mile Road. For much of its length, Eight Mile Road is the Detroit city limits. The Vanni Trucking Company was barely in the municipal jurisdiction, near Gratiot Avenue. It was a small wooden building on a large graveled lot, surrounded by a ten-foot cyclone fence. In the front of the lot there was a dormant excavation with a bulldozer parked in it and a large yellow front loader sitting idle by a pile of dirt.

A couple of automobiles were parked in front of the office building, and off to one side there were several automobiles and pickup trucks—evidently belonging to the drivers of the Vanni trucks. None of the trucks remained in the lot; they were all out on the job, Mulheisen supposed.

Mulheisen went into the little building and found himself in a single room divided by a low railing, so that there was a kind of lobby, beyond which were two desks—a large one for Vanni and a smaller one for Mandy Cecil. The lobby was obviously a place for the drivers to mill around and drink coffee from a big urn. Like the rest of the office, it was in imminent danger of being overrun by boxes of office supplies and filing cabinets. Clearly, the Vanni Trucking Company was a business that was rapidly outgrowing its quarters.

Vanni was on the telephone when Mulheisen entered, arguing volubly with someone about "down time" and "fleet prices." Mulheisen didn't mind; it gave him an opportunity to appreciate Mandy Cecil. He decided that raincoats were terrible things, although last night he had considered hers rather fetching. This morning she was wearing a one-piece jumper/slacks outfit in soft, form-fitting wool, with a long-sleeved blouse that had ruffles in the front and buttoned all the way up to the neck. It sounds prim and demure but it had an opposite effect. The form it fitted was worth fitting.

Mandy Cecil was one of those women who give

an impression of greater physical stature than they actually possess. She appeared to be tall and statuesque, but closer inspection revealed a somewhat busty, slender woman of average height. The main attraction was the fiery red hair that accented the fine ivory complexion of her lovely face.

Mandy Cecil smiled pleasantly at Mulheisen and continued to type. Vanni waved and continued to talk on the telephone. Mulheisen was content to sit and watch Mandy Cecil.

When he had finished his telephone conversation, Vanni came through the little gate in the railing and shook Mulheisen's hand. He led Mulheisen outside, where, he said with a nod in Cecil's direction, "We can be more private."

"You need a bigger office," Mulheisen said.

"We're building one," Vanni said, gesturing toward the excavation. "It'll be about four times the size of our present quarters, all stone and glass." He turned and waved a hand at several vacant lots that lay behind and to one side of the fenced-in area. "And I've bought some space there, so I can park more trucks, when I get them."

Mulheisen nodded at the idle excavation equipment. "What's holding things up?" he asked.

"The usual," Vanni said, "getting the financing, arguing with the architect and the contractor, and not enough time. But we'll get at it before long."

"You seem to be doing all right," Mulheisen said.

"Not bad," Vanni said with obvious pride. "I don't like to brag, but not many guys my age have come this far. And seven years ago I didn't even know how to drive a truck. Do I look like a truck driver?"

Mulheisen had to admit that Vanni did not. He was a tall, slender man with heavy black hair and a stylishly drooping mustache. It gave him a dashing look that went well with his strong, straight nose and flashing white teeth. Vanni dressed well. He wore a turtleneck sweater under a blue-and-white hound's-tooth jacket. His trousers were modestly flared and his shoes looked like $100 Italian.

Jerry Vanni was clean. He was so well shaved and scrubbed that he exuded an air of expensive soap and lotion. If Mulheisen had had to guess the man's occupation, he might have said "television producer."

"I rarely drive a truck anymore," Vanni said. "Only when a driver is sick and I can't get a relief man. I've got twenty-two double-tandem gravel trains now. We're hauling on that new interstate highway, plus I'm finishing up a runway contract at Selfridge Air Base."

"You did all this in seven years?" Mulheisen asked.

"It's not that fabulous," Vanni admitted. "The overhead is out of sight—you wouldn't believe what just one of those trucks costs, and fuel and maintenance are sky-high. They burn gas like a goddamn 747. But I take very little out of the business. Well, I bought a little cabin cruiser—Lenny and I went halves on it—but I still live in my parents' home, for instance."

"Your parents still live there, on Collins? I thought you said you lived alone?" Mulheisen asked.

"My parents died seven years ago," Vanni said.

"A head-on collision. They left me the house and some insurance money."

"Was your father in trucking?" Mulheisen asked.

"Oh, no. He worked at Dodge Main, in Hamtramck. Worked on the assembly line for almost thirty years."

"So how did you get into trucking?"

"After the folks died I dropped out of Michigan State and just sort of moped around," Vanni said. "Then a neighbor of mine got on my case, said I ought to get busy. He got me a job with a landscaper in Grosse Pointe. I had some money, so I bought an old dump truck and started hauling peat moss for the landscaper. Then I put in a bid for a city street job, hauling sand, and I got it. Next thing I know, I've bought a half a dozen used trucks and I've got some employees. Before you know it"—he gestured around him—"here I am. Lately I've been branching out into other things."

"Like what?" Mulheisen asked. He had lit up a fresh cigar and was perfectly happy to lean against Vanni's car on this sunny, crisp October morning and listen to tales of success.

"Last spring I won a jukebox in a poker game," Vanni said. "No kidding. This guy puts up a jukebox and I lay down three jacks. He had the jukebox in the Eastgate Lounge, over on Seven Mile. So I go in to check the machine out—you know, it's like a joke or something, right? Only the box is full of money! So I say to myself, Wait a minute, big fella! I start checking out the details of the business and I see right away that it's a license to coin money. So I bought some more machines, plus some cigarette machines. I've been living in this area all my life, everybody knows me, I get along. So pretty soon a lot of the bars around here put my machines in. But it takes up a lot of time. That's why I set up a new business: Vanni Vending. My buddy—you met him last night—Lenny DenBoer, he's going to run it. And Mandy, she's the secretary-treasurer."

"You've known her for a long time?" Mulheisen asked.

"Ever since she was a skinny little hillbilly kid. Her and me and Lenny used to play in the fields down on Mack and Conners, where that shopping center and everything is now. I never thought she'd grow up to look like that, believe me. She was skinny, and tough! Outrun most boys and beat the hell out of them if they caught her. She had a Kentucky accent you wouldn't believe."

"How long has she been working for you?"

"Not long. I lost track of her in high school. I went to Servite and she went to Southeastern. Then I think she got married or something. Then I guess, like she said last night, she was in the Army, for Christ's sake! Anyway, I bumped into her about three months ago. She was looking for a job. I had a secretary, but I let her go and hired Mandy. Believe me, the other gal was nothing compared to Mandy. Actually, Mandy's too smart to be a secretary. That's why I put her into the vending operation, as an officer."

"This vending business is interesting," Mulheisen said thoughtfully, "in the context of the shooting last night."

"How so?" Vanni said.

"I understand that operations like this have been infiltrated by the mob," Mulheisen said.

"I don't know about that," Vanni said. "The

Teamsters Union has put some pressure on. But so far I'm not big enough for them to bother with. Maybe if the business expands, I might have to deal with them."

"What kind of pressure?" Mulheisen asked.

"There's this guy from the Teamsters, or says he's from the Teamsters. I'm not sure. His name is Sonny something or other—I forget his last name. I see him at Forest Lanes, once in a while. He was bugging me a couple weeks ago about joining the union. I thought he was kidding. I laughed at him and he got pissed."

"Sonny DeCrosta," Mulheisen said. "He's got some kind of mob connection, but I don't know what it is. I don't know anything about this Teamsters routine. But what's this about a union? Don't you already have a union?"

"Sure, for my drivers," Vanni said. "No, this De-Crosta guy was talking about a vendors' union."

"Vending machines need a union?"

"The Teamsters have organized vending-machine operators," Vanni said. "But the way I look at it, I'm not an employee, I'm an owner. And Len and Mandy are officers of the company. Take, for instance, the trucking company: me and Lenny and Mandy don't belong to the drivers' union, do we? Ah, it's just another shakedown, if you ask me. My dad was a union man all his life; I'm not against unions. But this, this is just a racket. The trouble is, the vendor is vulnerable, if you know what I mean. You can't be everywhere at once, can you? I've heard these guys, if you don't join the union, they go around and screw up your machines. They fill them up with slugs, or break them somehow. But I haven't had any trouble so far."

Mulheisen made a mental note to discuss this with Andy Deane, at Racket Conspiracy. "I'm still trying to figure an angle on this gunman, Vanni. Maybe DeCrosta is involved. I'll check it out. Now, what about DenBoer?"

"I don't know anything about any gunman, Sergeant," Vanni said crossly. "As for Lenny, he's my oldest friend. He's been working for me for years and now I've just made him executive vice president of the vending company. I don't see any connection between him and last night's incident. You keep saying 'gunman,' but as far as I can see, the guy was just a thief who broke into my garage."

"I'm not accusing anybody of anything," Mulheisen pointed out calmly. "But the fact is, that guy was no ordinary burglar. He had a gun and I think he meant to use it. We turned up no evidence that the man tampered with anything in the garage, yet he was in there for at least ten minutes. He could have loaded up your van and driven away in that time. Instead, he just stands around. What was he waiting for? I'd say he was waiting for you. But you say you've never seen him before. And a half-hour later you show up with DenBoer and Miss Cecil. I don't think it's unnatural for me to wonder if there's a connection between this gunman and DenBoer."

"You'll have to ask DenBoer that," Vanni said.

"I will," Mulheisen promised. "Where is he?"

"He's out checking a project for me," Vanni said, smiling strangely. Then he frowned. "There is one thing . . ."

"What's that?" Mulheisen asked.

"Well, when Lenny came into the company, just as a matter of course we got this 'key man' insurance policy. It insures each of the officers for fifty thousand dollars, but the company is the beneficiary. It's part of our regular group insurance. I can't see anyone knocking off me, or Len, just so the company is fifty thousand dollars richer."

"Are you the sole owner of the two companies, or is it a public corporation?"

"The trucking company and the vending company are both wholly owned subsidiaries of a holding company called Vanni Services, Incorporated. I own most of the stock, but Lenny has some and so does Mandy. I see what you're driving at, Mulheisen, but if I die that doesn't necessarily improve Lenny's position. In my will I've left my stock to various relatives, some to Lenny and some to Mandy. But I don't think he'd be in a position to take over the company. Anyway, why are we talking like this! It's ridiculous. Lenny's my best friend."

Mulheisen agreed that DenBoer didn't seem to have much of a motive for hiring a killer. "There isn't anyone you know of, then, who would want to kill you? You said something about jealous husbands last night."

Vanni blushed. "That was just a joke, Sergeant. I'm sorry about that. I go out with girls, sure, and maybe one of them might have a husband, but I don't have anything serious going and I've never had any problems like that at all."

"How about an angry competitor in your business?" Mulheisen asked.

"We put in a sealed bid, like anybody else," Vanni said. "On a state job, or a federal job like the air base, the bids are opened secretly and the low bidder gets the contract. Not much room for bitterness there, is there? Anyway, all this talk about hired killers is awfully melodramatic, don't you think? It's kind of like TV, right?"

"It's no joke, Vanni," Mulheisen said. "I've met several hired guns. Some of them are in the penitentiary now, because of me. The guy in your garage was packing a gun that was so antiseptic he should have been wearing rubber gloves. He was real."

Vanni smiled. "If you say so, Sergeant."

"What's your deal with the mob, Vanni?" Mulheisen asked bluntly.

"What?" Vanni seemed outraged. "What are you talking about? I have no connection with the mob!"

Mulheisen shrugged, unconcernedly. "All right, then, who do you know in the mob?"

"I don't know anybody in the mob!" Vanni retorted.

"C'mon, Vanni, everybody knows somebody in the mob or, at least, someone who says he has mob connections. Who do you know?"

Vanni looked relieved. "Oh, well . . . you meet guys like that everywhere in this town. I stop by the local tavern for a quick one now and then—the Town Pump. There's guys in there who'll take a bet, who claim to be in the numbers racket, or they say they can get you a TV or even a car, cheap, meaning that it's hot. But nobody pays any attention to those bums. They're a dime a dozen."

"Name one," Mulheisen said.

"No. I mean, I don't really know them, right? Just a loudmouth here and there, trying to make himself important. Maybe some of the old-timers who sit around the tavern all day are amused. I'm not. Sergeant, if there's something else, let's have it. I've got a business to run."

"Where's this poker game?" Mulheisen asked.

"What poker game?"

"The poker game where you won your jukebox," Mulheisen said. "Is this a regular game?"

"Well, what the hell. I mean, everybody likes to play a little poker now and then." Vanni tried to laugh it off.

"So where's the game?"

"Oh, it's no big thing. Sometimes some of the guys come over, or someone calls and says there's a game. Sometimes I play with the drivers, after work. Just a little penny ante in the office. And sometimes, like we go to a blind pig or something, and there's always a game there."

"Which blind pig?" Mulheisen asked.

"Any blind pig! What difference does it make?"

Mulheisen sighed. "All right, Vanni. Go back to work. If anything comes up, though, like with De-Crosta, give me a ring, eh?" He gave his card to Vanni. "Ask Miss Cecil to step out here for a minute, will you? I won't keep her long."

Vanni seemed relieved. He stuffed Mulheisen's card in his pocket and went inside. A moment later Mandy Cecil came out. The autumn sun made her hair blaze, and Mulheisen realized for the first time what poets meant when they rhapsodized about green eyes. Cecil said hello and leaned against Vanni's car, waiting for the questions.

"I guess you've known Vanni for quite a while," Mulheisen began. "I understand that you've been out of touch for several years. What brought you back together?"

"I just happened to be driving through Detroit and I hadn't been here in a long time, so I thought I'd look Jerry and Lenny up. I was kind of surprised to find that they were both living in the same houses where they'd grown up."

"Why is that?" Mulheisen wanted to know. He lived in the same house he'd been born in.

"It seems like everybody moves around these days," she said. "That's all. My folks, for instance, they moved back to Kentucky years ago. Myself, I've lived in a dozen different cities." She folded her arms and waited for the next question.

"You were in Vietnam," Mulheisen said. "When did you get out of the Army?"

"About three years ago."

"What have you been doing since?"

"I went back to school, took some graduate courses at Berkeley on the GI Bill, and I lived with a guy who I thought was a genius—only, he turned out to be just a dope dealer, so I took off. I worked for a consumer-research outfit in San Francisco, I tried to manage a rock group called the Multiple Function, I even danced topless. All this was on the Coast. Finally, I thought I'd go to New York for a change, so I started driving. When I got to Detroit, I called Jerry and here I am. I don't know for how long."

Mulheisen had a wistful vision of Mandy Cecil dancing topless, but he suppressed it. He took a long drag on his cigar and released it slowly into the cool October air. "Vanni says he's made you an officer of the vending business. That sounds fairly permanent."

"It's not much of a business yet," she said.

"How do you get along with Jerry these days?" he asked.

"Fine," she said.

"Just friends, eh?" Mulheisen said.

"You mean, am I sleeping with him?" she retorted. "The answer is, when I feel like it, Sergeant."

Mulheisen didn't rise to that bait. "How about Lenny?" he asked. "Just another old pal?"

"Exactly," she snapped back.

"How does Lenny like that?"

"You mean, is Lenny jealous? Yes, I suppose he is. But would he hire a killer to bump off his best friend, who is also his rival? I doubt it, but you ought to ask him."

"I will," Mulheisen said. He tasted his cigar again and liked it very much. It was really a beautiful day. He said as much to Mandy Cecil and she agreed. It was nice just standing here, he thought, especially with Mandy. But he didn't tell her that. He just said good-bye and walked away.

FOUR

"**Y**ou know the phrase 'dead as a doornail'?" Joe Service asked.

Fatman nodded without looking up from the veal scallops. The two men sat at a table in the Seven Continents Restaurant at O'Hare International Airport, in Chicago.

Joe Service looked down at his own veal. He tried to remember what the menu called this dish and why it required melted cheese. He pushed the plate away untouched. "It's a very ancient saying," he said. "It dates from *Piers Plowman,* at least."

"Plowman? What is he, a farmer?" Fatman said, chewing slowly.

"Well, yeah. Actually, it's a book about a farmer. A very old book. From Chaucer's time."

"Chaucer? I heard of Chaucer. Don't look so surprised, Joe," Fatman said affably. "Just 'cause I got a lot of business, don't mean I never read a book."

Joe beamed. He was a short, muscular man. He wore cowboy boots and a denim leisure suit. He was deeply tanned and his blue eyes were startling. He had heavy black hair and thick eyebrows. He was not a handsome man. His features were too strong—an aggressive nose, solid jaw and wide mouth—but he wasn't ugly. He smiled a lot and that helped. Also, he looked intelligent, and people will forgive homeliness in a brainy man. In his trade Joe found that his home-liness encouraged other people's confidence in him, as baldness will do sometimes.

"So, this Piers is a farmer, right?" Fatman said.

"That's right. Anyway, it seems that in those days a doornail was probably the strike plate for the door knocker. So people are always knocking on this plate, or nail. The idea is, if you hit something on the head as often as a doornail gets hit on the head, why then, that thing gets to be dead."

Fatman had finished his veal. He looked at Joe's untouched plate. "You're not gonna eat?" he asked. "C'mon, I'm buying."

"I ate on the plane," Joe said. This was a lie. Joe had in fact arrived in Chicago on an Amtrak train from Montana and then cabbed out to O'Hare. He didn't mind that Fatman believed that he had flown in. "You eat it," he offered.

Fatman traded plates. "So what are you telling me with this little parable, Joe?"

"I went over to Detroit once before for you guys," Joe said. "I went through that door once and that was almost too often."

"You made out," Fatman said. "Sometimes, when there is a knock at the door, it's Opportunity."

"Sometimes it's the sheriff. But you're right, Fat. I did make out. Now I don't have to work."

"But you love to work," Fatman pointed out. He snapped his fingers at the waiter and ordered cognac for himself and Joe. "I don't understand this, Joe. You seemed interested. I come all the way over here to Chicago and you talk about doorknobs and farmers. What are you, scared or something?"

Joe watched a TWA 747 taxi ponderously toward the huge windows of the restaurant. "I'm just a fool," he said. "I like to travel. And it's always nice to see you, Fatman. Even if you always have harebrained schemes and impossible jobs. The last time I almost got shot. And then, there's a smart cop in your town by the name of Mulheisen, who nearly nabbed me with my hand in the cookie jar. And all this mindless stunting was because your outfit can't keep score in your own ball park. Hell, Fatman, you're the home team. You're supposed to win the home games. But me, I never get my last at bats."

Fatman laughed, his voice thick and moist. "I love talking to you, Joe. You got your own language."

The drinks came and Fatman said, "Waiter, how about some of that strawberry shortcake now? Lots of whipped cream. Joe?"

Joe shook his head and inhaled cognac fumes.

"Money, Joe," Fatman said. "Lots of it."

Joe smiled. His teeth were brilliant. "At last. How much?"

"Don't know yet. Carmine don't even know."

"Ah. Well, thanks for dinner, Fat, even if you did

eat it all yourself." Joe pushed his chair back as if to leave.

"Siddown," Fatman said. "It's plenty."

"Plenty," Joe said. "I like that word. I think it's from the Latin *plenus,* meaning 'full,' a sense of bounteousness."

Fatman beamed. "See? You got a language all your own, Joe. It's a treat to listen to you." The waiter brought the shortcake, a spongy little cake about the size and shape of a hockey puck, with racquet-ball-size strawberries on it and a mound of artificial cream that had been sprayed from a pressurized can. Fatman devoured the cake in three gulps. He wiped his lips and continued.

"Merchandise, Joe. Carmine has a deal with this guy. Young guy, shipping merchandise. Now this kid has come up with a Big Deal. At first Carmine doesn't take him seriously, so the kid says, 'Okay, I'll go it alone. But if it works out, can I count on you?' So Carmine says, 'Okay, keep in touch.' So, a little later it begins to look like maybe the kid can pull it off, after all. In the meantime there's some complications."

"God, I've heard that one before," Joe said.

Fatman shrugged. "So Carmine agrees to help the kid out, a little, with the complications."

"Only the complications don't get straightened out, they just get more complicated, right?" Joe said.

Fatman nodded.

"Is this dope?" Joe asked. "I don't do dope, Fat. Count me out. The people are too freaky."

Fatman waved the notion away. "No, no, it's not dope, Joe. This is hard goods. Carmine'll fill you in on it, if you come in. The deal is either a flat fee, or a percentage of the take."

"Last time I went for the percentage," Joe said, "I thought ten percent of twenty million would be two million. Only it turned out to be two hundred thousand."

"Joe, those were securities," Fatman pointed out. "We had to discount them. We sell them to a guy who sells them to a guy. So who makes out? The guy on the end? I don't know. Carmine tells me, 'Don't get us into no more securities.' This isn't securities, Joe. This is hardware."

Joe Service was pensive. "Hardware," he said at last. "I like the sound of that. It has a solid, sturdy, no-nonsense ring to it, like bullion. What kind of hardware, though? Cars? TVs? Guns? Diapers? There's all kinds of hardware, Fat. I heard about some guys out West who stole ten miles of pure copper wire, just stripped it off the power pylons."

"Where was this?" Fatman asked.

"Nowhere you know," Joe answered shortly. "Well, what's the deal?"

"Carmine says, you come to Detroit. He'll fill you in on the whole deal."

"Tell you the truth, Fatman, it sounds terrible. Sounds like you all have shit in your pants and you're all standing around grinning, waiting for the man to arrive with the toilet paper. What did this kid do, for Christ's sake?"

Fatman sipped his cognac. He got out a cigar and examined it closely, then looked all around him, turning his head with some difficulty on the short fat neck. There were two couples seated directly behind them, very solid middle-class people. Fatman sighed and tucked the cigar back in his coat.

"The kid hasn't done it yet," he said. "It's kind of complicated."

Joe groaned softly.

"There was a hit involved, but it got screwed up."

"A hit!" Joe leaned forward, very serious now. "Forget it," he said, almost hissing. "I am not a hit man, Fat. You know better than to tell me this crap."

Fatman held up chubby placating hands. "I know, I know. Nobody's asking you to hit anybody, Joe. It's just that a hit was scheduled, but it got botched: Carmine thought you ought to know."

"Why?" Joe Service was suspicious.

"It was somebody you maybe knew. A good man, one of the best, but he went down. Amazing deal. Some cops blasted him."

"Cops?" Joe said. "Working cops? You mean street cops took down the man? Who was it?"

"Sid," Fatman said.

Joe couldn't believe it. "Street cops took Sidney? Bullshit. Somebody must have turned him."

Fatman spread his hands. "I don't know, Joe. It looks straight. Sid was setting up and a neighbor lady spotted him, calls the cops. The cops come, Sid tries to walk, and the cops cut him in half with a shotgun."

Fatman had never seen Service look so strange. First he looked bleak, then he looked mean. Finally, he seemed to get hold of himself. "Sidney," he said under his breath, "I never would have believed it. Who are these cops?"

"Nobody," Fatman said. "Like you say, just working stiffs. They didn't know him from Adam, still don't. Just one of those deals. I guess Sid took a shot at one of the cops and didn't know the other one was behind him."

Joe sat back. "I don't believe that. Sidney wouldn't go down for street cops. It's not in the book. Somebody must have set him."

"Who could set him?" Fatman said.

"How about this guy, this kid?"

"No reason for it," Fatman said.

"Well, this is bad," Joe said. "Somebody could get Dunloped over this."

"Dunlop-ed?" Fatman said.

"Uniroyal-ed. B.F. Goodrich-ed," Joe said.

"You mean, like 'run over,' " Fatman said.

"I left out Michelin-ed," Joe said.

"Well, if you feel that way, forget it," Fatman said. "Carmine doesn't want you around if you're looking for blood."

"Don't tell me what to do, Fatman," Joe said mildly. "You did this on purpose, anyway, just to get me interested."

"Are you implying that we set Sid up?" Fatman was aghast.

"No, I don't mean that. Never mind. What kind of deal did Carmine have in mind?"

"About a hundred, Joe," Fatman said. "Maybe more if you work it right."

Joe smiled and doffed an imaginary cap. "Joe Service, at yo' service," he said.

"So you'll come? Fine."

"I'll come, if only to see what happened to Sid."

"What's Sid to you?" Fatman asked.

"None of your business," Joe said. "We were

friends, that's all. We went to school together, you might say."

"And what school was that?" Fatman asked.

"Smith and Wesson," Joe said.

Fatman laughed. "I love it." He hauled out the cigar again, and with a defiant look at the ladies at the next table, he bit off the end and lit up. Billows of rich blue smoke went up. There was some discreet coughing from the other table.

FIVE

Late in the afternoon, Mulheisen sat in Sergeant Maki's cubicle discussing Mutt and Jeff. Maki was a tall, rawboned man with a dour expression. He had a reputation for being tough on suspects. He didn't say much to a suspect, but one thing that enraged him was the suspect's asking him a question. When that happened, the suspect often got a kick in the shins, or worse. Maki's third wife was divorcing him because he wouldn't talk to her, but Maki didn't care. He had Mutt and Jeff now.

Maki was "married" to Mutt and Jeff, whose supermarket armed robberies stretched back nearly three years. Most of the robberies had taken place in the 9th Precinct; in some cases Mutt and Jeff had robbed the same market on more than one occasion. The robbers were a tall, lanky black man and a short, stocky black man—hence the sobriquet, awarded to them early on by the press. The robbers wore "stingy brim" hats under which were rolled-up nylon stockings that could be quickly pulled down as masks when the proper moment arrived.

Mutt and Jeff carried automatic pistols, but they had never fired them during a robbery. Not all of the Mutt-and-Jeff robberies had actually been committed by the "real" Mutt and Jeff. They had numerous imitators, most of whom had been caught. Some people believed that the original Mutt and Jeff had been caught as well, perhaps for an unrelated job, and were now in jail, quietly waiting to get out and dig up their buried thousands. Maki did not believe this.

Maki showed Mulheisen a graph he had drawn. "What do you think?" he asked.

Mulheisen didn't know what to think. "It's just a lot of dots and lines," he said.

"It's a 'Pattern of Criminal Activity Graph,' " Maki said. "I was reading a book by this psychologist. He says crooks act out of compulsive behavior patterns. They don't even realize they're doing things a certain way, or why. The trick for the detective is to chart as many factors as you can from a series of crimes. Then you make a graph. A pattern should appear. Sometimes you can predict when and where the criminal will hit next."

"What factors have you noticed?" Mulheisen asked.

"One: almost every robbery is Friday night, just at closing time; two: both robbers carry large automatic pistols, probably .45s; three: nobody has ever been hurt; four: the robbers speak very little, but give explicit instructions; five: they don't swear or shout; six: every time they come to separate check-outs at about the same time, with more or less the same items in their grocery carts."

"I didn't know that," Mulheisen said. "What's in the carts?"

"Corn meal, dried beans, smoked ham hocks, ketchup, vinegar, Mexican hot sauce and Stroh's beer."

"Then all you have to do is stake out the hot sauce shelf every Friday night," Mulheisen said, "and bust every middle-aged black male wearing a stingy brim hat who picks up a jar of Salsa Brava."

Mulheisen was saved from Maki's retort by the desk officer, who said he was wanted on the telephone. He took the call in his office. It was Jimmy Marshall.

"I found him!"

"Who?" Mulheisen asked.

"John Doe. At the Gratiot Health Spa. It's a little gym and swimming pool outfit on Gratiot, between Harper and Van Dyke. He was in here twice this past week. He worked out on the horse, ran a little, sat in the sauna, then finished off with a long swim. The proprietor never saw him before."

"Did he give a name?"

"Yes, indeed," Marshall said smugly. "He signed the register—Tom Brown, 23 Elm Street, Oshkosh, Wisconsin."

"Tom Brown," Mulheisen said. "Interesting name. Are you sure it wasn't Bill White? Or Vida Blue?"

Marshall's elation subsided audibly. "Pretty common name, hunh?"

"It's not his name," Mulheisen said, "but if you want, you can check with the Oshkosh police. Maybe they could take a run out to Elm Street for you. Well, don't let it get you down, kid. You did good. Now, what else should you do?"

Marshall was silent, so Mulheisen went on, "Find out how he was dressed. Did he speak with an accent? Did he talk to any of the regular customers? Did he come there in a car? Is there a parking lot with an attendant? Is there a cab stand nearby? Did he get off a bus? Maybe he walked. If so, he probably didn't walk from too far. Check nearby hotels. Check nearby restaurants, especially health-food restaurants and stores."

"Right! I'm on my way," Marshall said. "Oh, wait a minute." He sounded troubled.

"What's the problem?"

"I have to pick up Yvonne, my wife, at six."

"Go pick her up, then. Jensen and Field can handle this."

"But I could just take her home and then I could get back out here," Marshall said.

"Fine." Mulheisen hung up.

Detective Ayeh came into the cubicle and tossed his remaining post-mortem photographs of "Tom Brown" on Mulheisen's desk. "Nothing," Ayeh said. "Went to the Bridge, the Tunnel, talked to the bus company that runs the Windsor bus. Nobody knows him."

"Oh, well," Mulheisen said. "Lieutenant Johns was looking for you. Something about a whore that a cop hassled last night."

Ayeh groaned. "Another one of Buchanan's paranoia patrols."

Mulheisen went back down the hallway to Maki's cubicle. He passed a patrolman who was scolding a couple of worried-looking kids—something about broken windows. "Hang 'em, Larry," Mulheisen said in passing.

Maki looked up as Mulheisen entered. "The problem is to isolate the compulsive factor, or factors," he said. "Now all these are factors, but which ones are compulsive?"

"Does this system work when you have two crooks?" Mulheisen asked.

"A complicating factor in itself," Maki agreed.

"Do you suppose that Mutt and Jeff know that you're on their case?" Mulheisen wondered.

"Oh, they know it, all right," Maki said. "Senkbeil of the *News* wrote me up a while back."

"I wonder if it's as comforting to them as it is to you?" Mulheisen said. "Never mind. Let's grab some dinner at Cardinale's and hit the hockey game tonight."

Maki thought that sounded all right. He shuffled up his papers and graphs and stuck them in the desk. Mulheisen left word at the front desk that if Marshall called he would be at Cardinale's until seven-thirty.

Mulheisen and Maki devoured the lovely lasagna and drank Cardinale's red wine out of coffee cups. Nobody called. The two of them drove out Grand River Avenue to Olympia in Mulheisen's Checker. The parking-lot attendant greeted Mulheisen as "Fang," and cheerfully accepted a cigar as a tip.

The two detectives bought containers of Stroh's beer and stood in the ramp near the Montreal Canadiens' bench, talking to a uniformed cop and occasionally shouting encouragement to the beleaguered Red Wings. It was Mulheisen's favorite spot for watching hockey. The din was terrific. The skates made a sound like a knife being sharpened on a stone; the players screamed for passes and crashed headlong into the boards. Those on the bench kept up a constant barrage of insults directed toward the opposing team.

Mulheisen felt exhilarated.

SIX

It would be a famous night in the history of the Town Pump. Afterwards, Pump regulars would refer to the past in terms of whether so-and-so got married, won the Irish Sweepstakes or died before or after "the night the gunmen shot up the Pump."

The Town Pump was a fine specimen of a vanishing institution: the neighborhood bar. A bulwark of the ethnic neighborhoods, it is almost gone now.

The Town Pump in no way resembled a cocktail lounge. It was well lighted. It used to be a grocery store. In the display bays on either side of the doorway cardboard stand-up advertisements proclaimed the virtue of Stroh's beer.

The bar was oak and ornate, with a massive back bar, featuring a huge beveled glass mirror and fake pillars. On the back bar were stacks of clean glasses, many bottles of whiskey, and large jars of hard-boiled eggs pickled in beet juice. A sign on one of the jars said, "Boneless Chicken Dinner—10¢." There was also a jar of pickled kielbasa. Besides these viands, the proprietor, Dick VanLerberghe, had a grill on which he made what his customers called the world's best cheeseburger.

The mirror on the back bar was nearly obscured by comic signs that Dick and "the little woman" had collected on vacation trips in their camper.

Everybody's favorite sign was the one posted above the cash register:

SAVILLE DER DAGO
A TOUSSIN BUSSIS INARO
NOJO DEMER TRUX
SUMMIT COUSIN SUMMIT DUX

Strangers were encouraged to decipher this cryptic message. The regulars howled with delight at attempts to read the sign phonetically, or as if it were a kind of Pan-European language. At last, for the fee of a beer, a regular would consent to translate loudly: "Say, Villy, der dey go. A t'ousand busses in a row. No, Joe, dem are trucks. Some mit cows and some mit ducks." The recital was always followed by a good deal of cheerful chuckling, and often Dick would give the newcomer a scrap of paper and a pencil so he could copy this hilarious message.

During the week the Town Pump was a kind of social club for a dozen or more elderly men, mostly Belgian émigrés, who watched the ball game on the color TV, played euchre, and drank copious quantities of beer. On Saturday the Belgians would gather for pigeon races. They took their pigeons twenty-five miles north to Mt. Clemens, released them, then rushed back to the Town Pump to drink and wait for the judges. The judges went to each man's home mews and checked the automatic timer that stopped when the pigeon entered the cage. By the time the judges reached the Town Pump, everyone was drunk.

Tonight the television was tuned to the hockey game. Dick VanLerberghe watched the Red Wings score a goal while short-handed. "That's the way to kill penalties," Dick said, arms folded. At one table, four regulars played euchre, commenting freely on the folly of each other's play. The most loquacious of these players was Uncle Corny, a seventyish gentleman, originally from Rotterdam. He had a mild contempt for his companions, whom he called Buffaloes—they were from Liège and Brussels, respectively—and Polack—a skinny pensioner born in Cracow.

Two strange men entered the bar. They were about forty and looked quite a bit alike, dressed in blue overcoats and gray hats. They might have been brothers. Dick VanLerberghe took special notice of their noses. He considered that if it hadn't been for the presence of Uncle Corny, the two strangers would have had the largest noses in the bar. Their noses were formidable, Dick thought, but Uncle Corny's nose, that was a deformity: a square "bottle" nose, deeply pitted by a lifetime of daily alcohol consumption. It now resembled nothing so much as a stiff, square sponge.

The strangers looked the bar over carefully. They each ordered a shot of Jack Daniel's, with a beer chaser. Nobody ever drank Jack Daniel's in the Pump. Dick opened a dusty bottle.

The heavier man said in a high, mild voice, "You know a guy, Jerry Vanni's his name?"

"I have known Jerry since he was so high," Dick said, "and his father before him."

"That his jukebox?" the man asked.

Dick nodded and turned back to watch the hockey game. The two strangers stood silently at the bar. The smaller one stared at the SAVILLE DER DAGO sign, frowning. His lips moved soundlessly.

Uncle Corny crowed to his euchre companions, "When I see bot' a dem bowers fall, I know I got da rest."

The heavier stranger walked over to the jukebox. It was a big, fancy Seeburg. Dick noticed him and was annoyed. Couldn't the jerk see that the Red Wings were on? Nobody wanted to hear the jukebox.

The man fumbled in his pocket for change, then slipped a quarter into the machine. He ran his blunt forefinger down the list of titles. "Christ, all you got is polkas and Bing Crosby," he said in disgust. Dick shrugged. The man punched some buttons. The machine whirred and the strains of "She's Too Fat for Me" filled the room. Dick eyed the man with undisguised annoyance.

The smaller man had gone to the entrance. He stood just outside, then turned and nodded, holding the door open. There was a draft.

Dick was puzzled. Then he gawked.

The heavy drew an enormous pistol from his overcoat. With great care he took aim at the revolving record on the jukebox and then blasted it. The gun bellowed like a cannon. The jukebox slammed back against the wall, spitting glass and electrical sparks. Smoke issued from the gaping hole in the front.

Dick ducked down behind the bar. The skinny Polish euchre player leaped into the ladies' room. Uncle Corny, beer glass in hand, slowly eased his bulk around and stared solemnly at the gunman. Everyone else sat perfectly still, their ears ringing.

The gunman shouted, "Bartender! That cigarette machine. Is that Vanni's, too?"

Dick's muffled answer came from below the bar. "Yes."

The gunman took thoughtful aim and squeezed off four evenly spaced shots.

The cigarette machine bounced off the wall with the first shot and was knocked careening with the second. The third shot smashed it into the corner. It bounced forward and teetered precariously. The last roaring shot blasted its base out from under it, so that the machine fell forward onto its face, crashing to the floor, knocking over barstools. Quarters and dimes poured out softly and broken cigarettes were scattered about like straw.

Everyone was deafened. The smell of cordite hung in the air. The gunman strolled to the bar, swallowed the last of his beer wash with the pistol dangling from the end of his relaxed arm. Then he left, slamming the door behind him.

On the shelf over the end of the bar, the face of Detective Sergeant Mulheisen looked into the room. He and Maki were standing at rinkside at Olympia. The camera had followed the Canadiens' Yvan

Cournoyer to the bench as the Montreal team changed lines for an icing face-off. Mulheisen looked directly into the camera and pointed something out to Maki.

SEVEN

"I'm stupid," Mulheisen said.

"No shit," Maki said. They were both hunched over the bar at the Town Pump. Mulheisen had quit filling out a long investigative report form.

"I'm just plain dumb. I call in. Not every night. Some nights I go home. But if I'm in town, say I stop for a drink or two, maybe have dinner, then I almost always call in to the precinct before I head for home. Just out of curiosity. Curiosity and stupidity."

Mulheisen did not live in the city, which was against regulations. Like many officers he got around the regulation by maintaining an address in town, which was really just an answering service and a mail drop run by a creaky old hillbilly named Speed, on the near East Side. Speed charged each officer fifteen dollars per month, but it was worth it. If anyone called there, Speed made every effort to contact the officer, and he was good at forestalling suspicious superiors.

Maki drained off the rest of his beer and set the glass on the bar. Dick VanLerberghe filled up the glass promptly and waved away Maki's attempt to pay. He also filled Mulheisen's shot glass with Jack Daniel's. "That's what those thugs was drinking," Dick said to the detectives. "The first bottle of that I opened in months. And you drink it, too!"

"What does that sign say, for crying out loud?" Maki demanded irritably.

Dick looked at the sign over the cash register, then back at the two policemen. "Can't figure it out, eh? What kind of language you think that is?"

Mulheisen examined the sign for the first time. "Hmmmm. It's sort of like Latin," he said, "but not really. French? No. I don't know. Finnish, maybe? Nah, that's not right. I give up."

"Boy, a couple of smart detectives you are," Dick said. Then he recited the message smugly, grinning with vast amusement.

Maki stared at VanLerberghe with undisguised hostility. The bartender's smile faded. Mulheisen said, "Did someone call Vanni?"

"Here!" Jerry Vanni walked in the door accompanied by Mandy Cecil. The two looked like candidates for "Most Handsome Couple of the Year." Vanni wore a short fur-collared camel's-hair coat, extravagantly flared trousers and shoes with stacked wooden soles and heels that added an unnecessary two inches to his height. His white teeth gleamed and his mustache drooped stylishly. Mandy Cecil's hair was attractively windblown and her cheeks were rosy from the brisk October night. She wore a very woolly kind of fur jacket and voluminous pantaloons that stopped just below the knee where her high leather boots ended.

Maki eyed the pair sourly. "Hubba, hubba," he said under his breath.

Vanni stood with his fists on his hips, staring at the dark and wounded jukebox. "Now, what the hell?" he said.

Mulheisen watched Mandy Cecil as she examined the ruins of the cigarette machine. She asked what had happened. Mulheisen gave her a quick reprise while Vanni listened.

When Mulheisen finished, Vanni said, "I know what you're thinking, Sergeant. But I'll say it again, I have nothing to do with the mob."

"What about Sonny DeCrosta?" Mulheisen asked. "Hear anything more from him?"

Vanni shook his head. "No, but it looks like they might be trying to get some kind of point across to me, doesn't it?"

Mulheisen nodded. "You might call it a form of communication," he said.

"Well, what do I do now?" Vanni said.

"You might give DeCrosta a ring," Mulheisen suggested. "Talk it over with him, see what he knows about this. Maybe he'd be willing to guarantee you against this kind of loss. Then you'll know where you stand."

"I'm not going to pay off some slimy creep like that, if that's what you mean," Vanni said hotly.

"That's not what I was suggesting," Mulheisen said. "But it doesn't hurt to find out if DeCrosta's really involved. We might be able to work up a case against him."

"All right," Vanni said. "I'll call him. In the meantime, I guess I'd better clean up the mess." He took off his coat and began to sweep up the coins and cigarettes with a broom provided by Dick. Mandy Cecil took off her jacket and sat down at a table to separate the coins into different piles. She was wearing a satiny blouse and it was obvious that she wasn't wearing a brassiere.

Mulheisen and Maki sat at the bar watching her through the mirror. They discussed quietly the problems of pinning anything on the mob. Mulheisen said he would have to talk it over with Andy Deane tomorrow, for sure, and get a thorough check on Sonny DeCrosta. And, of course, the bartender would have to go downtown to Racket Conspiracy to see if he could identify the gunmen from Andy's gallery of known mob hardcases. Dick assured them that if the police had a picture of either man, he'd be able to identify them. "I'd know them noses anywhere," he said. "I'm a expert on noses."

The door swung open and a man came in. He was short and dark, with black hair and carried himself with a certain cheerful self-assurance. He wore a fleece-lined leather coat and Levi's. On his feet were cowboy boots. "Whew," he said, rubbing his hands together, "getting chilly out."

He looked around at the mess, now almost cleaned up. "Hey, looks like you had a brawl, eh?" He hopped up onto a stool.

"Brother, you wouldn't believe it," Dick said. "What'll it be?"

The stranger looked down the bar and noticed

the bottle of Jack Daniel's. "Black Jack Ditch," he said.

"Black Jack Ditch," Dick repeated, "which is . . . ?"

"Jack Daniels and water," the stranger said. He nodded to Mulheisen and Maki. "What happened here?" he asked. Maki turned away. He didn't like questions.

Mulheisen said, "Some guy came in and didn't like the jukebox, so he took a couple of shots at it."

"No kidding?" the man said. "He must have been packing a cannon."

Mulheisen nodded. "Probably a .44."

"I saw something like that out in Wyoming once," the man said, "in Sheridan."

"You from out West?" Mulheisen asked.

The man drank off his Black Jack Ditch and called for another, tossing a ten-dollar bill on the bar. "I've spent some time out there," he said. He seemed to lose interest in the conversation and gazed at Mandy Cecil for a while. She looked up and caught him. The stranger smiled at her. She smiled and went back to counting coins. The man drank down his whiskey again and picked up his change, leaving a couple of dollars on the bar. "Buy these fellows one," he said to Dick and strolled out.

"You know him?" Mulheisen asked Dick.

"Never saw him in my life," Dick said, pouring out a couple more drinks for the detectives. He glanced up at the clock on the wall, a promotional item from Hamm's Brewers that showed a continuously changing panorama of a Northern trout stream. It was 1:30 A.M., bar time. "Don't look like I'm gonna get much more business. Think I'll close her up. You fellows just sit tight." He went over to the front and turned out the tavern sign, then locked the door.

"Time to head home," Maki said. He didn't look very enthusiastic. Mulheisen wondered where he was living, now that he had broken up with his third wife. Maki had left behind him a string of furnished apartments. "Do yourself a favor, Mul, and don't go back to the precinct tonight. The blue boys got a report on this."

"I won't," Mulheisen said, "but I don't feel much like driving all the way out to St. Clair Flats. Nobody home, anyway."

"Where's your mother?" Maki asked.

"Texas."

"Texas? What the hell is she doing in Texas?"

"She belongs to some bird-watching outfit," Mulheisen said. "She's gone on a bird-watching tour. I think I'll cruise around town a little more tonight. Maybe I'll head over to Benny's and see what's cooking."

Maki got up and slapped Mulheisen on the shoulder. "Don't get caught in a raid," he said. "It'll look bad on your record."

"Nobody raids Benny's," Mulheisen said. "See you."

After Maki left, Mulheisen had another drink then strolled over to the table where Cecil and Vanni were both counting change from the jukebox and the cigarette machine. "I guess I'll take off," he told them. "Let me know if DeCrosta rises to your bait. I'll let you know if anything comes up on your hit man."

Mandy Cecil looked up from a pile of quarters. "Nothing new on him?"

"So far, all we know is that he liked to swim. Well, good night."

Dick let him out into the cold, windy night.

Benny Singleton was a short black man with a thick mustache. He was handsome, with large brown eyes and a neat round head. He wore his hair clipped short. "I'm too old for that Afro stuff," he'd once told Mulheisen. He was forty. He dressed himself in soft browns and grays, in good rich woolen cloth with quiet patterns. He wore oxford-cloth shirts with button-down collars and they looked right on him. With these he preferred silk ties and tweed jackets, silk hose and well-burnished old cordovan shoes in excellent repair. Benny moved with grace and spoke in a low, articulate voice that was audible yards away.

Benny Singleton had been a waiter most of his life. He started as a salad boy in a large downtown hotel, became a waiter, occasionally tended bar, and finally became maître d'hôtel, a position to which he seemed born. He was known, appreciated and even feared by those who dined well in Detroit. Eventually he became maître d' at the River Inn, a distinguished restaurant on the Detroit River. In this position he served for many years and was often tipped not with vulgar cash but with quietly uttered words of stock-market wisdom. Benny heeded this advice and in due time became wealthy enough to leave service, although he was honestly plagued with concern for his old patrons, who, he feared, would never find anyone to care for them adequately.

With his small fortune, Benny entered the twilight zone of Detroit night life. He opened a blind pig. Every city has its distinctive features. San Francisco has hills and refurbished post-earthquake houses; New Orleans has Creole food and hot jazz. Detroit has barbecued ribs and blind pigs. A blind pig is a tavern that opens after the legal closing hour, which is 2 A.M. In Detroit lots of people don't go out until the bars close.

The origin of the phrase "blind pig" is obscure. It has always meant an illegal drinking establishment. If one supposes that "pig" is a universal pejorative for policeman, and if one considers that no illegal saloon could possibly operate without at least the passive cooperation of the local constabulary, why then, a possible etymology suggests itself. Beyond that, however, one might consider the fact that during Prohibition (the Golden Age of the blind pig) the liquor retained in these speakeasies was often a volatile, unaged substance that was potent enough to blind a pig.

Whatever the origin, blind pigs are numerous in Detroit. Detroit needs them. Despite the fact that it is the fifth largest city in the nation, it has very little in the way of legitimate night life. There are jazz clubs and barbecue joints—sometimes on the same premises—and there are blind pigs. The Fords and the Fishers and the Liebermans go to the opera once a year when the Metropolitan comes to town, and there is a fine local symphony orchestra. But, by and large, after dark in Detroit it is jazz, ribs and juice. Detroit is a working town. It works shifts. When the midnight shift gets off, the boys want to go out and play. So Detroit stays open all night.

The police don't mind the blind pigs. Why should they? For the working cop on patrol it is a source of income. For the vice squad it is a source of income and information. For the Alcohol, Tobacco and Firearms Bureau it is a gold mine. Detroit is the terminus of an enormous bootleg and moonshine whiskey industry. The illicit booze comes in across the largely unpatrolled Canadian border, or it is driven into the city in what amounts to a continuous convoy of specially rigged tanker automobiles from Kentucky, Tennessee and West Virginia. Detroit is the marketplace for the South's cottage industry.

A blind pig has cheap booze and good booze; sometimes they come in the same bottle. It also offers prostitution, dope, gambling and what a sociologist might term an "interface" between the straight world and the criminal world. This interface is important, for the underworld has much to offer the law-abiding community. Besides whores, marijuana and a shot of whiskey at four in the morning, where else can one find a bargain on a hot car, a gun that doesn't have to be registered, or a hired killer? Even the most law-abiding citizen in Detroit seems to need a gun, and an unregistered gun is preferred. Why advertise to the cops that you are armed? And, anyway, the unregistered gun is a stolen gun and therefore cheaper than the one sold in the stores.

There are many kinds of blind pigs in Detroit, from filthy stews to fancy establishments like the one run by Benny Singleton. This is a pleasant, two-story frame house near Pingree Park, on the East Side, several blocks north of the River and north of Indian Village. Benny has never been raided. He liked to tell Mulheisen that "If it wasn't for me, none of you fellows could send your kids to college." Mulheisen would grimace and Benny would hasten to add,

"Course, I don't mean you, Mul. You always been square with me."

Benny's clientele was mostly white and well-off. He permitted no heroin or other heavy drugs on the premises. He allowed casual dealers to sell a baggie of marijuana or some tai sticks, but that was it. His whiskey was authentic Hudson's Bay scotch and Wild Turkey. He didn't deal with moonshiners. The prostitutes were young, expensive and free-lance. They sometimes looked like college girls, and were. Benny charged them fifty dollars a night to come into the house and they had to buy their own drinks.

"I been thinking, Mul," he said. "I ought to open a dining room. Just a little place, room for about eight people. I'd serve one or two parties a night. I'd make it as expensive as I could imagine—maybe seventy-five to a hundred dollars a head. Then I'd get me Alois Belanger, the chef at the Old Plank House, and pay him whatever he had to have. Or maybe I'd get different chefs on a one-week rotation. I bet I'd be booked solid within a week of opening. I already have a very good wine cellar, but I'd have to expand —it'd be a good excuse to go to France for a month."

"You've got a wine cellar here?" Mulheisen said, looking up from his Wild Turkey and water (he'd ordered a Wild Turkey Ditch).

"Hell, no," Benny said. "I ain't taking no chances. I never been raided yet, but I don't want the first raid to bag my good wines. I keep it next door, where I live."

"The restaurant sounds like a good idea," Mulheisen said.

"The question is," Benny said, "why do it here if

there ain't no question of legality. I mean, why not open up public?"

"Why not?" Mulheisen concurred.

"I don't know," Benny said seriously. "Somehow . . . I just don't like the idea of a legit business, you know? All them taxes and everything."

"I never thought about taxes," Mulheisen admitted. "What do you do about taxes?"

"My lawyer and my accountant are working a deal where I pay the IRS and the state on my investments. But it's hard to fudge investment income, and the IRS knows I have a bigger income than I'm claiming. I don't know if they know about this place, but when they find out, the shit is going to hit the fan. They ain't like no beat cop—you can't just slip them a few bucks to keep quiet."

Mulheisen thought about that. "You better open the restaurant, then. That'll give you a legitimate source of income and you can funnel your blind pig take through the restaurant."

Benny considered that for a while. "True," he said at last. "It's just that I hate going legit."

Mulheisen looked around the room. He noticed one of the mayor's assistants talking to a well-known mob bagman, but didn't think anything of it, since that sort of business would have been concluded hours ago, during "Happy Hour." They were probably just friends. A couple of girls looked lonely, and an inevitable drunk was sagging over his glass. Otherwise, Benny's was dead. "Where's all the action tonight?" Mulheisen asked. "Let's go someplace else, Benny."

"Let's see," Benny said. "You like music, we

could go to Brandywine's. He's got a new jazz group."

"Brandywine? Never heard of him."

Benny was shocked. "You don't know Brandywine? That's odd. He's a native. He was here when the Indians came."

"That long, eh?"

"Well, he's part Indian," Benny said. "His great-great-I-don't-know-how-many-greats-grandfather came here with the French explorers. That's right! There was some brothers with the French, you didn't know that?"

Mulheisen mused on this while they drove toward downtown in Benny's Cadillac. He had a vision of a giant cargo canoe hurtling through the rapids of the St. Lawrence, portaging onto the Ottawa, then into Lake Nipissing, onto the French River, thence onto Lake Huron. From Lake Huron the canoe would enter the St. Clair River and drift steadily past the site where Mulheisen's home would be built one day. Then it would ride out onto the smooth bosom of Lake St. Clair and float gently down into the Detroit River—*d'Etroit*, the throat itself—pass by Belle Isle and draw up on the shore where Cobo Hall now stood and the Detroit Pistons played basketball. In this imagined canoe was a tall, strong black man from Senegal now named Maurice Brandaouin after his master. Maurice would find love and comfort among the Chippewa in a heavily forested plain by the side of the river, in a country provisionally named New France.

Mulheisen and Benny pulled up in front of a duplex on Riopelle Street. Riopelle would be named for another French settler, of course—laid out along the ribbonlike edge of his farms as they ran back a mile or more from the river.

There was a fat black man at the door of the duplex. He grunted suspiciously at Mulheisen, but at Benny's gesture, he let the two in. There were thirty or forty people inside, in a somewhat dingier and smokier atmosphere than Benny's. This was more like a house party. People stood and talked with whiskey glasses in hand and passed around joints of marijuana. Mulheisen recognized a young vice-squad detective sitting on a sofa talking to two white girls who were evidently not prostitutes but just a couple of Wayne State University coeds out for a little fun.

Mulheisen and Benny stood at the flimsy dimestore bar and drank bottled beer. A pretty black woman in a blond wig came up to Mulheisen and rested her hand on the nape of his neck. It felt cool and dry. The hand slipped downward toward his hip, where the .38 nestled in its hip grip holster. Mulheisen stopped her hand with his right elbow and gently shoved her away. She drifted off.

About three o'clock, four black men entered the barroom, carrying musical-instrument cases. In one corner there was a low platform made out of plywood and covered with green carpet. A basic drum set was draped with a sheet. One of the men whisked off the sheet and settled behind the snare drum. He set about adjusting the cymbals. Another man took a tenor saxophone out of its case and installed a new reed he'd been soaking in his mouth. The third man blew short, breathy notes from the cornet. He was the oldest, a balding forty-five, and he wore dark glasses in the dimly lit room.

The youngest man switched on an amplifier/

speaker behind the chair on which he sat. He held a flat electric guitar on his lap and fiddled patiently with the knobs of the amplifier.

"Who are these guys?" Mulheisen asked Benny.

"I don't know their names," Benny said. "I believe I've seen that guitar player before."

The tenor man turned toward the drummer now and began to blow long looping phrases that caught the drummer's cadence on every fourth bar. He had a large, breathy tone and Mulheisen smiled involuntarily, remembering Lester Young.

The cornet man shook his horn to get rid of some moisture. He came along with the other two then, making precise little stabs in tempo.

Finally, the guitar chimed in and they all jammed along in G for a few bars. Then the guitar pointedly set out a brief chord progression and the two horns segued smoothly into "Last Year's Love." Mulheisen was suddenly very happy, and he hummed along under his breath.

A half-hour later, without warning, Mulheisen felt exhausted. He groaned and pinched the bridge of his nose, yawning into his palm. His eyes felt gritty and the beer was gaseous. He wanted to break wind, but didn't. "Aagh!" he moaned quietly.

"What's the matter, man?" Benny asked.

"I don't know," Mulheisen talked through a partially suppressed yawn. "I've had it. I've got to get the hell out of here, get some sleep." He got up and paced a few steps into the next room. A couple of young men sat in easy chairs talking spiritedly about ". . . marijuana laws, then all the big tobacco companies will. . . ." They fell silent when they saw him.

He drifted aimlessly through the room and into

a hallway that ought to lead to a bathroom. As he passed what must have once been a bedroom, he heard Spanish being spoken excitedly. He did not hesitate but went on to the men's room.

When he came out of the men's room, he saw a young woman standing outside the room where he'd heard the Spanish. She wore a fuzzy jacket and tall boots and she had brilliant red hair. She smiled as he approached.

"Hi," Mandy Cecil said.

EIGHT

"The last time I saw you," Mulheisen said, "you were counting quarters. Where's Tall-Dark-and-Handsome?"

Mandy Cecil shrugged.

"You mean you're here alone?" Mulheisen was aghast. Brandywine's was not exactly the place for an unaccompanied beautiful redhead, unless she happened to be a prostitute. It wasn't so much that she would be bothered by the customers, although she would certainly have no deficiency of lewd offers, but that when she left, the neighborhood was extremely dangerous.

"I'm not exactly alone," she said. She nodded toward the room outside which they were standing. The Spanish voices were as voluble as ever.

"Friends of yours?" Mulheisen asked.

"Sort of," she said diffidently. "But I spotted you passing by, so I—"

"Why don't you introduce us?" Mulheisen said. He pushed the door further ajar and stepped past her into the room. The talking stopped. There were about a dozen men in the room, most of them fairly young, sitting around a large poker table. They were not playing poker, however. It looked like an informal meeting of some sort. They were all drinking beer. All of the men turned to look at Mulheisen.

Mulheisen bared his fangs in a more or less friendly fashion and gazed back at them. Mandy rushed to fill the silence.

She spoke in Spanish, at first, something about *"muy buen amigo,* Señor Mulheisen." She took Mulheisen by the arm and led him forward, gesturing toward an extremely handsome young man in his late twenties. "Mul, this is Angel. And this"—she turned to a middle-aged man with a somber expression—"is Francisco." She went around the table, naming each man by his first name only. Each man stood and nodded slightly with a smile.

Angel grinned broadly, displaying gleaming white teeth under a thick mustache. "I am so happy to meet Mahn-dee's frans, señor. Weel you have a *cerveza?"* He gestured with a beer bottle. "Or tequila, perhaps." There was a bottle on the table.

"No, thanks," Mulheisen said. "I just bumped into Mandy in the hall. Sounded like you were having a party, but it doesn't look like it." He looked around innocently. "Business, is it?"

Angel laughed delightedly. "Oh, no, señor. It is much too late for business. We are indulging in that time-honored pastime of the exile—plotting *revolución!"*

The others laughed—uneasily, Mulheisen thought. The dour old man growled, *"Bufón."*

"Don't be so groucho, Francisco," Angel said gaily. "These *Yanquis* are well aware that we only plot. Only the CIA can make *revolución,* eh? But we have the luxury of talking about it."

"Where is this revolution taking place?" Mulheisen asked.

"Nowhere!" said Angel. "Only in our *cabezas.* Ha ha! But if the CIA will permit, we would have our *revolución* in that most far-flung province of Soviet Russia, otherwise known as Cuba." The latter statement had a bitter tinge to it.

The burly Francisco rose now and put a heavy hand on Angel's shoulder. "Angel," he said kindly, and the younger man subsided in his chair.

Francisco turned to Mulheisen with a sad expression. *"Mi amigo,* he is having too many of Cuervo Especial. It is as he says, señor: we have the luxury of talk."

Mulheisen nodded amiably. "You are Cubans, then?" There was a general chorus of *"Sí,"* but out of the corner of his eye Mulheisen caught someone who had risen quietly and was on the point of stepping out of the room. Mulheisen turned quickly. "And you? You are also Cuban?"

The man stopped halfway through the door. He was a slight, sallow-faced figure in a nicely cut blue pin-stripe suit, in contrast to the others, who wore bright shirts and tight pants. The slender man smiled slightly. "No, Señor Mulheisen, I am not Cuban."

"But you are South American," Mulheisen said.

"Yes, I am," the man said with scarcely a hint of an accent.

"Brazilian, perhaps?"

The man pursed his lips irritably, then replied, "Bolivian." He went out then, closing the door behind him.

Mulheisen turned to Mandy. "You about ready to go?" She picked up her large leather purse from a chair and slipped the strap over her shoulder. Then she waved to the circle of men.

"*Adiós!*" they chorused enthusiastically.

Mulheisen grinned. "*Adiós, amigos.*"

Mandy took his arm and led him from the room. Mulheisen liked her hand on his arm because it brought his arm into contact with a firm but unbrassiered right breast.

In the hall she muttered, "Always the snoop."

"I get paid to snoop," he said. "Which reminds me: why are you here?"

"It's a free country," she said.

"This place isn't free," Mulheisen said.

She smiled and leaned closer. He could smell her perfume, mingled with a sweet musty odor. "This isn't a raid, is it?" she asked.

"I haven't made up my mind," Mulheisen said.

"A one-man operation?"

"What's the matter, you don't think I could take them?" he replied.

"Oh, don't be silly," she said, losing interest in the repartee.

They walked into the little barroom where the quartet was still ticking along like a good clock. A rather fantastic creature was standing next to Benny. He was six and a half feet tall with a creamy-brown complexion and thick, velvety lips formed in a perpetual pout. He wore an enormous wide-brimmed hat with a long feather drooping out of the crown. He also wore a calf-length fur coat that appeared to be made out of an entire generation of Arctic foxes. He looked out at the world through huge, pale-blue spectacles and flourished a long ivory cigarette holder.

The creature waved his free hand languidly at Mandy and said, "Ah declayuh, Miss Mandy, ah'd sho love to jump on yo' bones."

Mulheisen flushed, but Cecil replied airily, "Jump, Mother Rabbit, jump."

The man laughed, displaying his gold teeth, and slapped Benny on the back. Benny coughed. "Benny," the man gushed, "this delicious kumquat is known as Mandy. Now, don't y'all wish you was Rastus? But this other person . . ." He frowned, looking at Mulheisen with obvious distaste.

"That's my friend I was telling you about," Benny said.

"I believe I've seen your friend before," the man said. He extended a bejeweled hand on a long arm and Mulheisen shook it briefly. "I'm Brandywine," the man said, "and you are Fang."

"Fang!" Mandy Cecil said. She looked at Mulheisen and laughed.

Mulheisen smiled, demonstrating his teeth. He stared into Brandywine's eyes. "Call me Mulheisen," he said.

Brandywine tossed his head extravagantly. "Do I have to?" he said.

Mulheisen laughed. "Let's go," he said to Cecil. "I think I've got a ride," he told Benny. "See you later."

It was very dark outside Brandywine's. Most of the streetlights had been broken by vandals, or perhaps on Brandywine's orders, to protect the anonymity of his customers. But it was not a nice neighborhood. Many of the buildings were abandoned and boarded up. A brisk breeze reminded Mulheisen and Mandy that it was late October. They set off in the direction of Mandy's car.

Almost immediately Mulheisen heard the gritty sibilance of footsteps on the pavement behind them. After a half block Mulheisen turned and stopped. The steps ceased. Mulheisen could see nothing. They walked on, and a few steps later he heard the sound behind them again. It sounded as if it were two people. He stopped and flicked his coat open, drawing his .38. He held the gun out before him so that if anyone could see, they would see the gun.

"Beat it," he told the darkness.

The only reply was a low chuckle.

Mulheisen was aware that Mandy Cecil had stepped away from him and he heard the sound of her purse being unsnapped.

"All right, then," Mulheisen said flatly, "come on."

After a few seconds they heard the footsteps of two people walking swiftly away. Mulheisen holstered the .38 and took Mandy's arm as they walked on.

She unlocked the driver's door of a large car and got in, leaning across the seat to unlatch the door for Mulheisen. He got into the car, and without closing the door he snatched up her purse. She reached for it, but he knocked her hand away. She glared at him in the yellow glow of the interior light.

"Relax," he said. "I just want to see what prompted you to open your purse back there." He fished inside the purse and came up with a .32 caliber

Beretta automatic pistol. "Damn nice piece," he said. "I suppose you know how to use it?"

"Of course," she answered. "Close the door. The alarm buzzer is giving me a headache."

Mulheisen closed the door and the interior light went out. He dropped the pistol back into the bag and set the bag between them. "You have a permit to carry that?" he asked.

"Yes." She started the car. It was a new Ford LTD. With the aid of power steering she swiveled deftly out of the parking space and accelerated down the street. "Where to?" she asked.

"My car's parked by Pingree Park," he said.

She stopped for a red light and looked up at the street sign. "I've always wondered why they would name a street 'John R.,' " she said.

"Local bigwig," Mulheisen said. "His name was John R. Williams. He already had one street named after him, but wanted another. So . . ."

She laughed.

As they drove out East Forest, Mulheisen said, "What were you doing with all those Cubans?"

"I wondered if you were ever going to ask," she said. "Nosy Parker, aren't you?"

"I can't help it," Mulheisen said.

"It's more than just the job, though, isn't it?" she asked.

"Maybe," he said.

"I thought so. Well, after Jerry and I finished with counting the coins, we went downtown to Mexican Gardens for a late snack."

"What did you have?" Mulheisen asked.

"Tostada," she said. "Anyway, Angel and his friends were there, as usual. We've seen them there often. I think Angel's got a crush on me, but he's so vain he can't admit it. He said they were all going to Brandywine's and why didn't we join them. Jerry was tired and begged off."

"Just you and twelve Cuban revolutionaries," Mulheisen said dryly.

"They're harmless," Mandy said. "They get all fired up and talk about overthrowing Castro, but it's all talk."

"Why are they so mad at Castro? Wasn't Batista as bad, or worse?"

"Who knows?" Mandy said. "It's all just a lot of politics. They were all with Castro, once upon a time. I think they're angry because Castro brought in the Russians. Angel was a pilot for Fidel, but he flew his MIG to Miami when *El Presidente,* or whatever he calls himself, executed some so-called traitors that were friends of Angel's. And Francisco rowed to Key West in a rubber dinghy because he didn't like the Russian railroad technicians that came in. He was an engineer."

"Some of those guys didn't look old enough to even remember the revolution," Mulheisen said.

"They're all quite young," she said. "Angel's got them all fired up. Him and Heitor."

"That's the Bolivian?"

"Yes. Heitor Casabianco. He claims he fought with Che. He says that Che broke with Fidel because Castro had perverted the revolution. They devour every word Heitor says."

"You're sure they're harmless?" Mulheisen asked.

Mandy laughed. "Whoever heard of a Cuban revolution in Detroit? They dream about getting aid from the CIA, or from right-wing groups, but that's just silly because they're farther left than Fidel."

"This is Pingree Park," Mulheisen said. "Named after one of our most illustrious mayors." He directed her around the block to his old Checker, parked across the street from Benny's blind pig. It was almost four in the morning and people were still going in and out of Benny's place.

Mulheisen no longer felt so tired. "You're a fascinating lady, Mandy," he said. "Why don't you come in for a drink?"

"I thought you'd never ask," she said. She parked the car and locked it.

The crowd in Benny's had swelled considerably. They found themselves a semiprivate corner of the bar. Mulheisen started right out with "Why do you have a gun?"

"This is a tough town," Mandy said. "Besides, I got in the habit when I was in the Army."

"You ever have to use it?" he asked.

"I've had to show it a few times," she said. "Like tonight."

"You know I'm going to check you out in the files first thing," Mulheisen said.

She seemed unconcerned. "I'd have thought you already did."

"No. I looked up Vanni. No record," he said. He sipped at his Wild Turkey. "Just how close are you and Vanni?" he asked suddenly.

Mandy looked at him in surprise, then laughed. "Why, Sergeant! You're jealous!"

"I am not," he retorted.

"And you hardly know me," she mocked. She sipped at her drink. "We have a little something going, that's all. It isn't anything heavy. Jerry's not the type to get involved."

"How about you?"

"I've tried it a couple of times. It was pretty hard to take when we broke up." She laughed suddenly. "I'm sorry. It all sounded so corny, like something we used to tell boys in high school—'I don't want to be hurt again!'"

They looked at each other with guarded amusement for a moment, then smiled. Mulheisen ordered another round of drinks. They didn't speak until the drinks came, then Mulheisen abruptly asked, "What's Vanni's involvement with the mob?"

Mandy looked exasperated. "Really! You are something, aren't you?" She shook her head. "As far as I know, he has no connections with the mob."

"Then why all this flourish of trumpets? Someone's being awfully obvious."

Mandy stood up and put on her jacket, then picked up her purse. "Got me, dearie. That's your job. Well, *ciao.*"

"Hey, wait a minute. How about dinner tomorrow?"

She glanced at her watch. "You mean tonight? I can't tonight. Tomorrow night. About eight. Pick me up. But call first."

Mulheisen curiously felt both annoyed and elated after she had gone. He had a couple of more drinks to celebrate this strange mood and was feeling quite cheerful when Benny came in. "Benny, old chap! How goes it?" he sang out.

Benny looked at him suspiciously. "How long's he been here?" he asked the bartender. He shook his head disapprovingly when he was told and then motioned for another round with a fatalistic gesture. "Mul, you ain't driving home tonight."

"No?" Mulheisen said.

"You're drunk," Benny said.

"An officer is never drunk," Mulheisen assured him.

Benny warned him to keep his voice down. After the drink was downed, he managed to convince Mulheisen that coffee would be in order. For this they went next door to Benny's house. The house was much more spacious than it appeared from the outside. While the coffee was brewing, Benny showed Mulheisen where he might put in the dining room, if he decided to do that. Some rooms would have to be combined and expanded, obviously. Benny thought that the living-room fireplace might be profitably remodeled with an ornate mantelpiece and a marble hearth.

Over coffee, Mulheisen asked about Brandywine. "He say anything about Mandy after we left?"

"A little," Benny said. "I guess she comes in there a lot."

"Who with?"

"I don't know, Brandy didn't say."

"What about those Cubans?" Mulheisen asked.

Benny didn't know what he was talking about. Brandywine hadn't mentioned any Cubans. Mulheisen dropped it.

After another cup of coffee Mulheisen asked what time it was. "Going on six," Benny told him.

"Good God! I've got to be in court at ten-thirty."

"You better crash here," Benny said. "I got plenty of room. I'll see that you get up in time, have a good breakfast, and you'll be all set. You don't want to be driving clear out to St. Clair Flats now."

Mulheisen protested, but Benny was adamant. The room was small but the bed was comfortable, and thirty seconds after he had crawled between the cool crisp sheets Mulheisen was out cold.

NINE

Mulheisen was awakened at nine o'clock by a stocky, middle-aged black woman who wore a housecleaning turban and a flowery cotton housedress with a plain white apron.

"Aagh," he groaned and clapped his hands over his eyes.

"You havin' a dream," the woman said matter-of-factly, "but it's over now. Benny said I s'posed to get you up at nine, and it's nine. You gone be all right?"

Mulheisen groaned again, sitting upright. "I don't know," he said thickly. "It was a good dream and a bad dream." It had been two dreams, actually, running more or less simultaneously. In one he had his arm around Mandy Cecil's waist and was about to kiss her; in the other—and already he could not remember which dream came first—they had been shooting at each other.

"You wants to remember your dreams," the woman said as she placed some folded clothes on the dresser. "I always looks mine up in the dream book, so's I can get my number for the day." She turned to go out. "I done washed your clothes, but I ain't got your shirt ironed yet. You wants a shower, it's right down the hall. Breakfast be ready in ten minutes." She closed the door. Mulheisen could make little sense of what she had said. He got up slowly, uttering low grunts of solace to himself. His head hurt, his mouth tasted like bile and his tongue had been attacked by some primordial fungus. He felt his throat and it seemed to him that it was swollen; he should have had his tonsils out long ago, he told himself again.

He wondered who the woman was. Benny's housekeeper, he supposed. Incredibly, she had washed and dried his underwear and socks while he slept. She must get here pretty early, he thought. He peeked out into the hallway and saw the bathroom just a few feet away. Naked, he flashed over there and quickly got into the shower. He was recovering nicely under the warm spray when he heard the door open and the woman's voice said, "I finished your shirt. They's a razor and a toothbrush there for you." The door closed.

A few minutes later he was back in the bedroom dressing. The woman had brushed his coat and pressed his pants. His change and other pocket items were arranged neatly on the dresser. Fortunately, he told himself, he'd had the wit to put his .38 under his pillow. Perhaps that was why he had dreamed about guns and shooting, he thought, and wondered if the form of a pistol pressing against one's head could induce the image of that pistol in the mind and, thus, dreams of violence. He laughed at himself.

A few minutes later he sat down to hot buttermilk biscuits, grilled ham and fried eggs with hashbrown potatoes. There was also orange juice, milk and hot coffee. The biscuits were soft and fluffy and Mulheisen wolfed down more than a half dozen of them with copious butter and homemade rhubarb preserves. "You make these preserves?" he asked the woman.

"Who else gone make 'em?" the woman replied. She sat across from Mulheisen, smoking a cigarette and drinking coffee. Occasionally she got up to fetch more coffee or more biscuits. Mulheisen couldn't tell if she was surly or was just one of those self-contained, self-sufficient women. He watched her with mild interest. She wasn't cheerful, but she wasn't sullen, either. She wasn't exactly indifferent, but she didn't seem to value Mulheisen's esteem. Irrationally, Mulheisen found himself wanting to be ingratiating, to gain her approval. But smiles and friendliness had no effect on her.

As he finished his coffee he decided that he had detected a family resemblance between her and Benny. He knew that Benny wasn't married, so maybe this was a sister or a cousin. But he hadn't the temerity to ask. He saw that it was ten o'clock, anyway. Time to get moving.

"Well, I've got to be going," Mulheisen said, standing up. "Thanks for the swell breakfast. I guess Benny isn't up yet?"

"Hunh!" the woman snorted. "Be three o'clock 'fore Benny gets up. Grown man, sleeping all day!" She huffed off into another part of the house. Mulheisen shrugged and went out, struggling into his coat.

It was a warm, sunny October morning with a high, milky overcast that made the sun weak. All the maples in Pingree Park were brilliant yellow and red, although some of them had already lost most of their leaves. There was the quiet peacefulness of midmorning, when all the working people are gone and few others are abroad. Squirrels raised hell in the piles of raked leaves in the park. Mulheisen suddenly felt very good, despite his lack of sleep and his frustration with the Collins alley affair. Obviously, the shower and the good breakfast had helped, he thought, as he drove downtown. As for the sleep, he wondered if it wasn't true that one only needs a couple hours of sleep, providing it is deep sleep. He had definitely slept well last night. It was only in the waking moments that the dreams had come. He pondered that, as he often had: do dreams really occupy only a few seconds of one's sleep? And then he turned his mind to more immediate matters.

He was due in court at ten-thirty, to testify for the prosecution in *The State of Michigan* v. *Robert Parenteau.* In every respect this case was more significant than anything he was now handling. The Parenteau case had been a minor triumph for Mulheisen. And yet he had very little interest in it anymore. He wished it were done with. Logically, he was committed to seeing the case through the justice system, but emotionally, he no longer cared what happened to Bobby Parenteau. For Mulheisen it was enough that he had caught Bobby, even if it wasn't really the killer that he had caught. It was the same boy, all right, and yet it wasn't.

Four years ago a dozen or more high school kids had gathered in the basement recreation room of the Parenteau home on Detroit's East Side. They were celebrating Bobby Parenteau's seventeenth birthday. About an hour after the party began, Bobby left the basement room and returned with his father's World War II souvenir, a smuggled-home Colt .45 automatic pistol. He opened fire from the basement steps and emptied the magazine. One girl of fifteen was killed by a bullet in the head. Four other teenagers were wounded, only one of them seriously—a bullet in the neck destroying part of eighteen-year-old Frank Witt's larynx.

And then Bobby had vanished. He disappeared for four years. Within a very short time the case was effectively dropped, though not officially, for lack of evidence and interest. There were just too many murders and other violent crimes clamoring for attention. And this was no burglar shot in an alley, no Wild West shoot-up in a tavern with the only casualty a jukebox. This was a fifteen-year-old blond girl named Lily Vargas with half her face blown away, and a kid named Frank who now talked like a throat-cancer patient after two years of extensive therapy. And three other kids with puckered circular scars that they didn't like to talk about. And yet the case had been allowed to molder quietly in the back files. Mulheisen very correctly assumed that he would not have much longer to play around with Vanni's dead burglar. For all he knew, there might be a homicide case waiting for him at the precinct even now.

He turned off Gratiot near the police headquarters and a few minutes later found a parking place near the courthouse. He went to the police detail office and was told which courtroom the trial was being held in. When he got there he found that the case had not yet been called. There were just a few spectators, despite the case's notoriety, and a full complement of reporters.

The assistant prosecutor was Ray Wilde, a thin young man who wore glasses that were light-sensitive so that they changed from clear to dark when worn in bright sunlight. For some reason, however, the glasses never got quite clear, so that Wilde always appeared to have dark circles around his eyes. He was glad to see Mulheisen, always a good, dependable witness.

"Something fishy's going on, Mul," Wilde told him while they waited for the judge to appear. "Epstein is pleading Bobby guilty on a reduced charge of unpremeditated, which we'd worked out, but now he's also going to argue that the boy had diminished responsibility during the shooting."

"Can he do that?" Mulheisen asked. "I thought that required a 'not guilty' plea."

Wilde made a wobbly gesture with his splayed right hand and grimaced. "It's iffy, Mul. Bobby refused to plead insanity, you know, and the psychiatrists were divided. But Epstein apparently feels that he has sufficient evidence to sway the judge. Brownlow's soft on this kind of argument. He's always saying crap like, 'The Law is a living thing. It isn't cut and dried.'"

"So Bobby may end up at Northville instead of the pen," Mulheisen said thoughtfully. "Well, honestly, Ray, I'm not sure that the kid wasn't nuts. The pen isn't going to be good for him. If I thought that the state hospital could actually help him . . ."

"I wouldn't be surprised if he got three years' outpatient at Lafayette Clinic, Mul. Those four years on his own will count big with Brownlow."

Mulheisen was startled and looked at Wilde questioningly, but the prosecutor shrugged.

Just then the prisoner was brought in. Bobby was now a tall and good-looking young man who wore dark-rimmed glasses. He had his hair cut neatly and wore a blue suit with a conservative tie and well-shined black shoes. He looked like a candidate for the Junior Chamber of Commerce's "Young Christian Businessman of the Year." But then, Bobby had never been a rebel. At the birthday party there had been no marijuana, no hard liquor and only a modest quantity of beer. No one was drunk. Bobby had no history of psychiatric disturbance. He was slightly above average on his IQ tests. He played the outfield and won his letter at Southeastern High School.

At the party Bobby had not argued with anyone. He had a girlfriend there, but she had not been shot at. Nor had there been any suggestion that he was jealous of her. Indeed, outside of insanity, no one could even begin to suggest a motive for the shooting.

Of considerable interest was the way that Bobby had lived during his four years as a fugitive. In effect, he hadn't hidden at all. One day Mulheisen had happened to be driving down Lenox Street and passed Bobby's parents' home. On impulse he stopped. He went to the door not knowing what he would say when it opened; he couldn't very well say, "Remember me? I was just wondering if you'd heard from Bobby." But he didn't have to. The door was opened by someone he had never seen before. The woman told him that she and her husband had purchased the

Parenteau home more than three years ago. She seemed not to know what had occurred in her basement, and Mulheisen didn't tell her. As far as she knew, she said, the Parenteaus had moved to the West Side, to Redford, she thought.

Curious, Mulheisen had found the Parenteaus listed in the telephone book, living in Redford. Out of what he later described as plain old orneriness, he drove out to Redford and asked around the neighborhood. The Parenteaus were well liked. They were a pleasant, middle-aged couple living in a neighborhood that housed mostly younger couples. The old man worked for Chrysler, the Mound Road plant. Occasionally their daughter visited them, with her husband. The daughter was very pregnant.

Mulheisen found that interesting: the Parenteaus didn't have a daughter. They had only one child, Bobby.

The next day a policewoman named Sandra Lewis called on Mrs. Parenteau. Officer Lewis represented herself as a door-to-door cosmetic salesperson. She sold Mrs. Parenteau some cologne and they talked a good deal about Mrs. Parenteau's daughter, and about baby showers. Officer Lewis obtained the address of Mrs. Parenteau's daughter.

That evening Mulheisen and Maki sat in Mulheisen's Checker, parked a few houses down from a small tract house in a new housing development out beyond Fifteen Mile Road. The owner-occupants of the house were listed as Robert and Evelyn Adamson. Adamson had been Mrs. Parenteau's maiden name. According to neighbors, the Adamsons were quiet, reclusive people. They didn't seem to go out much, they never had people over, except occasionally their parents. Mr. Adamson seemed very nice, the neighbors thought. He mowed his lawn and sometimes worked on his car, a recent-model Plymouth.

Mulheisen saw the Plymouth drive up and Bobby Parenteau got out. He went into the house carrying a lunch bucket. For a long moment Mulheisen considered that he held the future of this boy in the palm of his hand. Apparently, the boy was a good worker, employed at Chrysler, a job his father had gotten him. He had bought this house with his father as co-signer, and he never missed a payment. He had married a girl he had met at Chrysler and they were expecting a child in a few months.

The Adamsons didn't go to church, but they didn't party, either. They didn't read any books, as far as Mulheisen could tell. They watched their new color television a good deal. They didn't get a newspaper. They had no close friends, just a few other couples whom they saw once or twice a year. Mulheisen was appalled by their life. After the door closed behind Bobby, Mulheisen said "Let's go" to Maki and they went to arrest the boy.

When Bobby was brought in, he denied that he was Bobby Parenteau, which was not unusual, but he persisted in this denial long after being confronted with overwhelming evidence: fingerprints, visual identification and, finally, an admission of his identity by his parents. In fact, to date he had still to admit that he was Bobby Parenteau. Whether he maintained this curious fiction during the trial was something that interested Mulheisen.

He noticed that the canny defense attorney, Marv Epstein, had seen to it that Evelyn Adamson and her tiny baby boy were seated in the front row, where Judge Brownlow could not miss seeing them.

It was three o'clock before Mulheisen testified. Except for a couple of Coney Island hot dogs and a bottle of Stroh's beer, he had eaten nothing since breakfast. He was edgy and tired on the witness stand. His testimony was largely confined to a description of the crime scene and his interrogation of the defendant. Nobody was interested in Mulheisen's coup as an investigator.

"When you were questioning the defendant, did he seem sane to you, Sergeant?" Wilde asked.

"Objection," said a bored Epstein. "The sergeant is not a qualified psychologist."

"I know that," Wilde replied, "I'm just wondering if he *seemed* sane to the sergeant."

"Sustained," said the judge.

"All right, Sergeant. Was the defendant calm, or how did he appear to you, during interrogation?"

"He was very calm," Mulheisen said. "Unusually so. He persisted in telling us that he was not Bobby Parenteau."

"Would you say that this was a typical act, if you will, of a criminal who seeks to evade the law?"

"Objection," Epstein said.

"Sustained," said Judge Brownlow.

"Well, let me ask the sergeant if he thought the defendant was merely trying to be evasive," Wilde said irritably.

Mulheisen couldn't understand what Wilde was driving at. He shook his head sadly and testified that it didn't appear to him that Parenteau was merely trying to be evasive. It appeared to him that Parenteau *believed* that he wasn't Bobby. Shortly afterwards, the defense went back over the same ground with the witness, and it seemed to Mulheisen when he stepped down that Ray Wilde's glasses were tinted more darkly than ever, but that may have been caused by the waning light in the courtroom.

Court was adjourned until the next day, but Mulheisen was told that he probably would not be required. Wilde was taking a rueful but philosophical point of view as he walked across the street for a drink with Mulheisen. "I'll be damned if I know why I got onto that line of questioning," Wilde said. "I think I got confused there. I meant to draw out that Parenteau was calm and not insane, but now it looks like I've done just the opposite." He shook his head. "It must be overwork. My mind's snapped."

Mulheisen leaned on the bar and gazed into his drink pensively. "There was something strange about that kid, Witt, who testified this morning," he said, "but I'm not sure what it was."

"He wasn't much use to us," Wilde said. "You'd think if a kid got his throat messed up like that he wouldn't be too sweet on the guy who did it to him, but Witt was all 'Let's let bygones be bygones.' "

"Yeah," Mulheisen said, "I thought that was odd." He downed his drink and walked out.

At the precinct there was a note from Jimmy Marshall. He wanted Mulheisen to call him at home. Before Mulheisen could call, however, Lieutenant Johns came in. He was annoyed because he hadn't known that Mulheisen would be in court all day and apparently several people were trying to get hold of him. Also, the report on the Town Pump shoot-up was inadequate, and Buchanan had been brutal toward

Johns about it. Andy Deane had called twice and Marshall was as excitable as a blue tick hound under a coon-filled persimmon tree.

Mulheisen wondered out loud where Johns had picked up language like that, and Johns admitted that during the war he'd been stationed for a while in Mississippi.

"What's got Marshall so excited?" Mulheisen asked.

"I guess he might have found out where your John Doe was staying," Johns said. "It's a hotel over on Gratiot. I sent Jensen and Field to check it out."

"Fine," Mulheisen said. "Nice work for a kid. How long ago was this?"

"This morning. At first I told him to wait for you, but he kept calling back. He has to go on shift tonight, so I sent the Bobbsey Twins. They ought to be back soon." Johns left in a more cheerful frame of mind.

Mulheisen knew he ought to call everybody— congratulate Marshall, find out what Deane wanted, see what Jensen and Field had dug up—but instead he called Records and Firearms and asked for a complete check on Mandy Cecil and her gun. Then he called her at Vanni's office.

"I thought I told you I was busy tonight," she said in a low voice.

"Is the boss there?" Mulheisen asked.

"Yes."

Mulheisen grinned. He leaned back in his chair and stared at the ceiling, rotating an unlit cigar in his hand. "Well, I'll bet you just said that because you thought I wanted to see you on business. But I was thinking more about something a little friendlier. You sure you aren't free for dinner?"

After a moment she said, "For a while."

"You have to go someplace later, that it?"

"Yes," she said.

"You have to go home first, after work?"

"Yes, well, I guess not," she said.

"Good," Mulheisen said. "I'll meet you at five-thirty at Captain Shumway's. You know where it is? On Jefferson. Right."

Next he called Andy Deane. The Rackets man told him that the bartender of the Town Pump, Dick VanLerberghe, had been down, and from the description he'd given of the two gunmen, Deane had a strong hunch that they were a couple of Toronto-based hoods named Maio and Panella, but the only pictures he had of the two were quite old. He was trying to locate something more current through the RCMP and the Toronto police. "They're pretty heavy, Mul," Deane said. "I can't see them coming to town just to trash a jukebox. I've alerted the borders anyway, just in case they're still in town, but I imagine that they came in on a private boat, across the river. Soon as I get some fresh shots, I'll send you copies."

"Thanks," Mulheisen said. "What about this De-Crosta, now? And have you found any visible connection between Vanni and the mob?"

"DeCrosta has no official status with the Teamsters Union, Mul, but the word is that he's very close, especially on this vending-machine business. He has definite ties with the mob, through Rudy Percik and that bunch."

"Percik? He's not with Carmine Kusane, then?" Mulheisen asked.

"Nope. Carmine isn't into vendors. Carmine's into dope, prostitution, numbers, guns, you name it. Basic stuff. He likes to call it 'staples.'"

Mulheisen mused on that for a moment. Deane probably knew more about the mob in Detroit than anyone, including the mob itself. He was a clearinghouse of information and he pursued it with scholarly enthusiasm. It was widely assumed that Andy would one day write the definitive treatise on the structure and function of organized crime in Detroit. It would be a text of interest not only to thugs and cops but to social and political scientists the world over.

"As for this Vanni kid," Deane said, "none of my people know him. That doesn't mean too much. The mob has so much business in this town that no one could keep track of everybody who's involved."

"He says he gambles a bit," Mulheisen offered. "Plays cards at the pigs, now and then. What about blind pigs, since I've got you on? Is the mob into the pigs?"

"Strangely enough, they don't seem to be," Deane said. "Oh, I'm sure they've got good relations there, and they might run a card game or a numbers pickup, but as for actually running a pig, I've never heard of it. They're almost all run by blacks. I wouldn't be surprised if the mob bankrolls a few of them."

Mulheisen considered this information for a while after Deane had hung up. Presently Jensen and Field came in. As usual, Jensen did the talking, occasionally looking to his partner for support. Marshall had indeed found the hotel where the late John Doe had stayed, but, unfortunately, it hadn't helped the investigation much. Except for a change of underwear packed in an American Airlines flight bag, there was nothing in the room. The people in the hotel didn't remember much about the man. He had registered as Tom Brown. He had stayed for two days and had hardly spoken to anyone. No one noticed an accent. He had paid his bill in advance each morning. In the room they had found the key tag, which the man had apparently removed from the key.

"A very careful man," Mulheisen said.

Jensen and Field didn't comment. They left.

Shortly afterwards Mulheisen got his reports on Mandy Cecil from Records and Firearms. He stretched and began to put things in order. Maki stopped by to ask if he was interested in catching a beer somewhere, but Mulheisen said he had a date with a witness.

Mulheisen had already had two Jack Daniel's Ditches at Captain Shumway's before Mandy showed up. She looked simply smashing, as always. This time she wore an almost archaic but nonetheless elegant gray gabardine suit with a skirt that came below her knees and a coat styled out of the thirties. It was complemented by a large caricature of a gangster's fedora. The vee of the jacket was filled with an eruption of multicolored silk ribbons, like a corsage. It all went very well with her figure and her brilliant hair. Every man in the bar turned to watch her walk by, and most of the women as well.

"I haven't time for dinner, Mul," she said right away. "I have some very important engagements this evening."

"I'll bet," he said.

"I see you're still wearing the same clothes," she said. "Where did you spend the night?"

"Benny's," Mulheisen said. "It was very comfortable. What's so important that you have to skip dinner?"

"None of your business," she said. She sipped her drink, a stinger, perched on the barstool with legs crossed. Even with the long skirt there was a fine display of very glamorous legs.

"I ran a check on you today, through the computer," Mulheisen said. "You're almost clean."

"Almost?"

"You don't have that Beretta registered and you don't have a permit to carry it."

Mandy didn't say anything at first. She seemed impressed by Mulheisen's serious manner. "What are you going to do, confiscate it?"

"I should," Mulheisen said. "In fact, I ought to take you into custody and charge you."

She smiled alluringly. "Sounds lovely. Why don't you?"

Mulheisen bared his teeth. "I'm prepared to give you another chance. Stop in and register it at the first opportunity, eh?"

Mandy mugged a sigh of relief. "Gosh, thanks, Marshall."

Mulheisen looked at her for a long moment. "I keep thinking of you as a little girl playing hide-and-seek with Vanni and DenBoer. Then I look at you and the image vanishes."

"I'm glad," Mandy said. "Besides, we didn't play hide-and-seek, we played guns."

"Guns?"

"Several variations on a theme of violence: cowboys and Indians, cops and robbers, stagecoach, or war."

"And you were always the Indian," Mulheisen said.

"As a matter of fact, I wasn't," she said. "Jerry was always Roy Rogers, so I was Dale Evans. Lenny was the outlaw who got plugged. In war, however, we were all on the same side, against the imaginary Japs and Nazis."

"And in cops and robbers?" Mulheisen asked.

"That depends. Everybody wanted to be John Dillinger. Sometimes Jerry and I were Bonny and Clyde. But if the robber was just a crook and the cop was Sergeant Friday, then Jerry got to be Friday and Lenny got shot."

"Who were you?"

"I was Frank, Friday's sidekick."

"Poor Lenny," Mulheisen said.

"Well, he's just one of those guys," Mandy said. "Born to ride shotgun. But he didn't mind in the least. In fact, it always seemed to me that Lenny was the one most eager to play. He was still into that long after Jerry and I had outgrown those kinds of games."

"I suppose you and Jerry became interested in more sophisticated games," Mulheisen suggested, with a touch of malice that surprised himself.

Mandy didn't react the way he had expected. She smiled faintly without looking up from her drink. "Yes," she said. "I was just thirteen," she said. "It happened in our 'bunkhouse,' which was a kind of fortress built out of old tires and pieces of junk in an open field behind our houses. It was in the afternoon, in the summer. I cried."

She looked up at Mulheisen and laughed huskily. It made him nervous but aroused him. He ordered another drink for her.

"It was quite something," she went on. "We went at it pretty regularly for the rest of the summer. Lenny caught us once. I thought he was going to kill me. He went after me with a board, but I ran away."

"He was jealous?"

"Not on my account, I think. He was afraid he would lose Jerry. But when school started we all sort of broke up, and then a year or so later, my family moved back to Kentucky."

"But now you're all back together again," Mulheisen said.

Mandy looked at him for a moment. "You aren't getting nasty, are you, Mul?"

"I'm sorry," Mulheisen said. "I can't help being curious. It seems so cozy somehow, you and Jerry and Lenny over there on Eight Mile Road, doing a good business, thinking of moving into other things, none of you married. It all seems like an old movie. I keep waiting for the scene where the glamorous gal comes in to find Bing and Bob fighting over her and she declares that she's darned if she'll marry either one of those crazy galoots."

"And then the self-effacing Bing takes a job as a musician on a cruise ship, abandoning the field to Bob because he thinks Bob really loves the girl, and vice versa," Mandy elaborated.

"Only, even the wise-cracking Bob can see that the girl is really in love with Bing and he finally makes her admit it. In the last scene they're all on the cruise ship, sailing into the sunset." Mulheisen finished the scenario to Mandy's laughter.

"Except that I don't really see Jerry and Lenny as Bing and Bob," she said, still smiling. "In real life, Jerry wouldn't think of giving up the girl, and Lenny would sooner sink the ship with all aboard than surrender the girl if once he'd gotten her."

"Really?" Mulheisen said dryly. "But I take it that he has never gotten her?"

"Your mind is in the gutter, Sergeant," she said. "But I don't have time to sit here talking to you about it. I've got to get a move on."

"How about later?" Mulheisen asked.

"I won't be home before midnight, if then," Mandy said. "If you're still up, you could give me a call."

"I'll do that," Mulheisen promised. "But if I don't get hold of you, remember that we have a date tomorrow for eight."

She waved, and with every other male in the bar he watched her all the way out the door. He had another drink and let his mind wander back over what she had told him about Vanni and DenBoer. There was a danger, he realized, in thinking about people in terms of stereotypes. Vanni and DenBoer weren't Bing and Bob, any more than they were Laurel and Hardy. Imperceptibly, he found himself thinking about Bobby Parenteau. A few minutes later he dialed Ray Wilde at home.

"Sorry to interrupt your cocktail hour, Ray," Mulheisen said, "but do you remember if any of the psychiatrists ever questioned Bobby's relationship with Frank Witt?"

"No, I don't think so," Wilde said. "At least, I don't remember any mention of it in the reports."

"Well, it just occurred to me that the first two

shots that Bobby fired were aimed at Frank Witt. Only one of them hit him, the second. Then Bobby emptied the gun randomly at the rest of the crowd. Now, for no good reason . . . nothing that I can put my finger on, really, it struck me that Witt is a homosexual."

"He is?" Wilde said. "I never heard anything about that."

"No, nobody's mentioned it," Mulheisen said, "but I'm certain that he is. There's a possibility that he and Bobby may have had a thing, a relationship. Maybe Bobby wanted to break it off and Witt didn't. Maybe Bobby was horrified—his four-year history indicates that he isn't a homosexual, apparently. But young men will experiment."

"Yes, yes, I see," Wilde said thoughtfully. Then: "Mul, do you really think I should go into this? Won't it be opening a can of worms? I mean, we're in trial, right now! I suppose I could get a temporary adjournment, but Brownlow won't like it. Anyway, what would the consequence be?" Wilde was thinking out loud.

So was Mulheisen. "It may not change things," he conceded. "Well, I just thought . . . you know, the idea hit me. I guess it doesn't make any more sense to shoot a bunch of kids over a homosexual affair than for any other reason. Well, think it over, Ray. Give me a call if I can help on anything."

For once, Mulheisen got home before dark, to the white-painted clapboard house in St. Clair Flats. It was an old farmhouse and he had always lived in it. It was in good repair, with neatly painted shutters, surrounded by maple trees with a large oak in the back yard. Beyond the oak was an old barn that was now a garage and workshop. Beyond the garage, the low fields covered with tall brown grass sloped imperceptibly to the St. Clair River. A huge ore freighter was downbound in the channel as Mulheisen pulled into the driveway. Through some trick of the terrain, the channel was not visible and the freighter seemed to be sailing through a hayfield.

There was a lot of mail in the box, including a couple of postcards from his mother, postmarked Galveston, Texas. She seemed to be having a good time and was looking forward to seeing the nearly extinct whooping cranes.

Mulheisen got himself a cold bottle of Stroh's from the refrigerator and went up to his bedroom. He sat down near the window, where he could look out at the ships traveling up and down the Seaway. He had put on an Erik Satie record and he listened to the gentle tinkling of the piano as the light failed and the ship's lights grew stronger. He thought of smoking a cigar and actually got one out, but not lit, before he fell asleep.

TEN

At approximately 5:10 P.M., just as rush-hour traffic was beginning to pile up, two patrolmen from the 15th, or Conner, Precinct were approaching the station, northbound on Gratiot Avenue, near the Detroit City Airport. They were disgusted to see a locomotive of the Detroit Terminal Railways pull across Gratiot, blocking traffic at one of the busiest intersections in the city, just south of Conner Avenue.

Later one of the patrolmen said that the train had looked a little unusual to him, since there was a single boxcar in front of the engine and a whole string of loaded auto-carrier cars behind the engine. But mostly he was surprised that the railroad would choose this moment to transfer these cars. Usually they tried to avoid tying up street traffic during peak periods.

The patrolmen became even angrier when the locomotive pulled out of sight, into Gethsemane

Cemetery, and stopped. Its long train stretched back across Gratiot. A tremendous traffic snarl began to build as the train continued to stand. Finally, after five full minutes, the patrolmen pulled their squad car out into the empty southbound lanes and drove over to the tracks. They intended to issue a traffic violation to the train, which was their duty after five minutes of blockage. For this purpose the engine number was required. But just as the passenger patrolman got out and walked down the track toward the locomotive, the train began to reverse. The patrolman ran back to the squad car.

As the train rolled by he noticed the number— 1013—and also that the boxcar on the front was no longer attached. The driver of the squad car took advantage of the situation to cut across the tracks, diagonally across the avenue, behind the fleeing locomotive, in order to sneak into the precinct driveway ahead of the piled-up traffic.

"Did you see that engine?" the driver said to his partner. "There wasn't anyone in the cab."

"Sure, there was," the partner said. "You just didn't see him. He must have been standing on the other side of the cab. But he really did move out, once he made up his mind! I'm gonna write the son of a bitch up, anyway." He gestured at the sluggish Gratiot traffic that still had not begun to flow normally. "Arrogant bastards, who do they think they are?"

The train was now headed south, toward the Detroit River. Rush-hour drivers on the Edsel Ford Expressway were startled to see a dozen or more large auto carriers go thundering overhead on the overpass, highballing like a through freight. The Big 4, under the command of Dennis the Menace Noell was just coming up on the Conner exit on the expressway. "Lookit that son of a bitch go!" Noell exclaimed. "He's going into them Chrysler yards in a hell of a hurry!" He motioned the driver to speed up.

The Big 4 cruiser wailed down Conner. Near Mack Avenue, they could see the train flying along, at better than forty miles per hour, beyond the ball diamond. The train disappeared from sight behind some factory buildings. "Step on it," Noell yelled. "That fucker's a runaway! No engineer'd take her into this section at that speed!" He snatched up the radio microphone and told dispatch that they were pursuing a runaway train, southbound on Conner, and anticipating an emergency.

At Vernor Avenue he ordered the driver to turn and try to intercept the runaway, although, as he was to say later, there was really little he could do about it —"What am I gonna do? Jump on it and wrestle it to a halt?"

There was very little traffic on Vernor, a one-way artery westbound. The railroad barrier had automatically descended two blocks west. The driver of the Big 4 stood the Flyer on two wheels and fishtailed past a car waiting for the light, the driver of the car gaping in terror. The runaway train poured through the crossing before they reached it.

Noell yelled and signaled the driver to turn south on a narrow service drive that paralleled the tracks. They ran up alongside engine number 1013 at forty-five miles per hour. There was no one in the cab. Looking down the track, Noell saw that they were rapidly approaching Chrysler's Jefferson Avenue assembly plant, and smack in the middle of the track on which the runaway was rolling there was a long string of auto carriers, loaded with new Chryslers.

"Dispatch, Big Four," Noell shouted into the microphone, "we've got a derailment." He said it before the derailment actually occurred. "Give me every wagon you've got, plus the fire department. This is a code eighty-three!"

The Flyer dropped back as the train thundered across Jefferson Avenue, streaming past the cars patiently waiting at the barrier, and poured into the Chrysler yard.

And then the crashing started. The cars piled into the standing cars and began to jackknife and flip over, many of them crashing into buildings adjacent to the track on Jefferson Avenue. It was a scene that no Hollywood film director would dare to reenact: it would be too expensive. Hundreds of brand-new Chrysler automobiles were dumped out of their containers and junked instantaneously. The smaller boxcars in the yard were crushed and, finally, the impact sent a huge auto carrier arcing through the air, clearing several tracks to sprawl sideways, rolling over dozens of parked cars belonging to employees. There was a great cloud of dust and the air was filled with the clamor of shrieking metal.

The confusion was extreme at first. Dennis Noell was in immediate charge of the scene, at least for the first half-hour, since he was the ranking police officer present. To him belonged a great deal of the credit for the extraordinarily rapid recovery from catastrophe at the scene. He immediately notified dispatch of the existence of a disaster and said that he was initiating S.O.P. No. 1, the departmental disaster plan. He established a disaster headquarters in a building next to the Chrysler train yard. The other detectives from the Big 4 crew went to work directing traffic on Jefferson and Conner until squad cars arrived. Noell ordered the area blocked off, and policemen and firemen began to scramble through the wreckage, looking for bodies, while several ambulances stood by. At first they didn't find much.

A brakeman was found, pinned under the wreckage of a boxcar that had been toppled off its track. He was very lucky. There was a slight depression, formed by the grade of the track itself, and the brakeman had fallen in there, so that the car had merely trapped him instead of crushing him.

Shortly afterwards, five bodies were discovered in a wrecked Lackawanna boxcar. This boxcar had been coupled directly behind the locomotive, and when the collision occurred, the locomotive crashed through the boxcar, telescoping it and reducing it to kindling before the locomotive itself left the tracks and collided with yet another boxcar. The dead men were severely mangled. With some difficulty it was determined that they were, respectively: the engineer, who should have been driving 1013, the fireman and the two brakemen assigned to the train. The fifth man wore a private-security-service uniform, but his pistol was missing from its holster.

By the time Mulheisen arrived on the scene the district inspector, a calm, middle-aged man named "Ike" Weinberg, had taken over the command post from Dennis Noell. Weinberg detailed Mulheisen to question the terminal signalmen in the yard tower to find out how the accident had happened.

The signalmen were puzzled themselves. When

last heard from, 1013 was on the next section up the line, under the control of the Vernor tower. They had tried to contact the Vernor tower, but there was no answer.

"Ten thirteen should have been on break," one of the signalmen told Mulheisen. "Usually they knock off until street traffic dies down a bit. Then they'd come back into this yard and pick up the rest of the car carriers and take them out to the Grand Trunk yards to be broken up for different through freights."

Mulheisen tried to ring Vernor tower, but there was still no answer. "Must of knocked down our phone lines," said one of the signalmen.

"What happens when a runaway comes through a section, normally?" Mulheisen asked.

"Well, the tower would notice it. They'd see it on their display board. See here?" The signalman indicated his own electronic board, where colored lights indicated open tracks and the presence of cars and moving trains could be clearly seen. "All the tower man has to do is hit this button, and as soon as the train passes over this switch an electronic impulse will automatically trip the brakes on the locomotive and stop the train."

"Why didn't they do that in the Vernor section?" Mulheisen asked.

"I don't know," the signalman said.

Mulheisen went back to the district inspector. "I think I'd better go over there," he said, after he'd explained.

Surprisingly, it didn't take more than a few minutes to drive to the Vernor tower. When he arrived he noticed right away that the door to the tower was unlocked and hanging open. He drew his .38 and proceeded slowly up the stairs. The tower wasn't very tall, and long before he reached the control area he knew something serious was wrong. There was blood on the stairs. It dripped slowly down in a substantial stream.

Three men lay on the floor of the control area. All of them were lying face down, side by side, and all had been shot in the back of the head. Their blood had spread to the stairwell and then down the steps, one by one.

Mulheisen immediately called the district inspector. He explained what he'd found, then said, "That runaway was deliberate, Inspector."

Weinberg couldn't make any sense of it. Who would murder a tower crew and set a train on a runaway course with the train crew locked into a boxcar? Weinberg told Mulheisen to take charge of the murder scene and he would dispatch the necessary investigation team, along with the medical examiner, as soon as they could spare somebody.

A few minutes later, the district supervisor learned that a boxcar had been stolen from the Cadillac Gage Company, on Conner Avenue, just a few blocks from the 15th Precinct station house. The company was within the area controlled by the Vernor tower. The boxcar had been loaded with wooden crates containing Stoner rifles, which were manufactured by Cadillac Gage. The company had discovered the theft when one of the regular security men had gone from his front-gate position to the rear gate (where a spur railroad line entered the factory grounds) to find out why the rear-gate guard was not responding to routine calls. He found the guard post abandoned and the gate locked, but the newly loaded boxcar, which had been parked next to the loading dock, was gone.

It was nearly seven o'clock before Mulheisen and two detectives from the 15th found the missing boxcar. It was sitting empty in Gethsemane Cemetery. Company officials said that 2,400 Stoner rifles had been in the boxcar, along with half a million rounds of ammunition. The shipment was bound for a U.S. Marines camp in California, part of an experimental program to replace M-16s in rifle companies.

In short order the scene was invaded by federal agents of the Alcohol, Tobacco and Firearms Bureau, as well as the FBI. The men of the Scientific Bureau were on their third major crime scene of the evening, taking photographs, checking for fingerprints, and even making plaster casts of vehicle tracks in the dirt alongside the empty boxcar.

Frank Zeppanuk, from the Scientific Bureau, told Mulheisen that he had a nice print of the tread on a double-tandem truck. "It's nothing unusual, Mul. Probably ten thousand tires like this in the city, but none of them have quite these characteristics, because of stones they've been driven over, little cuts, gashes, things like that. Trouble is, unless you find the right tire right away, it won't do much good, 'cause continued driving will change the characteristics again."

"It's hopeless, then," Mulheisen said.

"Probably," Zeppanuk agreed, "but at least you know that the guns were almost certainly loaded onto a heavy truck, probably a semi."

Mulheisen thanked him and joined Lt. Del Moser, a detective from the 15th. Mulheisen explained what he'd learned from Zeppanuk and suggested that Moser detail some of his men to question nearby residents about heavy trucks that may have been seen in the cemetery.

Moser, a swarthy man with dark eyebrows and a hooked nose, took a long look around the darkened cemetery. Gethsemane was an old cemetery. The headstones loomed about them, dimly visible in the half-light of the commercial signs on the surrounding buildings and from the lights of traffic on the busy streets. A rear gate led out of the cemetery, onto French Street. French crossed Gratiot within a couple of blocks, and a few blocks later it passed over the Edsel Ford Expressway, with entrances onto the freeway both east and west. A truck leaving the cemetery had good routes for fast egress. It could be halfway to Chicago by now.

Mulheisen suddenly remembered his dinner date with Mandy Cecil. Well, he'd have to call and cancel. He left the scene crawling with officials from half a dozen jurisdictions and drove to a pay telephone booth near the City Airport. There was no answer at Mandy's apartment. He tried the Vanni Trucking Company, but there was no answer there, either. Disappointed and a little anxious, Mulheisen went back to the cemetery.

Moser had mustered several detectives and begun to canvass the neighborhood surrounding the cemetery. To the north there was nothing but the airport. A service road ran along the Detroit Terminal tracks around the perimeter of the airport and the hijackers' truck could have gone that way, but there were no exits into the airport itself, nor were there any good escape routes. Obviously, the best bet was through the neighborhood to the south of Gethsemane.

Mulheisen left the other detectives to canvass and went to call the cemetery corporation, to find out if there had been any funerals there during the day and what employees, if any, had been present. He learned that there had been no funerals that afternoon. As it happened, only a maintenance man had been present, except for possible unknown visitors to the grave sites, and he had gone home promptly at four-thirty, well before the activity had begun near the back gate.

Mulheisen was now at a loss as to how to continue. Moser and his crew were handling the canvass; Homicide was busy at the Vernor tower site and at the Chrysler yard; Robbery was busy at Cadillac Gage; and everywhere there were ATF agents, FBI agents, and God knows who else. Weinberg had informed Mulheisen that there would be a big meeting at police headquarters in the morning and he should be present. By then, it was hoped, everything would have been pretty well sorted out and the various agencies and departments could organize a proper approach to the whole case.

Tired as he was—it was now after eleven—Mulheisen didn't feel like going home. Too much was happening. It would have been unthinkable to head for bed, comparable to leaving a party just when they'd sent out for more beer. That reminded him that he could use a drink. It wasn't far to the Town Pump, he thought. Maybe the whole Vanni entourage would be there.

In fact, there was hardly anyone there. Only a short, dark man sat at the bar, amiably sipping beer and chatting with the bartender. Mulheisen thought the man looked familiar, but he couldn't recall where he might have seen him. The trouble with being a cop, he often told himself, was that after a while everybody looks familiar. It's because cops spend so much of their time just looking at everybody, watching what is going on around them. He took a seat at the opposite end of the bar. Dick said something to the man and made his way toward Mulheisen, wiping the bar as he came.

"Got everything all cleaned up, I see," Mulheisen said.

"Oh, sure," Dick said. "What are you having?"

"Black Jack Ditch," Mulheisen said.

"You too?" Dick looked at the Jack Daniel's bottle. *"Verdammte,"* he snorted. "This stuff is going like ice cream on the Fourth of July." He poured a heavy shot into a glass and splashed a little water over it.

"Well, I spent most of the day down at the police station," Dick said, leaning on the bar. "I been looking at pictures of hoods so long that they all look alike now."

"Did you make an identification?" Mulheisen asked.

"I think so. The fella there, what's his name, Lieutenant Deane, big fella with red hair, he got me some more pictures, more up to date. Boy, them noses! Those bums oughta get into another line a work. I recognized 'em right away. Maio and Panella, the lieutenant says. That's them, all right."

"So, you spend all day looking at mug shots and here you are back at work," Mulheisen said. "Don't you have a relief bartender?"

"I got a cousin, he works mornings," Dick said. "I can't afford a night man. Too expensive. Expensive in two ways, if you know what I mean. I never saw a bartender yet who didn't hit the till on you. And some of them, it's murder!"

He poured Mulheisen another drink. "On the house," he said.

"What about your cousin, the day man?" Mulheisen said.

Dick shrugged elaborately—a very Gallic gesture to Mulheisen's mind, although Mulheisen had never been to France or Belgium. "He's only alone for a few hours in the morning," Dick said. "And, he's family. He won't take too much."

Mulheisen changed the subject. "You haven't seen Vanni or DenBoer tonight, have you? Or the girl?"

"You're the second guy to ask that," Dick said. "I'll tell you what I told him. No."

"Who was asking before?" Mulheisen asked.

"That guy over there," Dick said, looking down the bar. "Now, where'd he go?"

Mulheisen turned. The man who had been sitting at the bar was gone, though neither Mulheisen nor Dick had heard him leave.

"Let's have another," Mulheisen said wearily. He took out a cigar and looked at it thoughtfully before clipping the end.

ELEVEN

Car 9-3 cruised along Conner Avenue before turning east on Jefferson. Jimmy Marshall was driving. Both he and Ray Stanos peered down the avenue to where all the action was still going on at the derailment scene.

"Damn," Stanos complained. "All hell breaking loose all over the goddamn precinct and we have to pull this crappy patrol."

The car radio crackled constantly with commands for various units to go to and from the sites of the wreck, Vernor tower or the Cadillac Gage Company. Out of that incessant chatter a different call rang out.

"Nine-three, dispatch."

Stanos grabbed the microphone eagerly. "Dispatch, nine-three."

"Go to Collins Street, that's a thirty-five-eleven."
Stanos didn't have to look that one up—3511 was

breaking and entering, in progress. "That's 3667 Collins, between Mack and Charlevoix. See the lady. Name is Fox."

"Nine-three, on the way," Stanos said. Then to Marshall: "I don't believe it. That's the same address!"

Marshall nodded. They were clipping along Jefferson very rapidly now, with the blue lights flashing. Stanos had already struggled into a flak jacket and had one ready at hand for Marshall. As soon as they approached Collins, Marshall cut the lights and they cruised silently to a parking place well back from the Fox address. Marshall radioed a 10-97 and he and Stanos approached the house with Marshall still snapping up the flak vest. Mrs. Fox was again on the porch. She was surprised to find that it was the same two young patrolmen who had answered her call a few nights earlier. She motioned both men into her living room. As usual, she was dressed in a bathrobe and slippers.

"I know you won't believe it," she said, "but I saw someone sneak into Mr. Vanni's house." While watching the Johnny Carson show on television she had gotten up during a commercial break to get herself a drink of water. As usual, she hadn't turned on the kitchen lights, relying on the little bit of light that came from the living room. She got her glass of water, and while drinking it she saw a man come to the rear door of the Vanni home. The man stood and fiddled with the lock for a moment, then the door opened and he went inside. She thought it was rather strange, since the man obviously wasn't Mr. Vanni and, besides, he hadn't turned on any lights.

"Why couldn't it have been Vanni?" Marshall asked.

"Mr. Vanni hasn't come home yet this evening," Mrs. Fox said, with the assurance of a woman who knows when her neighbors are home. "Besides, Mr. Vanni is tall and this man was short. And you can see that there still aren't any lights on in the house." She pointed out the window.

Marshall and Stanos drew aside to confer. They agreed that there was probable cause to believe that a crime was in progress and it would be proper to enter the house, but under the circumstances it might be as well to simply wait for the intruder to leave and arrest him then. They felt that a house is a far more complicated situation, somehow, than a garage. Marshall thought that given what had happened just a couple of days earlier, they ought to call in to the precinct; possibly the duty officer would be able to advise them. In the meantime, of course, they could watch the house.

They moved Mrs. Fox out of the kitchen, and Stanos went back to the car to get a shotgun while Jimmy kept watch from the window. It was reasonable to assume that the intruder would leave by the same door he'd entered. When Stanos returned, Jimmy suggested that Stanos station himself by Vanni's back door while Jimmy called in.

The duty officer, when he heard the news, promptly referred the decision to Mulheisen, who had just strolled in. Mulheisen listened to Marshall and concurred on the action taken. "You watch the front of the house," he told him, "and I'll be right over."

It took Mulheisen five minutes to drive to Collins Street, and another three to find a parking place. He walked casually up the street toward the house, hands in his raincoat pockets. In his right hand was the .38 Chief's Special.

The house was completely dark and there was no sign of movement. He scanned it carefully without breaking stride and walked on by, even though he had noticed Marshall crouching in the shadow of some shrubs near the porch steps. Once out of line of sight of the house, he turned and came back, using Mrs. Fox's house as cover until he was close to Marshall.

"Nothing doing?" he whispered to Marshall.

Marshall shook his head.

"Stanos still out back?" Mulheisen asked. At Marshall's nod he said, "I'm going back there. After I talk to Stanos I'll signal you, so watch for me. Stanos and I will go in. After I signal, you wait until the lights go on in that back room—I'd guess it's a kitchen. Then you go onto the porch here and wait by the door—not in front of it. Understand? We'll work through the house, turning on lights as we go. When we get to the living room, if nothing is happening, I'll let you in and we can make a systematic search upstairs and down."

A few seconds later Mulheisen explained the same procedure to Stanos. "One thing that bothers me," he said, "is that the door wasn't forced. Whoever went in either had a key or knew a lot about locks. Does this Fox woman seem reliable to you?"

"She was right before," Stanos said.

"Unh-hunh," Mulheisen grunted. After a moment he said "Here we go." He stepped to the side of the house and waved to Marshall, then he and Stanos went up the little back steps and tried the door. It was locked.

"What the hell?" Mulheisen was surprised. He looked at Stanos. "You ever heard of a B and E man who locked the door behind him? Neither have I. This changes things. You stay here."

Mulheisen went to the front of the house and stepped onto the porch. "Back door's locked," he said to the surprised Marshall. He tried the front door. The storm door was unlocked, but the main door wasn't. Mulheisen hadn't expected it to be. Since the storm door only locked with a hook, it suggested that someone had gone out that way. He presumed that Vanni normally left the house by the back, to get to his car in the garage.

"Well, do we break in or not?" he said to nobody. Suddenly he heard voices at the back. "Stay here," he said to Marshall and ran back alongside the house, .38 in hand.

Jerry Vanni stood on the path from his garage, hands in the air, looking frightened at Stanos's shotgun. When he saw Mulheisen he lowered his hands and his face darkened. "What the hell is going on here?" he demanded.

Mulheisen sighed and waved Stanos off. "We have a report of an intruder here," he explained. He filled Vanni in quickly, then suggested they use his house key to enter and check the house. If he liked, Vanni could wait outside.

"I've got a better idea," Vanni said. "You wait outside and I'll go in and look things over. If there's anything wrong, I'll invite you in."

"What if the burglar's still in there?" Mulheisen asked. "He might shoot."

"From what you say, it doesn't sound to me like there's any burglar inside," Vanni said, "and from all the noise we're making, I'm sure he knows I'm coming."

"All right," Mulheisen compromised, "why don't you and I go in together. Okay? The fellows can wait outside."

As Vanni had said, there was no one inside. They went through the entire house turning on lights, even checking the attic. When they were back downstairs in the living room, Vanni said, "All clear, Sergeant. Now if you'll excuse me, I'm kind of tired."

"I've got some questions," Mulheisen said. He pulled out a cigar and clipped it. "Mind?"

"The cigar? No. The questions, I'm not so sure. All right, go ahead."

"I've been looking for your partner, Miss Cecil. Any idea where I can reach her?"

"You might try calling her at home," Vanni said. "I haven't seen her, if that's what you mean. Why?"

"I've been looking for you and your partners, actually, but none of you were home," Mulheisen said. "I wanted to go over some information about the shooting in the alley and the shooting at the bar. You didn't see DenBoer this evening, did you?"

"No. He took off from work about the same time as Mandy. As for me, I had a date. Satisfied?"

Mulheisen was suddenly too damn tired to fuss with the case anymore. "I'll wait until tomorrow," he said, "when your partners are available."

He stalked out and collected his subordinates. He was feeling very irritated with Mandy Cecil at the moment. His irritation was aggravated, he knew, by a vague sense of guilt for not getting in touch with her.

He supposed she thought that he had stood her up, but then, where the hell was she? Why hadn't she been home?

He stopped to interview Mrs. Fox. She could provide little information, except that the person who had entered Vanni's house was a short man who moved with great assurance. She was sorry if she'd caused a fuss. Mulheisen assured her that she had been a good citizen. He also satisfied himself that she was not just a hysteric who was imagining men sneaking into houses. Evidently, someone had broken into Vanni's house, but whoever it was had been very careful and hadn't wasted any time. No doubt he had left the house before Marshall could cover the front door. Mulheisen wondered who it had been and what he'd wanted. He had an uneasy feeling about it. Someone was poking around in things that perhaps they hadn't any right to poke around in.

And with that, he went home to bed. It was after two in the morning before he crawled between the wrinkled sheets of the bed he had not made that morning and he slumped down with grateful relief. He was just about to lose consciousness when he sat up, muttering to himself. Reluctantly he got up and put on his robe. He picked up the telephone and dialed Mandy Cecil's number, one more time.

A man's voice answered. "Hello," said the voice crisply.

Mulheisen was surprised. "Uh, is Miss Cecil there?" he asked.

"Miss Cecil isn't home at the moment," the voice replied. "Who is calling, please?"

For a moment Mulheisen did not reply. He was impressed with the style of the person answering

Mandy Cecil's telephone at two o'clock in the morning.

"Hello?" the voice said. "Are you there? Can I help you?"

Mulheisen started to hang up, then he considered the situation. "Are you a friend of Miss Cecil's?" he asked.

"Yes, I am," the voice said. "Mandy isn't home just yet, but she asked me to take any messages. Can I say who is calling?" The voice was deep and smoothly insistent.

"Just a friend," Mulheisen said, and hung up. He sat there staring blankly at his toes for a moment. Then, with a groan he heaved himself to his feet and began to dress.

It was a fifteen-minute drive to Mandy Cecil's address in St. Clair Shores, a city downriver from Mulheisen's home. He drove down her street slowly, noticing the nondescript Chevrolet parked in front of the small apartment building where she lived. There was a man sitting at the wheel of the car. He glanced at Mulheisen as he drove past, but didn't seem too concerned or interested. Pretty bold, Mulheisen thought.

The street ended a half block farther on, at the chained entrance to a marina. Beyond the chain a hundred or more boats bobbed in restless water, agitated by a steady breeze off the lake. Mulheisen found a parking place and got out. He walked to the nearest alley and disappeared into its darkness. He found the apartment building without trouble, but now the problem was how to get in without being seen by the sentinel out front? He wondered idly when was the last time he'd had such a long and busy day. What would Dennis the Menace do in a situation like this? Kick the damn door down and go in with guns blazing.

He decided there was no easy way to do it. So he might as well do it the hard way. He walked around to the front of the building, unholstered the .38 and approached the parked Chevrolet. He bent down and rapped on the window with the .38. The driver looked around and his jaw fell open. Mulheisen opened the car door and slipped in. He grinned, showing all of his teeth, and fished out his credentials, which he flopped open for the driver to see, along with the .38, which the driver had already seen and continued to keep well within his periphery of vision.

"What does it say?" Mulheisen asked the man.

"It says 'Detroit Police Department, Sergeant of Detectives,' " the man read. He was young and tall with a short haircut. If he had been scared at first he no longer showed it. Mulheisen leaned over and patted the man's chest, then removed a .38 revolver from a shoulder holster. He slipped it into his own raincoat pocket.

"I'm going to get out of the car now, and so are you," Mulheisen told the man. "And we're going into this building. Let's not do anything silly, eh?"

"Sure," the man said calmly. He got out and closed the door carefully, then walked around the front of the car and preceded Mulheisen to the lobby of the apartment building. Inside, Mulheisen made him lean against the wall on his palms and spread his legs, then worked him over carefully. Apparently the man had carried only the one gun. Mulheisen took out the man's wallet and flipped it open. He read the identification card and gave a soft groan.

"Okay, Agent Deegan," he said, "you can rest easy." He handed the man his wallet and his pistol. He shrugged. "Sometimes it has to happen this way," he said. "Sorry."

Deegan looked indifferent.

"Who's upstairs?" Mulheisen asked. "Your boss?"

"That's right," Deegan said. "Agent-in-charge Phelps."

"I guess I'd better go up and see him," Mulheisen said.

"I'll wait in the car," Deegan said, and turned to leave.

"Any special signal?" Mulheisen asked.

"Just two quick jabs on the button," Deegan said, and left.

Mulheisen turned to the board on the wall of the lobby that listed the names of the occupants with a buzzer next to each one. Mandy Cecil was number 401. He gave the buzzer two quick jabs. Almost immediately the entrance door buzzed and Mulheisen pushed through. The elevator was right there and empty, so Mulheisen got in and pressed the button for the fourth floor. Now it's their turn, Mulheisen told himself. He walked out on the fourth floor with his hands up. Sure enough, a man was there with a gun in his hand.

"I knew that Deegan would lie to me about the signal," Mulheisen said with a sigh. "Agent Phelps? My name is Mulheisen, Detroit Police."

Phelps was another tall one, and slender too, like a movie star, with close-cropped silver-gray hair. He had a hard face but it was a handsome one. He held out his left hand and gestured with the long fingers. Mulheisen took his meaning and dropped his identification folder into the hand. Phelps looked it over carefully, then lowered the .38, tossing the folder back. "Agent-in-charge Phelps," he said in his deep voice. "Alcohol, Tobacco and Firearms."

Mulheisen nodded and got out a cigar. He followed Phelps into Cecil's apartment. He looked around. It was an ordinary modern apartment, no doubt overpriced, with a living room, a tiny kitchenette with breakfast area, and a single bedroom. He gathered from the darkness beyond the picture window that Mandy had a good view of Lake St. Clair.

"You were the guy who called a little while ago," Phelps said.

"That's right." Mulheisen looked at him. "I saw you earlier this evening, down at Cadillac Gage."

"You were there?" Phelps said. "I didn't notice."

"My precinct," Mulheisen pointed out. "At least, the derailment area is, and the Vernor tower. Cadillac Gage and the cemetery are in Connors Precinct."

"That's nice," Phelps said. "What's your interest in Cecil?"

"Unrelated, Phelps. Has to do with another case, also in my precinct." Mulheisen had his cigar going by now. "She was supposed to meet me at eight o'clock this evening, but she didn't answer her phone. Actually, I was trying to break the date. But then I got kind of concerned. Especially when a man answered her telephone at two-thirty in the morning and wouldn't let me talk to her. I take it she isn't here?"

"No, she's not here," Phelps said. Without saying so, his eyes made it clear that he wished that

Mulheisen weren't there, either. "How much do you know about this Mandy Cecil?"

"This Mandy Cecil?" Mulheisen said. "Not much. She works for a trucking company and her boss is in a little trouble with the mob right now. I think she might have some information for me about the boss. No big deal, yet. Why is ATF interested in this Mandy Cecil?"

Phelps leaned back in the overstuffed easy chair, stretching his long legs out before him. He had the irritating mannerism of fixing one with his piercing gray eyes. Mulheisen didn't like that game; he studied his cigar. After a long moment Phelps said, "I suppose you'll be in on District Inspector Weinberg's big briefing this morning?"

"I've been asked to attend," Mulheisen said.

"No harm in telling you, then," Phelps said. "Mandy Cecil is an ATF agent."

"She what!"

Phelps smiled, obviously pleased by Mulheisen's surprise.

"Oh, yes," he said. "We've had her on Vanni for about three or four months. She didn't tip herself to you? Good."

"But, why in hell . . . if the ATF is after Vanni, why didn't you come to us, let us in on it? What's the point of all this goddamn secrecy?" Mulheisen was irritated.

"It's our experience that the police are not good at keeping secrets, Sergeant. No offense, I hope."

"Oh, no offense. Why were you after Vanni?"

"Right to the point, eh?" Phelps said. "Well, I guess there's no harm telling you now, since you know so much already. The answer is guns."

"Guns," Mulheisen repeated.

"That's right. Several months ago a hundred M-16s disappeared from Selfridge Air Force Base. We think we know who the actual thief is, an air police sergeant. But we couldn't figure out how the hell he got the guns off the base. Their absence was noticed right away and the barracks were searched, as were all cars leaving the base. It's pretty hard to hide a hundred rifles, but they seemed to just vanish. Then we discovered that a couple of dump trucks had been seen in the vicinity of the base armory. They were hauling sand for a runway construction job. The two trucks were driven by Jerry Vanni and his partner, Leonard DenBoer. Next thing we find out is that this air policeman is a native Detroiter. He lives off base and he sometimes plays pool with a bunch of guys at a blind pig. One of the guys he plays pool with is Jerry Vanni."

"I'm beginning to get a picture," Mulheisen said.

"Right. So we still don't have anything on anybody. So we look around for an underground agent, preferably one with a Detroit background. Bingo! Turns out we've got a woman in San Francisco who was from Detroit, and better yet, she actually knows the target, Vanni. It was a heaven-sent opportunity. Cecil's been on it ever since."

"Only, lately she's disappeared," Mulheisen said.

"Yeah. Now she's disappeared and we still don't have anything on Jerry Vanni. We were thinking of pulling her off pretty soon, if something didn't happen. Maybe something's happened."

"You figure it has anything to do with this Cadillac Gage operation?" Mulheisen asked.

"Vanni? No. This sort of operation is far beyond

him," Phelps said, waving his hand dismissively. "No, we were thinking of a group of Cubans that I believe you met the other night with Miss Cecil."

"You know about that?"

"I know a lot that you don't, Mulheisen," Phelps said. "She mentioned it the last time she called in."

"Where was she supposed to be tonight?"

"Don't know," Phelps said. "I assume she was meeting with the Cubans again. At this juncture, since she hasn't returned, I'm prepared to go on the assumption that the Cubans have learned of her ATF affiliation and have acted accordingly."

Mulheisen didn't like the sound of that. "What have you got on the Cubans?" he asked.

"We've got a full file on the three major figures: Angel DeJesus, Francisco Morazon and the Bolivian, Heitor Casabianco. We've got identifications and some information on the others, but they're not so important."

Mulheisen thought back to the smoky poker room at Brandywine's. The bright-shirted Cubans sitting around the table with beers in hand, cigarillos dangling from mustached lips, their hair combed elaborately, and talking cheerfully of revolution. They looked like movie Mexicans. Surely murder and hijacking were not games for romantic poseurs.

"I know what you're thinking"—Phelps' deep voice cut in—"but they're a serious group of men. And they have the skills. Morazon was a railroad engineer, you know. Do you know how he escaped?"

"Something about rowing a dinghy to Florida," Mulheisen said.

"Oh, that. Well, the point is, Castro brought in a bunch of Russian railroad technicians to help the

Cubans. The Russians were all diesel men, they'd never worked on steam engines before. Morazon took them on a little tour, then when he'd got up a good head of steam he came roaring back into the roundhouse at full speed—only, he bailed out. The Russians were all killed and the roundhouse was nearly destroyed, along with many of Cuba's remaining steam engines. Sound familiar?"

"Vaguely," Mulheisen said. "I'm surprised the CIA didn't give him a medal."

"The Russians just replaced all the steamers with diesel," Phelps said. "It didn't help the cause that much. Anyway, Morazon's a devout Marxist. He wasn't against communism, just Castro and his Russians."

"Sounds like a brave man," Mulheisen said.

"He's a bold man, and a desperate one. He and DeJesus are fully capable of pulling off this thing, with a little help. Hell, when DeJesus left Havana with his MIG, he buzzed Castro's office!" Phelps laughed. "We like to think of them as harmless, ignorant peons, but they've got skills, guts and desire. And unless I'm dead wrong, they also have about a million dollars' worth of Stoner rifles and ammo. Enough for a small army."

"And they may have Mandy as well," Mulheisen said softly.

"Could be," Phelps agreed. "Though I reckon they've dumped her by now, if they're on to her."

Mulheisen thought he'd never heard such a cold-blooded statement in his life.

"Of course, there's an alternative," Phelps added. "She could have turned. It's happened before, though usually in drugs, where there's a lot of ready cash involved. Sometimes, though, the agent starts to identify with his or her quarry. They get too close to them."

"Who is Mandy close to here?" Mulheisen asked. "The Cubans? Or Vanni?"

"Not Vanni," Phelps said. "Vanni's just a two-bit hustler, as far as I can tell. But the Cubans have a Cause. That's what makes them interesting. Impassioned men with a Cause." Phelps said it with consummate cynicism.

"And Vanni doesn't come into it?" Mulheisen said.

"Not as far as I know," Phelps said. "Oh, Cecil met the Cubans through him. They met at a blind pig. She didn't take them seriously—not seriously enough. She worked on the premise that the Cubans were trying to buy some guns, maybe some of those M-16s, from Vanni. But so far, she hadn't turned up anything definite along those lines.

"One of the Cubans, however, took a shine to her. DeJesus. He thinks he's God's gift to women, according to Cecil. She strung him along at our suggestion, hoping to penetrate their group. Sort of a spin-off from the Vanni investigation. It sometimes works that way."

"I take it that these revolutionaries have vamoosed," Mulheisen said.

Phelps nodded. "I admit I didn't connect them with the hijack at first, but as soon as it began to look like Cecil was missing I had every one of them checked out. Result: there isn't a one of them available in Detroit and all their friends and relatives are saying nothing. If that doesn't confirm that they're involved, I don't know what does."

Mulheisen agreed. "So you don't have any leads right now?" he asked.

"I wouldn't say that," Phelps insisted, sounding defensive. "Thanks to Cecil we've got a good list of everybody involved and we've got a substantial list of places that have to be checked. We'll get them, don't you worry. They may have pulled this just as slick as greased glass, but there's too many of them. No discipline in the world can hold that big a gang together."

"A pretty ruthless bunch, if it was them," Mulheisen said. "I went to Vernor tower. There wasn't any reason to gun those men down."

"Yeah, same with the poor bastards in the boxcar," Phelps said. "Well, the *Free Press* has already received a statement—bogus, I believe—from a left-wing group calling itself the 'Black American Red Army,' and claiming credit for the raid."

" 'The Black American Red Army'! That's pretty absurd, isn't it?"

"A dozen of them spring up every day. You have to take them seriously, no matter how childish they sound. The Symbionese Liberation Army sounded pretty childish until they got hold of some automatic rifles. That's what I don't like about this. All those guns floating around." Phelps shook his head. "In this case, however, we think the Cubans faked this claim to put us off the scent until they can get the guns out of the country. In a way, I wouldn't mind letting them take them. It's better than having them on the street. All I'm hoping is that they didn't tumble to Cecil's cover and put her out of circulation."

Mulheisen felt very gloomy. He was tired, exhausted even. He didn't like to think about Mandy Cecil lying in a ditch somewhere with a bullet in her head. But the longer she stayed gone, the worse it looked for her.

"What are you going to do about Vanni?" he asked Phelps.

"Nothing. What can we do? We don't have a case against him, as far as I know. And if we don't get Cecil back we sure as hell won't have any case. We're pretty sure he was involved with that air police sergeant, but we have nothing concrete on him. Naturally, we wanted to know his movements tonight, and that's originally why I tried to contact Cecil, thinking she'd know that, at least."

Mulheisen told him about the B & E at Vanni's. "He said he had a date and I had no reason to question him," Mulheisen concluded, "but I'll get on him again, tomorrow—or today."

"It sounds like he's in some kind of jam with the mob," Phelps said finally. "We don't know what it is, and neither did Cecil. The burglar was probably one of theirs. Kind of odd, though, coming just at this time."

Mulheisen had to agree with that. He asked Phelps about DenBoer.

Phelps scratched his chin thoughtfully. "We're not sure how much Vanni confided in DenBoer." Mulheisen noticed that Phelps had a habit of saying "we" when he was uncertain, but "I" when he was on firmer ground.

"We think DenBoer is just a spear carrier for Vanni," Phelps went on. "He's obviously deeply involved in whatever Vanni is up to, but we're not even certain what that is."

Mulheisen said he would check out DenBoer as soon as he could get to it, this morning. "I've been wanting to talk to him, anyway, about these other matters," he said, "but he never seems to be around. What time have you got?"

Phelps looked at his watch. It was after four. "I think I'll make some coffee," he said, "and settle down here to wait for Cecil. Not much point in sleeping. Inspector Weinberg has his big show scheduled for nine. Maybe there's a good movie on the Late Show."

Mulheisen said he'd stay for a cup of coffee. He told Phelps that he figured he'd go over to Vanni's office first thing. "They probably open pretty early," he said. "I'll talk to Vanni and DenBoer."

Phelps thought that was a good idea. He made it clear to Mulheisen, however, that this was an ATF operation now, and anything Mulheisen found out must be relayed to ATF immediately. Mulheisen didn't complain. He was still trying to deal with the image of a beautiful redhead lying in a ditch.

TWELVE

By 6 A.M., Phelps was making another pot of coffee and Channel 50 was showing *Jubal*, the fifth in its Glenn Ford Festival of Films. Mulheisen couldn't take it anymore, and left. He drove over to Gratiot and Eight Mile and found an all-night restaurant sandwiched between a paint store and a jewelry store. The café had a long counter and a tall, loosely filled blimp of a cook in white shirt and pants with a paper hat on his head. The scene reminded Mulheisen vaguely of Hopper's famous painting, "Nighthawks."

He ordered ham and eggs and read the morning *Free Press*, while construction workers and truck drivers piled in and out of the little café. Nearly every customer excitedly discussed the Cadillac Gage caper. Their attitudes ranged from frank admiration for the way it had been executed to anxiety about the potential increase of guns on the street.

"Man, it don't bother me," one burly fellow in a

watch cap declared. "They come around to my house, I'll blow the bastards away."

"He will, too," said the man's smaller companion. "Frank's got more guns . . . whatta you got, Frank? About a dozen?"

"I got the 30-06," Frank said, ticking items off on his thick fingers, "I got the .270, I got the little popgun for the old lady—that's a .32 automatic—I got the Hi-Standard .22 'Sharpshooter,' I got the .357 magnum Ruger, I got. . . ."

Mulheisen couldn't stand any more. He called for another coffee and moved to a booth. But in the next booth another customer was saying, "I never even heard of a Stoner rifle. I wish I had one. It sounds like a great little gun."

The man's companion exclaimed, "What the hell you want with a machine gun, for Christ's sake? They're illegal."

"Well, if the niggers got 'em, I don't see why . . ."

"What the hell you talking about? What niggers?"

"It says right here," the man told his companion, "the 'Black American Red Army' took the rifles and killed all those guys. That's niggers, ain't it?"

There was a silence from the booth, then the companion said wearily, "Howard, you're dumb." Nothing else was said. A little later a wiry man with red hair left the booth with another, stocky man in a leather jacket. Mulheisen couldn't decide which one was Howard.

It was daylight now. He decided to check on Vanni. He drove down Eight Mile Road to a spot about a block from the trucking company. The gates

of the high cyclone fence were open and the last of
the dump trucks were rolling ponderously out, trail-
ers bumping emptily behind them. In the yard near
the office a man was operating a front loader. He was
collecting dirt from a pile next to the excavation for
the new building and dumping it into a truck and
trailer that stood by.

Mulheisen drove into the yard and parked next
to Vanni's shiny new Oldsmobile. He was about to go
into the little wooden shack when he realized that the
man operating the front loader was Vanni. Mulheisen
stopped and watched. The dirt was piled quite high in
the truck and trailer now. Vanni backed off in the
front loader and lowered the bucket to the ground,
then cut the engine. He jumped down and noticed
Mulheisen for the first time.

"Hi," he called. He was wearing slacks and a
dress shirt, with an old poplin jacket. He looked very
boyish and handsome, like a photo magazine's idea
of an aggressive young executive.

"Like to keep my hand in," he said to Mulheisen. He seemed in good spirits. "C'mon inside, I got
the coffee pot going."

"Looks like you're overloaded," Mulheisen said,
indicating the dirt heaped over the top of the truck
and trailer.

Vanni looked back. "Maybe. But I know a place
to dump where I don't have to pass over any scales to
get there."

They went inside. The coffee was hot but weak.
"Sorry about that," Vanni said. "That's usually
Mandy's job."

"Where is Mandy?" Mulheisen asked.

"Got me," Vanni said. He flopped down behind

his desk and put his feet up. "She's probably still in bed." He glanced at his watch. It was only seven-thirty. "She never gets here before eight-thirty, nine. Why should she? Nothing starts happening until then."

"Why are you here so early?" Mulheisen asked.

"They start these construction jobs early," Vanni said. "I get the boys on the road."

"Where's DenBoer? Doesn't he come in early?"

Vanni frowned. "Yeah, he's usually here. I don't know where the hell he is. Well, what can I do for you, Sergeant?"

"Did Cecil give any indication of where she was going when she left work yesterday?" Mulheisen asked.

"No," Vanni said. "She left about the same time as Leonard. About four-thirty. Why?"

Mulheisen ignored the question. "How about DenBoer? Where was he off to?"

"That I know," Vanni said. "He was taking one of the trucks down to a garage, to have the differentials checked."

"And you haven't seen or heard from him since?" Mulheisen asked.

"That's right," Vanni said. "Why should I? I'm not his keeper. What is this? Is Lenny missing?"

"I don't know," Mulheisen said. "But I'd like to see him as soon as possible. I've got to get going now, but I'll be back at the precinct by noon, I think. How about if you and DenBoer drop by this afternoon and chat? And bring Mandy, too, if she shows."

"I guess you're pretty busy with this Cadillac Gage thing, eh?" Vanni said. "I read about it in the paper. Pretty far out! What'd they get, a thousand guns or something like that?"

Mulheisen watched Vanni closely but could detect no special interest. "It was a pretty slick operation," he said.

"I'll say. Like a goddamn commando strike! You have any idea yet who did it?"

"Not so far," Mulheisen said. "Well, I'll see you this afternoon, then?"

"Okay, Mulheisen. But let this be the last of it, all right? I'm a businessman. I've got work to do."

Mulheisen stood up and set his coffee cup down on Vanni's desk. "It's not my garage that's broken into, Vanni. It's not my jukebox that's shot up. You come and see me."

He left without waiting for a reply.

"We feel that we now know all the significant aspects of yesterday's events in Precincts Nine and Fifteen," said Ike Weinberg, the district inspector. He was speaking to some seventy men who had gathered in a conference room at police headquarters. These men represented nearly every bureau of the police department, plus representatives from the health department, the medical examiner's office and public utilities. The mayor was present, and, of course, the police commissioner. Mulheisen was there, too, nearly asleep in a theater-type seat next to McClain of Homicide and Deane of Racket Conspiracy. Phelps sat up front on the little stage, next to some display boards that were covered with organizational charts and a blowup of the area served by the Detroit Terminal Railway.

Before the meeting started, the mayor had

stopped to shake hands with Mulheisen and had in-
quired about his mother. Inspector Buchanan, standing nearby, had watched this exchange with interest.
The mayor did not speak to Buchanan.

Weinberg continued: "At first we did not connect the derailment with the Cadillac Gage hijacking,
but with the killing of the signalmen and the security
officer at Vernor tower, we began to understand that
all three events were part of a coordinated plan. Here
is how we reconstruct the sequence of events." Weinberg turned to the display boards. "Apparently, at
about 1645, yesterday, the crew of train 1013 prepared to take a break. They were then located right
here." He pointed with a sort of conductor's baton to
a section of track near Vernor tower. "The crew included Engineer T. Hanson, Fireman L. Ruybal, and
two brakemen, K. Briggs and K. Bangert. The very
moment they left the train, which, besides the locomotive, included two empty boxcars and a dozen
loaded auto-carrier cars, Hanson and his crew were
intercepted by gunmen who forced them into the
empty boxcar located just behind the locomotive.

"At about 1700, the hijackers took possession of
train 1013," Weinberg went on. "This was precisely
coordinated with an attack on Vernor tower by another group of gunmen. Obviously, the attackers
knew that the railway security officer, an eighteen-
year veteran named Raymond Carver, was due at the
tower at 1700. When he unlocked the tower door, the
attackers appeared and took him at gunpoint up to
the control deck, where he and the two signalmen, M.
Crawford and C. Kinder, were shot and killed. The
gunmen then operated the electronic switch system,

clearing the track for 1013 to proceed on track number three. All other tracks were closed.

"At 1705, train 1013 was under way and at 1712, it arrived at the locked rear gate of Cadillac Gage. This required entering a small spur off track number three. The switch is a manual one. The gatekeeper at Cadillac Gage, a long-time employee of Silver Security, named John Keester—"

"Ike," interrupted the police commissioner, "do we have to keep hearing these names?"

"No, no," the mayor said, "I want to hear them, John. These were brave men who died in the line of duty and I think the City of Detroit owes them a debt of gratitude and condolences to their loved ones."

"Well, this is what I'm going to release to the press, sir," Weinberg said to the commissioner, "and, naturally, they want all the names. As it is, I'm leaving out the ages of the victims. I didn't think you'd want that."

"Very well," the commissioner said, "go ahead."

"Now, where was I?" Weinberg looked at his papers. "Oh, yes . . . the gatekeeper—Keester—was presented with a bill of lading, possibly, or else he was threatened with a weapon. At any rate, he opened the gate. There is no evidence of a struggle, nor did he make any attempt to signal for help."

"Is there any chance that this Keester was collaborating with the hijackers?" the commissioner asked.

"Well, since he was murdered by the hijackers, it doesn't look likely," Weinberg said, "but, of course, sir, that is a possibility we did not ignore. But Keester seems to have been a very stable, circumspect employee of Silver Security. He'd been with them for twelve years. He was happily married and had seven children—"

"Possibly he needed money," the commissioner said, "with seven kids."

There was dutiful laughter throughout the conference room. The commissioner smiled complacently. Even the mayor smiled.

"Possibly," Weinberg said, "but he worked another job as well. He was a night guard at a liquor store on Dexter Boulevard. So we think he was able to support his large family, all right. Shall I go on?"

The commissioner nodded and Weinberg continued. Mulheisen drowsed. It was warm and close in the conference room, and the heat had caused him to dream about summer. He dreamed that he was repainting the hull of his catboat, a gaff-rigged nineteen-footer. The sun was warm, but occasionally a cool whiff from the river would chill him. He woke up, feeling gritty-eyed and foul-mouthed. There was a bead of sweat under his chin. He groaned softly. McClain looked at him and grunted, apparently in commiseration. "You look like ten pounds of shit in a five-pound bag," McClain whispered. Mulheisen nodded weakly.

"Once the guard was safely stowed in the boxcar, along with the train crew, another man in uniform took Keester's place in the guard shack, at least for a few minutes while the train entered the Cadillac Gage rear yard and coupled onto a loaded boxcar that was sitting next to the loading dock. In this boxcar there were twenty-four hundred Stoner rifles, of the type designated the Stoner 63 Weapons System, along with five hundred thousand rounds of ammunition for the weapons." He went on to explain just what the Stoner 63 Weapons System was, and estimated the value of the shipment in excess of $2.5 million. During this portion of the briefing, ATF Agent Phelps stood and pointed out salient aspects of the Stoner 63 on a large chart illustrating the weapon in a cutaway drawing.

Weinberg now described how the boxcar had been moved to Gethsemane Cemetery, next to the City Airport, and unloaded into at least one truck, probably a semi-tractor trailer. As yet, no witnesses had come forward to describe the truck, and it was uncertain how the hijackers had dispersed from that point, unless it was in the phantom truck itself.

"The boxcar was uncoupled and left in the cemetery," Weinberg said, "and train 1013 was put into reverse, the throttle locked into a 'full' position, and the train abandoned by the hijackers. We presume that the hijackers who operated the train escaped with the rest in the semi. We also believe that the act of sending the unattended train back down the tracks at high speed, with the tragic result of the derailment that killed five men, was a vicious, callous, premeditated act of murder for the casual purpose of diverting police attention from the robbery.

"Ordinarily a runaway train can be stopped by automatic braking devices. In this case, however, since the hijackers were still in control of Vernor tower, the train was not stopped. The train hit the Chrysler loading yards at full speed, with the tragic results that we all know. All of the men in the boxcar were killed outright. It was, as I am sure you all appreciate, a particularly brutal and callous act on the part of the hijackers."

At a signal, Phelps rose and addressed the audience. "I have established to my satisfaction the identity of the hijackers," he said. Everyone sat up, except Mulheisen.

"A few months ago an undercover Alcohol, Tobacco and Firearms agent established contact with a group of Cuban displaced persons, all young men who had lived here in Detroit for some time. These men were part of a South American–organized conspiracy to invade and overthrow the Castro regime in Cuba. They were attempting to purchase guns here in the United States. The agent was to be part of the undercover gun deal, but the agent was never taken fully into the confidence of the conspirators. As of yesterday, the agent has disappeared, and so have the Cubans. For obvious reasons, I don't believe that it would be politic to disclose the name of the agent at this time."

"That's the understatement of the week," McClain muttered to Mulheisen. A chill spread over Mulheisen as he realized that what McClain said was true: just the bare statement by Phelps had seriously endangered Mandy Cecil's life. Whom else could the conspirators suspect, when they came to read Phelps's statement in the newspapers? Mulheisen shook his head in disbelief.

"I have issued an all-points bulletin for the arrest of twelve men whom we have identified from our agent's reports."

Phelps then read a list of names, including DeJesus, Morazon and Casabianco. "We have prepared a brief bio on each man and it will be appended to the handouts you will receive after this briefing."

"Pretty slick, eh?" McClain whispered. "These Feds like to do it up brown."

Weinberg was back on his feet. "That's about it," he said. "As of now, there is no civil emergency. Conditions have been returned to normal, and we feel fortunate that there was not more damage or loss of life from the derailment.

"Homicide is in charge of the murders, with assistance from ATF, the FBI, and some precinct detectives. ATF has taken command of the hijacking itself. What you have heard this morning is basically the information that will be released to the media"—he glanced at his watch—"in a few minutes. If any of you feel that you need more information, please contact the proper bureau or agency, or myself. Thank you."

There was a moment when Mulheisen thought that applause would break out in the audience, but it passed.

Phelps appeared at Mulheisen's side. Mulheisen didn't quibble: "You sure blew Mandy's cover, didn't you?"

Phelps didn't react. "If her cover isn't blown by now, it means she isn't with the hijackers. Did you see Vanni?"

"I stopped by his office," Mulheisen said, lighting a cigar. "Cecil wasn't there, neither was DenBoer. It was kind of early, though. Vanni was irritated, but not alarmed. He didn't see either of them after they left the office yesterday afternoon, he says. I asked him to come in to the precinct this afternoon, with Cecil and DenBoer."

"Well, I'll leave Vanni and DenBoer to you," Phelps said. "We're pretty busy hunting for DeJesus and his pals." He looked pensive for a moment. "It would be nice to know if Vanni is really a part of this or not."

"Why don't you pick him up?" Mulheisen suggested. "Federal business sometimes scares punks like him."

"I don't have time," Phelps said. "Besides, it's your case. You're legitimately investigating him about the dead burglar, the shoot-out, and now this break-in last night. You can reasonably lean on him a little. All I've got on him is the fact that he was on the air base at the time the M-16s were stolen. For that matter, DenBoer was there, too."

"He was! You didn't tell me that," Mulheisen said.

"He was driving one of the trucks for Vanni. I didn't mention that?" Phelps shrugged. "I tend to overlook DenBoer sometimes." He glanced at his watch. "Gotta go. Good luck, Sergeant." He patted Mulheisen on the shoulder. The gesture annoyed Mulheisen; it seemed patronizing. Phelps was back across the room shaking hands with the mayor and the commissioner.

Lieutenant Moser, from the 15th, came up to Mulheisen. "What a load of crap! Now I have to attend a 'mini-briefing'! You ever hear of such a thing? These guys are organization-happy. After the mini-briefing I suppose they'll want us to break up into encounter groups."

Mulheisen laughed. "Find anything else at the cemetery, Del?"

"Not much. We're calling funeral homes about a funeral party."

"There wasn't any funeral yesterday at Gethsemane," Mulheisen said. "I thought I told you that. I checked with the corporation."

"You did tell me, but maybe you better check again. Half a dozen people in the neighborhood saw a small funeral procession in the cemetery, or near it, at about the right time."

"That could be the way the hijackers dispersed," Mulheisen said. "Who are you checking with?"

"I had the boys start with nearby and most frequent users of the cemetery, among the funeral homes. There's a hell of a lot of undertakers in this town, Mul!"

Mulheisen agreed. "Who's running this mini-briefing?" he asked Moser.

"McClain. Phelps is supposed to drop in, to 'coordinate our activities,' as he put it."

Mulheisen smiled. "Ask Mac—or Phelps—if anyone checked the City Airport out."

"You think they might have escaped by airplane?"

"Phelps mentioned that one of the Cubans—DeJesus—had been a pilot. It's worth a try. Well, see you later. Have fun at the mini-briefing."

Mulheisen was glad to be outside, even if it was a windy, chilly day. The sun was out and there were a few ragged cumulus clouds being chased past the towers of the Renaissance Center, a few blocks away. He began to revive in the brisk air. Passing by the Recorders Court, he decided to pop in and see how the Parenteau case was progressing.

He met Ray Wilde just coming out of the courtroom. "All over?" Mulheisen asked, surprised.

"Yep," Wilde said. "Bobby skated. Brownlow bought the whole package. He hasn't announced his sentence yet, but I don't have any illusions. It'll be the State Hospital at worst, and possibly outpatient."

"You didn't use the homosexual angle," Mulheisen said.

Wilde shook his head. "It wouldn't have helped. Brownlow's hip enough to believe in insanity, but he wouldn't believe that a fag could kill someone out of jealousy. To him, homosexuality is itself an indication of insanity. Oh, well, that's the last time Epstein gets a break from the prosecutor's office. Thanks for the testimony, anyway, Mul." Wilde hurried off.

Mulheisen trailed slowly after him, thinking about Bobby. He shivered in the wind when he got outside, whether from the breeze or the thought of the state hospital he wasn't sure. He found his car in the parking lot and drove away, still thinking about Bobby Parenteau. It was almost a welcome distraction from worrying about Mandy. It seemed to him that Bobby's case had been a much simpler, easier one. True, it had taken four years to wrap up, but really only a few weeks of investigation. Mulheisen hoped that whatever had driven Bobby to open fire at Witt and the other youngsters wasn't still bothering him. Obviously, the four years of exemplary behavior had impressed Judge Brownlow.

But here, the ATF had already spent several months investigating Vanni and his friends with little result except the fortuitous "spin-off," as Phelps called it, of the Cuban investigation. It was all a tangled and confusing mess, as far as Mulheisen could see. He didn't expect that it would ever be completely sorted out. But he was used to that. Hardly anything is ever completely explicable when it comes to criminal investigation. Even when a case is more or less satisfactorily concluded, as with Bobby Parenteau, the nagging little mysteries remain. How much more so would it be in the present case?

Normally, there was a powerful tendency for investigators to abandon old, unproductive cases in favor of new, active ones with interesting new leads and unfamiliar witnesses to interview. To be sure, the sheer pressure of the horrendous caseload made that necessary. But Mulheisen knew that many detectives were adept at avoiding complicated or controversial cases in favor of "grounders"—typically, the crime that comes equipped with its own solution, as when the wife telephones the precinct to inform them that she just shot her husband to death and will they please come and get her.

Mulheisen turned up Vernor Avenue en route to the precinct, and shortly afterward drove by the signal tower where three men had died. It looked normal and routine this morning. A switch engine rumbled down the track, looking for something to hook on to.

Mulheisen mused on. There were other detectives, of course, who looked for sensational cases. It was one way to get ahead. You took a chance, naturally. If the case couldn't be solved in good time, you were on the spot. Some guys didn't mind the heat. But most, he thought, preferred routine. "It's just a job," they would say, although he didn't know any detective who really believed that his job was ordinary. No detective thought of his job in the sense that an assembly-line worker, a mailman or a garbage collector thought of his job. Detectives thought of themselves as something special. It was an important job. Routine, at times, but still not "just a job."

Come to think of it, he told himself, probably the mailman and the garbage collector feel the same way. Why shouldn't they? But he doubted they had the same intensity of feeling about their jobs.

At the precinct there was a note from the medical examiner's office. They wanted to know if "John Doe number nine–eighty-nine" could be released from the morgue. The medical examiner wanted to dispose of the cadaver. It would go either to the Wayne State University Medical School or to a private research organization upstate. Mulheisen talked to Dr. Brennan, the autopsist.

"I don't see why we can't clear this one, Mul," Brennan said. "There isn't any legal action pending, is there?"

"No, but I'm working on some related material. Can't you just bury him? Then if we have to, we can dig him up again."

"We could, but that costs the county money. The other way we make money."

"You mean you're selling corpses?" Mulheisen said.

"I wouldn't say 'selling,' " Brennan replied. "We are compensated. It isn't much, but it helps to keep the refrigerators running. Have you gotten anywhere on an identification? If he had some relatives, or even some friends, we could cheerfully release the body for burial."

Mulheisen admitted that he hadn't been able to identify the man. Probably there was no reason to hold the body, but somehow he was reluctant to let it go.

"If he goes to the med school or this other place,

this research outfit, he'll be all chopped up and disappear, won't he?" Mulheisen asked.

"Sometimes, Mul, you have a way of making things sound worse than they are," Brennan said in a wry tone. "Your John Doe won't 'disappear,' but he will get scattered, certainly."

"Doc, I feel terrible. I haven't had much sleep, not much breakfast, too much coffee . . . this conversation is gagging me."

"How have you been feeling, generally?" Brennan asked, with evident concern. "Why aren't you sleeping?"

"Every time I go to bed, the telephone rings."

"You're sure that's all it is?"

Mulheisen was surprised by the doctor's interest; he knew Brennan, but they weren't close friends. "How's your stool?" Brennan asked.

"My stool's fine! What is this? A little loose, maybe."

"You been drinking a lot lately?" Brennan asked.

"No more than usual," Mulheisen said.

"Do your hands feel puffy? Any heaviness in the legs?"

"Doc, I'm okay," Mulheisen said. "I'm sorry I mentioned it. I'm just not getting enough sleep. As soon as this case I'm on is wrapped up, I'll go to bed for a week. Okay?"

"When's the last time you took a vacation?"

Despite himself, Mulheisen reflected. "My God! It's over three years."

"You're working too hard," Brennan said. "What for? You ever ask yourself that? Keep it up, Mul, and I'll be looking at you on my table one of these mornings. You're getting into the forties, aren't you?"

"I'm thirty-nine," Mulheisen muttered. "All right, I'll put in for a vacation. I've got a couple months coming. I'll go to Florida or something." Yeah, Florida, he thought. They've got Cubans there, too.

"Are you taking any kind of medication?" Brennan asked. "Any speed? Something to just keep you going?"

"Caffeine," Mulheisen said.

"Go see a doctor. Get your blood pressure checked. Hell, come down and see me. I'll do it for free."

"Thanks, Doc. I'll do that, I mean it. In the meantime, hang on to John Doe for me, okay?"

"I'll give you a week," Brennan said, "but only on the condition that you stop by to see me. I don't get to do much live-people doctoring. I need the practice." He laughed and hung up.

THIRTEEN

"Where's DenBoer?" Mulheisen asked.

"Search me," Vanni replied, shrugging.

Mulheisen looked at the man. He felt a growing discontent with Vanni. He didn't like to show his irritation with him, however. He said mildly, "All right, let's go back to my office."

As soon as they reached the cubicle Vanni started right in, without sitting down. "Sergeant Mulheisen, I don't have much time. I've been waiting ten minutes already. DenBoer didn't come in this morning, and neither did Mandy. I'm swamped! I got the agency to send over a girl to answer the telephone and type a few letters, but I've got to . . ." Vanni faltered under Mulheisen's baleful stare.

"Sit down, Vanni," Mulheisen said. He himself was slumped in his chair behind the gray metal desk, one foot deposited in the open bottom drawer. He dragged shallowly on a cigar. Vanni sat down stiffly.

For several seconds Mulheisen watched him. The man was infuriatingly fresh, despite his complaint of a harried morning. He looked so clean and dapper that Mulheisen had a fleeting vision of Vanni as a raccoon, daintily rinsing his lunch by the streamside. The notion was amusing enough to quell Mulheisen's impatience.

"Have you tried to get hold of DenBoer or Cecil?" Mulheisen asked.

"Yes. There was no answer at either number," Vanni said.

Mulheisen made some notes on a note pad. "Let's see," he said, "DenBoer lives where?"

"He lives with his parents, on East Canfield," Vanni said. He gave Mulheisen the address and the telephone number from memory.

"And there was apparently no one at home? What time was this?"

"Well, no one answered the telephone, anyway," Vanni said. "I called about ten o'clock, I guess. And then I called Mandy and there was no answer there, either. Do you want her number?"

"I've got her number," Mulheisen said. He picked up the telephone and dialed DenBoer's number. There was no answer. He hung up the telephone and sat back in his chair, drawing thoughtfully on his cigar.

"Vanni," he said finally, "I'm afraid you are in heavy water." He lifted a hand quickly to forestall Vanni's indignant reaction. "No, no, don't give me any bullshit. I don't want to hear it. One"—he ticked off on his fingers— "a gunman is surprised and shot to death behind your garage. Two, a couple of mob soldiers come into the Town Pump, a bar you are

known to frequent, possibly looking for you. Not
finding you present, they shoot up a couple of vending machines that they have taken the trouble to find
out belong to you. Three, a burglar breaks into your
house but doesn't steal anything; in fact, there's
hardly any trace that he was there—just a lucky eye-
witness account."

Mulheisen looked across at Vanni, who sat upright, noncommittal.

"Okay, four," Mulheisen went on, still ticking on
his fingers, "your secretary is seen in a blind pig with
members of a gang now being sought for a spectacular gun hijacking which, incidentally, included the
brutal murder of eight men and considerable danger
to the public when a train was deliberately derailed."

Vanni looked surprised at this statement.

"I'm glad to see you're paying attention," Mulheisen said. "Now. Five, the secretary disappears. Six,
perhaps coincidentally, one of your most trusted associates disappears at the same time. Both of these
disappearances roughly coincide with the time of the
hijacking."

"Sergeant, I—" Vanni started to interrupt.

"No, one minute"—Mulheisen held up his hand
—"I'm not through yet. Clever detective that I am, I
have discovered that you also knew the suspected hijackers. That, in fact, it was through you that Mandy
Cecil came to know them. I have also discovered,
rather belatedly, I'm afraid, that Mandy Cecil was no
ordinary secretary. She was an undercover agent for
the Alcohol, Tobacco and Firearms Bureau. I see
you're shocked. Well, just let me say a few more
words and then I'll listen to you.

"Apparently, the ATF believed that you had

something to do with the robbery of some M-16s from Selfridge Air Force Base several months ago. In telling you this I am violating the confidence of the ATF, but I don't give a damn about that. They haven't done me any favors lately. I don't care whether you were involved in the Selfridge deal or not. It's none of my business. I'm just putting my cards on the table.

"You're a poker player, Vanni. Tell me I'm bluffing. Better yet, call me."

Mulheisen watched the young man. Outside of the show of surprise at the revelation of Mandy's undercover role, Vanni did not display any emotion. Mulheisen saw that the man was a good poker player, after all.

"I now have to ask you some questions. The answers to these questions may, in one way or another, tend to incriminate you and your answers could be used against you in a court of law. You are not, at this time, being accused of any crime. Still, it may be advisable for you to have the benefit of professional counsel. Do you have an attorney?"

"Yes," Vanni replied.

"Do you wish to contact him?"

Vanni unbent a little. "Uh . . . what kind of questions?"

"They're questions about Mandy Cecil, about Leonard DenBoer, about the hijacking suspects. I'm not asking anything about the Selfridge deal, but I do want some straight answers about your relationship with the mob."

"I can tell you right now," Vanni asserted firmly, "that I have no connection with the mob. As for the rest, I guess you might as well ask the questions and

I'll consider whether I want Homer when I hear
them."

"Homer? Is that your attorney? Homer
Ferman?" Mulheisen asked. Vanni nodded. Homer
Ferman was well known to Mulheisen. He was a
pleasant, fat man with a deep and reassuring voice.
He always reminded Mulheisen of a jovial innkeeper,
but he was also the most respected criminal lawyer in
Detroit.

"Okay," Mulheisen said, "but you do understand
that you may have your lawyer here, if you like, and
that if you do answer it is of your own free will?"

Vanni nodded. Mulheisen got up and went out.
He came back a few seconds later with Maki and, in
his presence, repeated the whole litany again and got
Vanni's agreement. Then, with Maki lounging against
the wall, Mulheisen proceeded.

"First of all, do you know where Mandy Cecil is,
or what might have happened to her?"

Vanni said no.

"Do you know where Leonard DenBoer is, or
where he might be, or what might have happened to
him?"

Again Vanni said no.

"Do you know, personally, any of the following
persons: Angel DeJesus, Francisco Morazon, or
Heitor Casabianca?"

Vanni said that he knew all three of the men, but
that he knew them only casually and socially. He had
met them at a restaurant and had later seen them at a
blind pig, known as Brandywine's. To further prod-
ding, he said that he had no business dealing with the
men and that he did not know they had intended to

rob the Cadillac Gage Company, nor that they had intended any kind of criminal activity.

"Did you know, or do you **kn**ow, of any reason why the man presently referred to as John Doe number nine–eighty-nine—the man apprehended and killed at the scene of your garage—was in that garage?"

"No," Vanni said.

Mulheisen looked at Maki and shook his head wearily. Maki scowled at Vanni. Vanni sat calmly upright, as unperturbed as a boy scout.

Mulheisen sighed. "Can you account for your whereabouts between the hours of four-thirty P.M. yesterday and one A.M. this morning?" Mulheisen asked.

Vanni sat silently, considering. Then he said, "I'm afraid I can't answer that."

Maki leaned forward abruptly, his face only a few inches from Vanni's. He shouted, "Why not? What are you covering up?"

Mulheisen jumped up and took Maki by the arm. Maki angrily shrugged his arm away. "Look at him, Mul! He's lying, the son of a bitch! Why doesn't he answer."

Vanni smiled. "Don't pull this old 'Mutt and Jeff' crap on me, fellows," he said.

" 'Mutt and Jeff'? I'll give you 'Mutt and Jeff'!" Maki shouted.

"Don't mind him," Mulheisen said calmly. "He's working on a case, you've probably heard about it— the 'Mutt and Jeff' robberies? Yeah, well, why can't you tell us where you were yesterday, Vanni? What's the problem?" He sounded very understanding.

Vanni sat very straight, with a stubborn expression. "I just can't," he said. "It's . . . it's a matter of honor."

"A matter of honor?" Mulheisen said, puzzled.

"A woman's honor," Vanni said stiffly. He clamped his mouth shut.

It was Mulheisen's turn to be outraged. "Woman's honor? You talk about woman's honor?" he shouted. "I'm talking about a woman who's been missing for twenty-four hours! A woman whose life may be in danger! Don't give me this bullshit, Vanni! You fucking Lothario! Where the hell were you for eight hours yesterday, and let's have names!"

Vanni leaped to his feet. "Did you hear that?" he demanded hotly of Maki. "You heard him! He called me a name. He thinks I'm some kind of dago, or wop, that he can insult! I don't have to put up with that! I'm an American! I own my own company! I want my lawyer, right now!"

Mulheisen and Maki both looked at him with surprise. They looked at each other. There was a long moment of silence, then Mulheisen said placatingly, "Okay, okay, sit down. Take it easy."

Vanni looked furiously from one to the other, then he sat down and was silent, his arms folded defiantly across his chest. Mulheisen sat down, too, and fiddled with his cigar, which was out. He got out another and clipped it, then lit it. "Go get us some coffee, Maki," Mulheisen said. "You want some coffee, Vanni? What do you take—black? Two blacks, Maki." Maki left. The two men watched each other in silence until Maki returned with the coffee in paper cups.

Finally, Mulheisen said quietly, "Now, what's all this about a woman?"

"You called me a name," Vanni said petulantly, sipping at the hot coffee.

"I called you a Lothario," Mulheisen pointed out. "It's not necessarily an insult. I meant no slur on your nationality or anything else. A Lothario is, well, it's used to connote a lover. You're pretty popular with women, aren't you, Vanni?"

Vanni permitted himself the hint of a smile.

Mulheisen said reassuringly, "Of course you are. Why not? That's no crime. You're young, good-looking, successful. Now, what's all this about a woman's honor? Come on, spill it. Who is the woman and where did you spend eight or nine hours with her yesterday?"

Now Vanni smiled outright. "Actually, it was two women," he said smugly.

Mulheisen nodded. "At the same time or separately?"

"Separately, of course," Vanni snapped. "I don't go for that kinky stuff." He then revealed his activities for all of the preceding evening. He had left the trucking company office at 5 P.M. and had driven to a bar on Eight Mile Road, where he met one Shyla Lasanski, who was a married woman. They had dinner together in a restaurant connected to the bar, and afterwards they had driven to a nearby motel, where Vanni had rented a room. By 9:30 P.M., he was out of the motel, parting from Mrs. Lasanski, and had driven downtown to an apartment near Wayne State University, where he had visited with one Kari Wordlaw, a student at the university. He had left Wordlaw's apartment by midnight, alone. He had stopped at the Alcove Bar, on Woodward Avenue, for a drink and around one o'clock had arrived home, where he found Mulheisen and two patrolmen.

"The thing is," he explained, "Shyla's married to one of my drivers. I don't want to get her in trouble with her husband."

Or yourself in trouble with her husband, Mulheisen said to himself. "What about this Wordlaw woman? You're not worried about her?"

"Kari can take care of herself," Vanni said. "But Shyla, she's had a hard time with Dick, her husband. Hell, she already feels so guilty that she wants to tell him all about our affair, for Christ's sake!"

Mulheisen said that he would have to check it all out. He asked for the names and addresses of the two women and copied them down on a sheet of notepaper. "Now, when did you last see Mandy Cecil?" he asked.

"She left the office about four-thirty. She and Leonard both left about the same time."

"Together?"

"Well, more or less. See, Lenny's always after Mandy, if you know what I mean. Always asking her to have a drink with him after work, that sort of thing. So I guess he finally talked her into it. Anyway, he had to drive one of our trucks down to LaCasse's garage, to leave it for some repair work. Mandy was supposed to meet him at LaCasse's and they were going on from there."

"What's LaCasse's number?" Mulheisen asked.

Vanni consulted his pocket secretary and read out the number. Mulheisen dialed it.

"I'm calling about a truck that was supposed to be dropped off yesterday, from Vanni Trucking?" Mulheisen told the man who answered the phone.

"Yeah," said the man, "where is it? If you get it in here real quick I'll try to slip it in this afternoon."

Mulheisen looked up from the telephone. The guileless face of Jerry Vanni gazed back at him.

"I'll see what I can do," Mulheisen said into the telephone. He hung up and turned to Maki. "Get a stenographer, have him make a full statement and sign it."

He got up and left.

FOURTEEN

"After many a fretful hour I know why I'm here," Joe Service said.

The Fatman seemed pleased. They were sitting at lunch at the Villa Di Roma, in Bloomfield Hills. They had just returned from the buffet, heavily laden with Italian delights. "This is a lot better than that gyp joint in Chicago, eh, Joey?"

"I'll say," Service replied. He plunged into the ravioli with a good appetite.

"That joint," Fatman said contemptuously. "What prices! You know that lousy dinner cost me thirty bucks! And what did we get? A coupla skinny dabs of veal. Look at all this." He gestured lovingly at the array of soups, salads, antipastos and assorted entrées that he had trucked back from the buffet with the aid of two lackeys, who had taken a nearby table. "Here," he said, "a man can *eat.*"

They occupied themselves with the food in relative silence for several minutes, then Joe said, "I still can't get over how Sidney got nailed."

"It was those cops," Fatman said.

"But what was Sidney doing there?"

"Obviously, he was working," Fatman said, not looking up from the mostacioli.

"For you?" Joe asked.

The Fatman shrugged and reached for a hunk of garlic bread. "That doesn't concern you, Joe. What concerns you is getting those guns. You see now what a bright man Carmine is? He was afraid of something like this. So now he's got you on the job. You get the guns, there's a hundred big boys in it for you."

"I haven't seen the hundred yet, Fatman," Joe said.

"I give you twenty last week," Fatman protested.

"I need all of it," Joe said. "My contract is to find the guns. *You* have to get them. I just find them. And the deal is, I get a hundred whether I find them or not, right? Now, I never guarantee a job like this, but I always come through. So before we go on with this conversation, let's count the money, okay?"

The Fatman belched quietly into his fist and pushed himself away from the table, with the result that the table slid closer to Joe. Fatman picked up a glass of Valpolicella and drank thirstily, watching Joe. Then he crooked a finger.

One of the lackeys at the nearby table quickly wiped his mouth with a napkin and hurried over. He leaned down with his ear next to Fatman's mouth. Then he straightened and went out. A few minutes later he was back with a cheap blue vinyl briefcase that had a folding flap that snapped shut. It looked like a door-to-door salesman's sample case. After a nod from the Fatman the lackey handed the case to Joe.

Joe started to open the case.

"Not here!" the Fatman hissed.

"Why not?" Joe said, grinning, but he contented himself with only cracking the case open a little, so as not to embarrass the Fatman by displaying all the money arrayed within. There were many packets of banknotes. Joe slipped his hand inside the case and withdrew a single bill from the center of one packet. He laid the bill next to his plate on the table and set the briefcase down next to his foot. He studied the bill while he ate pasta. It had a picture of William McKinley on it.

"They aren't all five hundreds, are they?" Joe asked.

"No, mostly they're hundreds and fifties," Fatman said. He went on eating while Joe rummaged through the briefcase again and examined specimen bills.

"What are you, counting it?" Fatman said, annoyed.

Joe looked up. "It's all here?"

"It's all there," Fatman assured him.

"I believe you. I was just making sure that it was all good money. Had that happen to me once, in Reno." Joe chuckled.

Something in the chuckle made Fatman uneasy. "You got it all straightened out, though, eh?"

Joe looked at him with his clear blue eyes. "Oh yes," he said. He took another bite of ravioli, chewed for a moment, then said, "You remember I was talking about people who might get Dunlop-ed?"

"You mean, you run this guy over, in Reno?" Fatman said.

"*These* guys," Joe amended. "There were three of them involved. But, no, I didn't Dunlop them. In that case I Hillerich-ed them."

"Hillerich-ed?" Fatman raised an eyebrow.

"Hillerich-ed and Bradsby-ed," Joe said, stuffing his mouth with ravioli.

"I don't get it," the Fatman said.

"You must not have been born in this country," Joe said, looking at the Fatman with interest. "Every American boy knows who Hillerich and Bradsby are. They make Louisville Sluggers."

"What's that, a baseball team?"

"Baseball bats," Joe said. "Now I have the money, so all I need is some information."

The Fatman was glad to change the subject. "What do you want to know?"

"I take it that Carmine didn't have any kind of deal with these Cubans," Joe said. The Fatman's look of disgust answered that. "I didn't think so. So who did you deal with?"

"You know, with the punk. Like I told you."

"Then how did these Cubans get involved?" Joe wanted to know.

"How the hell do I know?" Fatman said. "That's your job. I told you things had gotten complicated."

Joe nodded, then shook his head in disgust. "If the public only knew how fucked up the mob really is, they wouldn't have any respect for you at all. If you guys didn't have all the money, I'd never do another job for you. Well, the fat's in the fire now. Have you even heard from the punk?"

Fatman got a pained expression on his face.

"You haven't even heard from him," Joe said, shaking his head again. "Your two heavy troopers still in town? The guys who had such a dandy time at the bar? They are? I thought so. What's the deal, Fat—if the kid doesn't come up with the guns, you're going to waltz over there and provide him with some ballast, that it?"

"Something like that, Joe," the Fatman said. He had begun to eat again.

Joe Service sat back in his chair and picked up the briefcase. He held it on his lap. "In the meantime, I go on looking?"

"That's right," the Fatman mumbled through a mouthful of pasta.

"Let's see, then. The kid engineered the job, the Cubans helped him, and now you don't know where the guns are and the kid hasn't called yet. By the way, I guess you knew that the girl was a ringer?"

"Yeah, we knew that," the Fatman said complacently. He mopped his mouth with an already stained napkin. "That was only one of the complications I was telling you about. We thought we had that taken care of, but . . ." He shrugged.

Service stared at him for a moment, then he said, "Oh, no." He slapped his forehead. "Am I stupid! Well, I'm not the only one, am I?" He started to get up, then sat back and asked, "How long do I have?"

"The deal was the kid would contact us as soon as he had the guns in a place where he could make a delivery. So maybe he'll come through, after all. That don't mean that you should stop looking. If you find the guns, who knows? We might be able to get them a little cheaper than we bargained. There'll be a bonus for you, of course."

Joe smiled grimly. "Just remember, Fat. I'm not going to deliver the guns. I'll find them. That's the deal, okay?"

"Okay. Whatever you say, Joe. Carmine has the greatest confidence in you."

"Just a couple more things, Fat. What was the idea behind that shoot-out? Was that your idea?"

"No, no," Fatman waved his hand. He belched quietly. "That was just a little back scratching, that's all."

"Must have been a powerful itch," Joe said. Then: "Just for my own information, Fat, who was Sidney's contact here?"

The Fatman thought for a minute, then said, "This is private? It won't involve Carmine?"

Joe nodded agreement.

"His name is Lorry. Lorry the Shoe."

FIFTEEN

Shyla Lasanski lived on Cadieux Road. It was a small one-story white house with blue painted shutters and trim, surrounded by a sturdy wire-mesh fence. Inside this fence was a dog. This dog gave every appearance of living up to its billing, a sign posted on the gate which read MEAN DOG! There was a mailbox on the gate post, so that explained how the mailman coped. Mulheisen wondered how Vanni coped, assuming that Vanni occasionally visited here.

The dog was apparently a mixture of Labrador and Alsatian. It was a male, thick-chested with powerful legs, but one of the legs was injured, so that the dog walked with a limp. Mulheisen was willing to bet that the leg had been injured in a fight. The dog did not bark. It limped slowly over to the fence and stood there, out of reach—not that Mulheisen had any intention of reaching. The dog cocked its head slightly and uttered a low growl. Mulheisen felt the hairs on

the back of his legs prickle and he was sure there was
a draft somewhere.

Mulheisen stood there, undecided. Maybe he
should go see the other woman? No, he was here and
he ought to go in. He noticed that the fence ran all
the way around the house, so there wasn't any point
in trying an approach from the rear. He could just
haul out the iron and shoot the damn dog; probably
save someone's britches, he thought. At last he decided, Oh to hell with it, and was turning to go when
the front door opened. An attractive woman leaned
out the door and called to him.

"Can I help you?" She was clutching a bathrobe
together at the throat and her hair was somewhat
disheveled. Mulheisen took out his identification
folder and held it open. At this distance she'd be able
to see the badge, at least.

"Police. I'd like to talk to you," he said. She was
fifteen feet away and he noticed the look of terror
that swept her face.

"Wh-what's it all about?" she asked plaintively.
She had a low, quiet voice.

"I'm investigating a man named Jerry Vanni. Do
you know him?"

"Yes." She looked around. There was nobody
else on the street, but cars were passing. She was
obviously aware of her state of undress. "You'd better
come in," she said.

"What about the dog?" Mulheisen asked.

"Oh. Yes. I'll get him." She came out and called
the dog, whose name was Ivan.

". . . the Terrible," Mulheisen appended, under
his breath. Attila would have been as appropriate, he
thought—or Hitler.

The dog came to her reluctantly and she stooped
to catch hold of the collar, releasing the throat of her
robe briefly. That was all it took for Mulheisen to be
treated to a fleeting view of two very large, bulbous
breasts with large pink nipples. She led the dog away
to the back. A few minutes later she reappeared at
the front door and beckoned to Mulheisen.

Once inside, Mulheisen explained his purpose
again and introduced himself. He couldn't help noticing that Shyla Lasanski was a very attractive woman
and she was naked under the robe. She had a lovely
face—gray eyes and a straight, fine nose, a small
mouth but rather sexy lips that were full and almost
translucently pink, like a child's. Her hair was fluffy
and blond. She said she had just come from the
shower. She said it with some embarrassment. Mulheisen thought it was odd that someone would take a
shower in the middle of the afternoon, but he didn't
say so.

"What is it you wanted to know about Mr.
Vanni?" she asked. "He's my husband's employer,
you know."

"That's what I understand, Mrs. Lasanski."

"Oh, don't call me Mrs. Lasanski. It's so horrible. Call me Shyla." She smiled, and Mulheisen
wasn't positive but he got the feeling that she was
being seductive. He eyed her curiously. She was
about forty years old, but they hadn't been brutal
years. At the same time she possessed a definite girl-
ishness that was very appealing. It wasn't just her girl-
ish face but also her short, almost fragile stature. In-
congruously, perhaps, her fragility was accentuated
rather than marred by her extreme bustiness. She
looked lost and lonely and wistful, in need of some

strong, kindly man. It made Mulheisen feel avuncular, but he fought the feeling, telling himself that she was probably his senior by a couple of years.

"I hear that you're rather close to Vanni," Mulheisen said bluntly. He added, "Shyla."

She suddenly looked frightened and Mulheisen's resolve softened. "I mean, uh, Vanni told me that you had dinner with him last night." Ordinarily, he would not tell a witness the source of his information; it helped to make people think that you knew more than you actually did.

"Yes, we did have dinner," she said. "Why do you want to know?"

"It's a matter of establishing Mr. Vanni's whereabouts yesterday," Mulheisen said. "Now, what time did you meet Mr. Vanni last night?"

"About five-thirty, I think. Dick—my husband—was supposed to be there, but he never showed up. We were just going to meet for a drink, that's all. But when Dick didn't show, I accepted Mr. Vanni's invitation to dinner."

Mulheisen made some notes of this, then asked, "What time did you leave Vanni?"

"About nine-thirty, I guess."

"Long dinner," Mulheisen said.

She flashed the seductive smile again. "We were hungry."

"And where was your husband?"

"He went bowling, he said. But Jerry told me there was a poker game at the office. Sometimes the drivers sit around the office after work. Jerry buys them a case of beer."

"Was this the first time you'd had 'dinner' with Vanni, Shyla?"

Shyla Lasanski sat in an easy chair across from the sofa, where Mulheisen was seated. She had been sitting very primly, feet and legs together, her hands in her lap. Now, after a short pause, she sat back and crossed her legs. The movement exposed a great deal of white leg and in repose the hem of the garment barely came to her knees. Mulheisen found the view of her slender legs very appealing.

"I've had dinner with Jerry before," she said.

"Does your husband know about this, uh, 'dining arrangement'?" Mulheisen asked.

She looked down and spoke softly. "I don't think he does. Perhaps. I'm not sure it would make any difference. We've been married a long time, Sergeant."

Momentarily Mulheisen was at a loss for what to say, and before he could begin, Mrs. Lasanski went on. "I used to love my husband. When we were married, I was the happiest girl in town. He used to be a musician, you know." She looked up and smiled wistfully. Mulheisen didn't say anything. He just watched her.

"He played the C-melody saxophone. He played in lots of very good bands. Actually, he could play almost any instrument—tenor saxophone, trumpet, even piano. I met him at a dance at the old Greystone Ballroom. He was almost thirty and I was only eighteen. He was wearing a white jacket with a red carnation and I thought he was the most handsome man I'd ever seen."

She stopped and chewed on her lower lip pensively.

"But then the big bands went out of business, soon after we married. He was on unemployment a lot. He wanted to get into recording studios, but you have to be in New York, or L.A. for that, and he was afraid to leave Detroit, I guess. He always drank a lot. I think he went out with other women. In fact, I know he did."

She looked defiantly at Mulheisen. "We hardly speak to one another, Sergeant. I'm here all day, of course. I cook supper and he doesn't come home till late, but if he comes home on time and supper isn't ready he gets in a vile mood. Sometimes he doesn't come home until I'm in bed. I pretend I'm asleep. I have to take sleeping pills—otherwise I get migraines and I can't sleep."

She was speaking very freely, almost distractedly. Mulheisen listened gloomily. It sometimes happened this way. You get a witness talking and the next thing you know they spill their guts and the whole life story comes tumbling out.

"Sometimes he makes love to me in my sleep," she said.

Mulheisen cleared his throat uncomfortably. This was going too far, he thought.

"I wake up in the morning and discover that I've been . . ." She waved her hand to indicate that she couldn't supply the necessary word. "It's even worse if I'm only pretending to sleep. Then I have to let him do it without revealing that I'm awake. That's difficult."

She finally noticed Mulheisen's pained expression.

"It isn't love!" she insisted. "We haven't made love—real love—in years. I don't think he can bear to put himself in a position that would even suggest affection toward me. He can't say anything nice to me, especially if someone is around."

Mulheisen was struck by the lack of rancor in her tone. There was no hint of self-pity, either. It was a rather clinical description of a horrible relationship. Nonetheless Mulheisen felt compelled to mutter, "It's a two-way street, isn't it?"

"What? Love, you mean?"

"Well"—he waved his hand airily—"marriage, anyway."

"You've never been married, have you?" she said. "I didn't think so. But yes, yes, it is a two-way street. It's other things, too. It should be children. I thought we'd have children."

"Why didn't you?"

"We can't. He says it's because I'm sterile. But the doctors never found any evidence of that. He won't go to the doctor, of course."

"You could have adopted a child," Mulheisen suggested.

"I wanted to. He wanted to, once. But . . . for some reason it was never the 'right time,' if you know what I mean. We were always too broke, we had to buy a new car, the furnace needed to be replaced . . . it was always something."

She stood up and walked nervously to the front window. The robe was rather thin and the sun shone through the window. Mulheisen watched as she stood with her back to him and looked out the window. Her body was quite visible, her legs slightly apart. She turned slightly and her large breasts swung against the thin cloth of the robe. Mulheisen was aware of a growing movement in his groin.

"Your husband sounds like a regular bastard,"

he said, to dispel the dangerous charm of the moment.

Shyla Lasanski turned to face him. "He's just an ordinary man. Would you like some coffee? I have some on the stove—just made it before I got in the shower."

Mulheisen welcomed the change of mood. He followed her into the kitchen. It was very neat and clean. The stove and refrigerator were several years old, he noticed, and the Formica counter tops were scarred here and there with cigarette burns and knife cuts. But the room was light and cheerful, with dotted-swiss curtains and green plants hanging in macramé slings. They sat at an aluminum and plastic table. The coffee was fine.

"Freshly ground," she said. "I like to do things like that. I bake my bread. I bake a lot, actually. Cookies, mostly, for the kids in the neighborhood, although most of them are grown up, now. There used to be a lot of kids around here. I still bake. It helps to fill up the day."

"What kind of cookies?" Mulheisen asked.

Shyla Lasanski blushed. "I don't have any right now."

Mulheisen sipped his coffee. "I see," he said. "Maybe you should get a job."

"I wanted to," she said. "But . . . 'No wife of mine is going to work,'" she mocked her husband's voice. "I guess I could, now. He couldn't stop me. Maybe I will."

"Have you, uh, talked to anybody about this? I mean, someone professional?"

"You mean 'the clergyman of your choice,' or a marriage counselor, or a psychiatrist? Yes. All of them. In fact, I even went to two clergymen, a Catholic and a Protestant. I'm not Catholic, but Dick is—or was. It didn't help. I couldn't take them seriously—dressed in their funny collars and black suits. What do they know about being a woman? And then, the psychiatrist wanted to sleep with me."

"Isn't that unethical?" Mulheisen said.

"Well . . . it wasn't as bad as it sounds. He helped me more than the others. We talked a lot about sex. I feel I understand it better. He suggested I should have an affair. So I did, but not with him. Actually, I've had several affairs besides Jerry, though he's about the best." She smiled lasciviously at Mulheisen.

"I made it with the furnace man, once. He called me up several times after that, but I wouldn't see him again." Her voice dropped and she said softly, "He called me a whore the last time he called. Maybe I am a whore."

Her hand strayed across the table and stopped next to Mulheisen's, not quite touching. He did not move. He looked at the robe where it had fallen open to reveal all but the nipples of her breasts. It was very tempting.

Mulheisen had a feeling of great lassitude. It was quiet in the kitchen and the sky had clouded up, filling the room with rich, warm shadows. He could faintly hear cars passing on the street.

"Do you think I'm a whore?" she asked softly.

Mulheisen stood up, even though he had a partial erection. Shyla stood up as well, and took a tentative step toward him.

"So you can positively state that Vanni was in

your presence from five-thirty until nine-thirty?" he said.

Shyla stopped and smiled her wistful, little-girl smile. Mulheisen could have sworn that her eyes got larger and mistier.

"Yes," she said quietly. "We had dinner and then we went to the motel. I think it's called the Pines, or something like that. It's on Mack. We made love. Twice. Jerry's quite a boy. A little dumb, sometimes, but ambitious and healthy."

Mulheisen made some notes. "Okay," he said crisply. "I guess that should do it." He started for the door.

"What's Jerry done?" she asked.

Mulheisen looked back at her. She stood in the kitchen doorway, leaning against the jamb. Her robe was open now, the ties held in each hand. Mulheisen thought, What the hell, might as well look, anyway. He took a long and eye-filling look. Her pubic hair, he noticed, was light and fluffy, so he guessed she was a natural blonde.

"Very nice," he said.

"Thank you."

Mulheisen opened the door and went out. It was cool and sunny, a nice day in detroit. He looked around nervously for Ivan the Terrible, but evidently she had locked him in the back somewhere. He walked down the sidewalk to his car, thinking, God, I hope the other one's easier than this.

SIXTEEN

Mulheisen stopped at a telephone booth to call the DenBoer home and realized that he had left DenBoer's number at the precinct. He looked in the telephone book and discovered that there was an L. DenBoer listed, on E. McNichols, and a Leonard DenBoer on Canfield. He remembered then that Vanni had said that DenBoer lived on Canfield. He dialed the number and got no answer.

He called the precinct then and asked if there were any messages. There was one from Phelps: he said that he appreciated the tip about the City Airport and was pursuing it. As yet there was no trace of the hijackers.

Mulheisen asked for Maki, who told him that Vanni had obediently signed the statement and had left. Mulheisen thanked him and asked if Dennis the Menace had been around. "He's right here," Maki said, and put him on.

"Mul, baby, what's shaking?" Dennis asked.

"You were telling me about an old con you knew, a gunsmith. Remember?" Mulheisen asked.

"Yah. Ol' Earl. I ain't seen him."

"I thought you were going to look him up. Well, I was thinking, maybe he knows something about this Cadillac Gage caper. Rattle his chain a little, eh?" Immediately Mulheisen was sorry that he'd even remotely suggested that. Dennis came back with enthusiasm.

"Good idea! I'll go out and find him right now. I was feeling a little restless, anyhow. Time for me and Ol' Earl to jawbone."

The verb "jawbone" had an unfortunate connotation for Mulheisen. He was always reminded of his Sunday school class, in which Samson was depicted slaying the Philistines with the jawbone of an ass. Dennis the Menace's use of the word, as a verb, suggested something considerably more active than a friendly conversation.

"Look, uh, Dennis, I didn't mean to literally 'rattle his chain.' Maybe you could just rap with him, eh?" Mulheisen hung up, then, thinking that even "rap" could take on uncomfortable overtones. He pondered this as he drove over to Mack Avenue and stopped at a motel called the Pines.

A quick check of the register showed that a "Mr. and Mrs. R. Lasanski" had checked into the motel about eight o'clock.

"What did Mr. Lasanski look like?" Mulheisen asked the clerk.

"I don't know. My wife signed them in," the man said. He went off to get his wife.

"He looked like that Olympic swimmer," the

wife said, "the one who won all the medals, what's his name?"

"Mark Spitz?" Mulheisen said.

She snapped her fingers. "That's the one. Yep, looked just like him. The woman, she was old enough to be his mother."

Mulheisen thanked her and left. He drove downtown to see Kari Wordlaw. It was an old brick duplex, now converted into several apartments, near the university. Kari had a roommate named Heidi, who was out. Right away, Mulheisen noticed that Kari shared several qualities with Shyla: she was short, she had a pretty, little girl's face, and she had very large breasts. Mulheisen was starting to get a general impression of Vanni's taste in women.

There were some differences, however: Kari Wordlaw was only twenty, she had long dark hair and she wore glasses. Unlike Shyla, she did not project an aura of sexy dreaminess or helplessness. On the contrary, she was a self-assured, self-aware young woman. Like Shyla, though, she was not reticent on sexual matters.

"Sure, he came here about ten or so, and stayed until after midnight. We fucked a couple of times, then I kicked him out because I have this paper due in Poli. Sci."

"A couple of times!" Mulheisen couldn't help exclaiming.

Wordlaw grinned. "Oh sure, he's a real stud, didn't you know? I had to love him up a little to get him going the second time, but then he was fine. He took a long time to come." She was obviously enjoying Mulheisen's embarrassment. "There's no law against fucking, is there?"

"There are a few, but they don't apply in this case," Mulheisen shot back, recovering his equilibrium. "It's just that I'm from an older generation, Kari. It sometimes catches me by surprise when a pretty young girl like yourself uses language like that. But no matter. I just wanted to verify Vanni's whereabouts, and you've taken care of that. Thank you." He backed out of the apartment without allowing her to ask what Jerry had done.

Since he was running pretty close to the rush hour, Mulheisen did not stop to telephone DenBoer, but drove straight to E. Canfield. The traffic on the Edsel Ford was beginning to jell when he got off and he was feeling a bit harried by the time he pulled up in front of the pleasant frame house. The front door was opened to his knock by a woman in her late fifties, wearing a cloth coat. Obviously, she had just come in, for next to the door was a wire two-wheeled cart with a grocery sack in it. A stalk of celery stuck out of the top of the sack.

Mrs. Leonard DenBoer, Sr., was a pleasant, motherly sort of woman. She talked to Mulheisen while she put away the groceries in the kitchen. She had about her a scent of fresh-baked bread. Her face was soft with powder and lightly made up and her hair was waved in a permanent. It was black with many strands of gray. Despite the baking scent, she did not remind Mulheisen of Shyla Lasanski in any way. There had been no such scent about Shyla or her kitchen. Of course, Mulheisen reminded himself, Shyla had only *said* that she baked a lot. She hadn't offered him any cookies.

Mrs. DenBoer was quite alarmed about "Junior's" continuing absence. "Of course, he's a big boy, now, but . . ."

"Your son lives here, at home?" Mulheisen asked. "I see. And has he always lived at home?" He took notes.

"He was in the Navy for four years," Mrs. DenBoer said, "but since then, he's been at home."

"And he's never stayed away this long before?"

"Usually he calls. As a matter of fact, he often doesn't come home at night, but he always calls to say if he'll be here for dinner. I never say anything to him about it; he doesn't like people keeping tabs on him. Confidentially"—she leaned toward Mulheisen and actually touched his arm, almost whispering—"I think he has a couple of women friends. But I don't like to pry."

They sat at a large old wooden table, drinking coffee. To give Shyla credit, Mulheisen thought, she does make better coffee. This was a large kitchen, with a high ceiling and many cupboards. There were nearly twenty feet of counter space. Pots and pans were on the stove and something that smelled like a roast was in the oven. It looked like a working kitchen. Mulheisen was reminded of his own mother's kitchen; it was more like this than neat like Shyla's. There were stray crumbs under the toaster and at least one milk-clouded glass next to the sink.

"You have other children, then?" Mulheisen asked.

"I have two grown daughters, and four grand-children. They just live down the block. The little ones are in and out all day. But I've been out most of the afternoon."

"That reminds me," Mulheisen said. "Were you here this morning? About ten?"

"Yes, why?"

"I wonder if you received a phone call from Jerry Vanni?"

"No," Mrs. DenBoer said. "I was right here. I don't think Jerry would call in the morning; he knows that Leonard, my husband, works midnights—at Budd. He's always sleeping during the day." She glanced at the clock. "He'll be getting up in about an hour."

"I called about one. There was no answer."

"I guess I must have just gone out. Leonard is a pretty heavy sleeper, once he gets to sleep." She poured some more coffee for Mulheisen and forced some chocolate-chip cookies on him. They were very good.

"I don't want to mislead you, Mrs. DenBoer, but I'm afraid that your son may be in trouble. We're looking for him in connection with our investigation of the Cadillac Gage Company holdup."

"Why, that's just down the street!" Mrs. DenBoer exclaimed. "I'm sure Junior wouldn't be involved in anything like that!"

"We're not sure he was. But we think he may have information that could assist us. That's why it is essential that I get in touch with him as soon as possible."

Mrs. DenBoer looked quite upset, naturally, and very fearful. "I can't help you," she said. "I would if I could, but I don't know where he is."

"You mentioned that he might have a girlfriend. Do you know her name?"

"Oh, no. Junior would never mention a girlfriend to me. He's very private about that sort of thing. He has a few friends, but mainly they're Jerry's friends, too. Junior and Jerry are very close. They've been pals since before they went to school." She prattled on in the safe territory, eager to avoid a return to troublesome topics. Mulheisen listened patiently, nibbling at a cookie. At last he broke in.

"Is there any place he might go, if he were in trouble, Mrs. DenBoer? Do you have a summer cottage, perhaps?"

"Yes, we do. It's way up north, on Duck Lake. That's near Interlochen. But the cottage is all closed up now."

Mulheisen got all the information down. It would have to be checked. "Do you think I could look at his room, Mrs. DenBoer? It might help."

She led him upstairs, cautioning him to be quiet, since her husband was still asleep. She stood in the doorway of Leonard Jr.'s room while Mulheisen looked around.

It was a boy's room. Mulheisen, who still lived at home, of course, hadn't seen anything like it since his youth, unless it was in a Walt Disney film. There was a model of a red, tri-winged Fokker airplane dangling from a string over the bed, with a model Spad in pursuit. There were plastic model sailing ships on the dresser and Detroit Tiger pennants on the wall. In one corner there was an old Springfield rifle that had been lovingly restored; in another corner, a fishing rod and a baseball bat. Mulheisen wondered if there was a football in the closet. There was, lying next to some old tennis shoes and a baseball glove.

"When he was in the Navy I kept it just like he left it," Mrs. DenBoer whispered. "In his letters he always asked if I had messed with his stuff, but I didn't."

"I don't see any correspondence or anything like that around here," Mulheisen said. "Doesn't he get his mail at home?"

"Yes. I guess he just doesn't like to keep things like that lying around."

There was a boy's desk in the room, but its drawers contained nothing but modeling tools and a few old *Popular Mechanics* magazines. There was not a single picture of a woman, not even a *Playboy* centerfold in the room.

"Did he ever say anything to you about Mandy Cecil?"

"You talk about him as if he were dead," Mrs. DenBoer said fearfully.

"I'm sorry," Mulheisen said.

"I remember Mandy so well. They were all such good friends when they were little. Junior, Mandy and Jerry. They were the cutest things. She was quite a little tomboy. My heavens, it must be ten or fifteen years since her family moved away."

"He hasn't mentioned her lately?" Mulheisen asked as he followed her down the stairs.

"No, I don't believe so." Mrs. DenBoer looked at Mulheisen expectantly, waiting for Mulheisen to enlighten her. He didn't.

There was nothing to do here, he felt. He declined another cup of coffee and left.

Mulheisen drove back to the precinct with his mind in turmoil. It was twenty-four hours since the hijacking, and as far as he knew, they were no closer to apprehending the hijackers than before. As for Vanni and Company, he had to confess that he was confused. The death of the man in the alley was still a complete riddle; the motive behind the shoot-up at the Town Pump eluded him; he now realized that he had gravely neglected Leonard DenBoer in his investigations; and the personality of Jerry Vanni still had him puzzled. The main problem, of course, was, Where is Mandy Cecil?

There were messages waiting from Phelps, McClain, Andy Deane, the prosecuting attorney's office and half a dozen more. It was after six o'clock; there was no point in calling back on most of the messages. McClain wasn't in, nor was Phelps, but the duty agent at the ATF office said that the airport investigation had turned up some promising leads. Mulheisen said he'd check back with them.

He called the state police and asked them to check out the DenBoer cottage on Duck Lake. Then he called Del Moser at the 19th. Moser told him that the funeral-home investigation had not panned out. They were at a loss to account for the presence of a funeral party in the Gethsemane Cemetery yesterday. So there was another dead end.

Dennis the Menace loomed in the doorway of the cubicle. He made a bugle of his fist and blew a kind of fanfare. "Well, I saw him," he said heartily. His voice, like his presence, was too evident. Mulheisen made a hushing, calming gesture with the palms of his hands.

"You saw who?" Mulheisen asked.

"Ol' Earl," the Menace replied.

"Ol' Earl?" Mulheisen couldn't place the name.

"Yeah, Ol' Earl. You asked me to look up Ol' Earl and I did," the Menace said with some exasperation.

"Okay, okay. I remember now. Well . . . how's Ol' Earl?"

"Ol' Earl's all right," the Menace said.

"He doesn't have any broken bones or anything?" Mulheisen asked. He got out a fresh cigar and clipped it.

"Broken bones? I wouldn't hurt Ol' Earl. I respect Ol' Earl. No, I was just jawboning with him, nothing fancy. Amazing how these ol' cons get back in the swing of things, Mul. Here Earl's been in the pen for five years and he's only out a couple weeks and already he knows more about what's going on around town than I do." Noell shook his head thoughtfully. He was walking back and forth in the cubicle, which meant he could take two steps in each direction. He had his hands on his hips with his sports jacket pulled back, revealing the huge .357 in its Western-style holster on his hip. His elbows practically grazed Mulheisen's head in his passage.

"We got to rapping about guns and ammo and stuff," the Menace went on. "He was telling me about Jurras, the guy who invented the Super Vel—"

"What the hell is a Super Vel?" Mulheisen interrupted.

"Cartridge," Noell said with mild surprise. "A jacketed hollow point. Everybody uses them. You don't use that issue crap, do you? They're no good. Anyway, here's this guy Jurras who practically revolutionizes pistol ammo, doing a good business—hell, he can't keep up with the demand—and then he has to go out of business. Know why?"

Mulheisen blew out a long plume of smoke. The cigar comforted him. "Tell me," he said.

"He ran out of brass. Couldn't get enough! Not

enough brass! Is this the United States of America, or what?"

"So that's all Ol' Earl had to say?"

"No. He said I should switch to Winchester 158 grain JHP for the Python, unless I load myself, or I could get it from him. I think I might have him load me some. I just don't have the time for it. On the other hand, Earl thinks I ought to go to a bigger caliber, maybe S and W's Model 29, .44 mag. Then I could use the Remington 240 grain JHP."

"What the hell are you talking about?" Mulheisen said.

"Say, that guy who got shot by Stanos? Earl never heard of him—he *says*. Maybe he's not lying. Why should Earl lie about something like that? Anyway, he gave me another name. Lorry the Shoe. That name ring a bell?"

Mulheisen thought for a moment. "Down on Woodward? Hangs out in those bars around Sibley, that area? He's a hustler. He hustles shoes."

"You win a cigar," the Menace said. "Lorry is your genuine character. He specializes in getting you a pair of shoes, cheap. But he can also get you other things. In fact, just about anything you want, except a woman. Lorry hates women. But guns, that's his best item, according to Ol' Earl. Hell, he might even get you a guy to shoot the gun for you."

"Where does Lorry hang out, when he's not in the bars?" Mulheisen asked.

"He's usually in the pigs pretty late, but I wouldn't look for him there tonight."

"Why not?" Mulheisen asked.

"We're going tipping tonight," the Menace said, grinning cruelly. "Your buddy Phelps is fed up with no results. He doesn't like the press he's getting, so the ATF is going to do something spectacular. He's planning to hit a whole shit pile of pigs tonight. It's bullshit, I know, but it sounds like fun, too."

"You're going out with them?"

"We all are," the Menace said. "Fact is, I think I better take a little nap if I'm going to be up all night." He smacked a huge fist into his open palm. "Hot times tonight! We're gonna whack 'em!"

"Do you know if they're hitting Brandywine?" Mulheisen asked. "Or Benny?"

"Not Benny. But Brandywine, it looks like it."

"Do me a favor," Mulheisen said, "if you run across Lorry in any of these raids, let me know. I'd like to talk to him."

"Run across him? Hell, I'm liable to run over him." The Menace guffawed. "Well, I got to split. Time for my beauty sleep. Bye!" He waved a huge paw.

Mulheisen immediately dialed Benny Singleton.

"Hey, Mul, I was just thinking about you," Benny said. "Is what I hear on the level?"

"What did you hear?" Mulheisen asked.

"About a bunch of blind pigs gonna get tipped over tonight," Benny said.

"It's a possibility," Mulheisen said. "But I don't think you have anything to worry about, Benny."

"I wasn't worried, Mul. I was just thinking, I might better put out more stock tonight and get me another bartender. If everybody else is closed, I might have a big night." He laughed.

"Benny, do you know a guy named Lorry the Shoe?"

"Lorry the Shoe? No, I don't. Where does he hang out?"

Mulheisen told him.

"Brandywine'd know him," Benny said. "Want me to give him a call?"

"I'd like to talk to Brandywine anyway," Mulheisen said. "Do you think you could invite him over? It would be to his advantage, you can tell him."

"You mean right now? Well, I'll try. Say, you had dinner yet? Well, I'll tell you what you do," Benny said. "My sister, who keeps house for me here, she's gone and cooked up a whole pile of ribs. I was just sitting down to them when you called. Why don't you come along and have some and I'll try to get the 'Big Buck' over here. That's what I call him. He says he don't like it, but I think he does."

"I'm on my way," Mulheisen said.

SEVENTEEN

The French fries were a trifle soggy, but Mulheisen didn't mind. He was there to eat ribs, and they were delicious. He didn't even look at the coleslaw. "Nothing in my long experience has conditioned me to appreciate shredded cabbage mixed with a watery dressing," he explained to Benny. There was a murmur of agreement from Benny, muffled by the sound of barbecued ribs being devoured.

Eating barbecued ribs is a messy process. It took several towels to clean up afterwards. "Got to keep the kitchen clean," Benny explained. "My sister come back from the movies and find the kitchen a mess, I'm done for." Afterwards they went next door to "the club," as Benny liked to refer to it. Brandywine was already there, sipping a brandy Alexander he had made for himself.

Brandywine looked particularly outrageous, with a great green velvet cape slung over his shoulders. He wore the large black slouch hat and it had a green feather in it, about a foot and a half long. Below a shimmering silverish blouse with voluminous sleeves, green velour knickers gave way to knee-high yellow boots that laced all the way up the front and featured three-inch stacked soles and heels.

Mulheisen could hardly refrain from whistling. Brandywine smiled slowly. "Hey, baby, have a drink."

Mulheisen obliged and Benny mixed him a Black Jack Ditch. It was still fairly early. The blind pig was not open for business yet, since the bars were not closed. Very likely, Benny's would be crowded tonight.

Mulheisen thought the raids would probably start early, because there were going to be so many of them. Ordinarily a blind pig wouldn't be raided until three, at least, and usually later. There had to be time for the drinkers to get from the bars, get themselves another drink and for things to sort of get under way at the blind pig. In the meantime the vice squad's undercover man would get inside, make a purchase and examine the layout. If he had a partner, the partner would leave and tip the raiding party outside that things were ready. At a prearranged moment the inside man, or men, would take up stations watching the bar, watching the back door and keeping an eye on the toilet (so nobody could flush dope down the drain). The outside men arrived with the warrant, everybody was informed that it was a bust, and from that point on, things went their usual orderly way. The paddy wagon carted everybody off to the local precinct and booked them. In the morning the prisoners were transferred downtown, their fingerprints and records were checked, and off they went to

Morning Court to plead guilty to "loitering," or maintaining an "illegal occupation." The fine for the first offense was usually $10; for the second, $30 to $300. Usually, everybody paid and went home and the following night found them back at their favorite blind pig.

Tonight it might be a little different, Mulheisen thought. The ATF was along, and they tended to be more serious about these things. Also, they were looking for dangerous criminals, or leads to them. They weren't just shutting down blind pigs whose half-life had expired. Mulheisen had little doubt that the ATF would find no trace of the hijackers.

"My man Benny says you want to talk to me, Fang," Brandywine said. "What about?"

"I was in your place the other night and ran into Mandy Cecil. You seemed to know her. How come?"

"She comes in from time to time. Just a customer," Brandywine said.

"Always with the same people?"

"I don't know who you mean."

"Well, who does she usually come in with?" Mulheisen asked.

"Let's get one thing straight, Sergeant Fang. I'm here talking to you because Benny says you're a friend of his. But you ain't no friend of mine, you dig? I have myself a little place down on Riopelle and I don't have no trouble there. Nothing heavy going down in my place. So I ain't worried about you. What my customers do is they own business. It ain't mine, it ain't yours."

"What about the Cubans? Do they come in often?" Mulheisen asked.

"I told you . . ." Brandywine mocked a look of theatrical exasperation. "I don't know no Cubans."

"You know Mandy Cecil, though," Mulheisen pointed out, "and she has disappeared. I just wonder if you know anyone else who has disappeared lately."

Brandywine finished his drink with a loud slurp and put it down on the bar. Benny, who had withdrawn to the other end, came along and picked it up. "You want another?" he asked.

"I do, if Dr. Fang here is buying," Brandywine said.

"Sure, I'll buy," Mulheisen said. "Let me have another, too, Benny." When the drinks were mixed and Benny had gone back down the bar, Mulheisen said, "I'll do better than buy you a drink, Brandywine. I gather that you pull in quite a nice piece of change at your place most nights. How much do you think you'll net tonight?"

Brandywine glanced at him through hooded eyes. Mulheisen realized that the man wore quite a bit of makeup, including eye shadow.

"I know what you're talking about, Fang. As a matter of fact, I decided to take a little vacation tonight."

"That's smart, Brandywine. Except that you won't have much income for the night."

"Comme ci, comme ça," Brandywine said, with a toss of his elegant head.

"In exchange for a little information, I think I could arrange for you to be open tonight," Mulheisen said.

Brandywine thought about that for a while, then said, "Make the arrangement."

Mulheisen went into Benny's back room and di-

aled the ATF. Phelps was finally in. He was very excited. He had learned that someone approximating
the description of Angel DeJesus had flown out of
City Airport at 5:45 P.M. on the afternoon of the hijacking in a leased Apache. Apparently, the aircraft
carried two other passengers, who were not named.
The flight plan had been filed for Green Bay, Wisconsin, but the aircraft had not arrived at Green Bay.
Instead, the pilot had radioed for an amended flight
plan while en route, naming Lafayette, Indiana, as his
destination. From Lafayette the airplane had been
tracked as far as Dallas, Texas, via Memphis, Tennessee, and Little Rock, Arkansas. There was a VFR
clearance out of Dallas, naming San Antonio as the
destination. From that point on there was no trace of
the aircraft. Phelps was very hopeful, however.

Mulheisen asked him if he still intended to raid
the blind pigs. Phelps affirmed that he did. The operation was all geared up and it would be difficult to
cancel now, even though it no longer looked like such
a worthwhile project.

"Still, you don't know, Sergeant, it could pro-
duce something."

"I'd just like one name left off the list, if you can
manage it, Phelps. There's a possibility of getting
some good information on Cecil, as well as DenBoer
and the Cubans."

Phelps balked when he heard that it was Brandywine's place, one of his prime targets, but he gave in
when Mulheisen pointed out that the City Airport
lead had been Mulheisen's contribution.

"You're back in business," Mulheisen told Brandywine. "Now, let's have it."

"Well, usually she comes in with Mark Spitz,

that's what I call him. And another dude I call Po'kchop."

Mulheisen gathered from the descriptions that Brandywine meant Vanni and DenBoer. It amused him to think that Brandywine's identification of Vanni with Mark Spitz was shared by a fat, middle-aged white woman who ran a hot-sheet motel.

"Tell me about the Cubans," Mulheisen said.

"They come in a lot, not always all together and not always with Cecil. Fact is, I mostly seen just three of them: Angel, Frank, and Heitor. Sometimes they ask for a room, like they was going to play cards, but they don't play no cards. They sit in there and talk to Mark Spitz and Po'kchop."

"What did they talk about?" Mulheisen asked, suppressing his interest as best as he could.

"I don't know. Revolution, I guess." Brandywine grinned. "Man, them revolutionaries is bad business. I don't go for no revolutionaries."

"Why is that?"

"Let's face it, baby, I'm Establishment. It may not be up-front Establishment, but it's still business. I see they still ain't no casinos in Havana, and that's gettin' on to twenty years that Castro been in power."

"Tell me about guns, Brandy. Did the Cubans ever ask you about guns?"

"You mean like 'Where can I get one?' That kind of thing? Man, everybody asks where they can get a gun. Sure, they asked. I told them to go see Lorry."

Mulheisen felt a little thrill run along his spine. "Lorry the Shoe?" he asked.

"That's the only Lorry I know about," Brandywine answered.

"Did they see Lorry?"

"You have to ask Lorry that."

"Good idea," Mulheisen said. "Where do I find him?"

"He ain't been around the last couple of days," Brandywine said. "Somebody mentioned he was in the Detroit House of Correction, picked up on some chickenshit peddling charge."

"So Lorry's a gun dealer, is that it?"

"That's what they say." Brandywine yawned. "Anyway, your Cubans, they don't need no guns. They got all the guns they need—I just throw that one in for free, Fang." He winked lewdly. "Now, some of the brothers, they'd like to talk to them Cubans, too. Lots of people would like to get their hands on those guns."

"I know," Mulheisen said. "You haven't heard anything about Cecil, then?"

Brandywine shook his head slowly. Mulheisen had to accept that. If there was any news about Cecil, Brandywine would know about it. The only question was, Would Brandywine tell him about it? Well, why not? Mulheisen decided that Brandywine would tell him, providing it didn't involve himself or any of his people.

Benny came and gave them a couple more drinks while Mulheisen pondered. Brandywine grew restless and wandered across the little barroom to play the jukebox. Soon the strident tones of a Motown group filled the room.

So, what did he have? He had pretty good evidence that Vanni and DenBoer were involved with the Cubans on the hijacking. But in what way? The Cubans had needed guns, obviously, in order to carry out the operation. Perhaps they had gotten them from Vanni. Mulheisen presumed that DenBoer had been the go-between, the gun bearer. And now DenBoer was absent. Quite possibly the Cubans had accepted the guns and then had decided to dump DenBoer as well, as a possible threat to their security. If Mandy Cecil was with DenBoer, she would have been dumped, too, whether the Cubans knew she was an ATF agent or not.

Brandywine was jigging about by himself, next to the jukebox. Mulheisen watched him without paying real attention. He was reminded, inevitably, that all of Vanni's sudden surfacing in the public eye could be due to an attempt by the mob to pressure him on account of his vending-machine operation. Mulheisen felt that he had strayed dangerously from this initial and orthodox view of the whole affair. It was always a mistake to find complexity where none existed, he knew. But for him Mandy Cecil had changed everything.

"Who else did the Cubans talk to?" he called out to Brandywine.

The tall black man paused, as if irritated, then posed in a mockery of Thought, with one hand on his hip and a long forefinger poking into his lip. He started to say something, then just flipped his hand. "Just about anybody." He turned back to the machine.

"Wait a minute," Mulheisen said. "Satisfaction guaranteed, remember? I still have time to put you back on the list."

Brandywine didn't turn around. "If I open up and I get tipped, you gonna owe me, Fang. We made our deal. You gonna owe me bad."

"Ask Benny if I'm straight," Mulheisen said calmly, knowing that Brandywine already had been thoroughly assured of that or he wouldn't be here. "I'm just looking for a straight end to my deal. But I'll make it easy on you. Angel talked to an undertaker, right?"

Brandywine smiled his grand, lovely smile. "The way you say it amuses me," he said. "I'll give you one name, and that's it."

"Shoot."

Two minutes later Mulheisen was on the telephone to the 19th Precinct. It was his luck that Lt. Del Moser was still there. "I didn't think I'd catch you this late," Mulheisen said.

"They got us roped in on this blind-pig raid," Moser said wearily.

"Can you get away for a bit? It may not take long," Mulheisen said. "See if you can run down a Jabe Cook, he's a black undertaker, over on Dexter. There's a possibility that DeJesus or one of the other Cubans may have rented a hearse from him. Check it out, you know what to look for."

Mulheisen hung up and dialed the Record Bureau. He asked for the file on Lorry the Shoe.

"That shouldn't be hard," the officer assured him. Mulheisen held on the phone. It took almost fifteen minutes. Benny brought another Black Jack Ditch.

"Hello, Sergeant Mulheisen? Sorry I took so long. It's all in the computer now, so it's supposed to be faster, right? Only, now you have to stand in line for an open terminal. Well, here it is. You want to copy?"

"Let's have it."

" 'Lorry the Shoe.' Real name, Lorenzo Shmuel Feinschmecker. How about that?" The officer spelled the name. "Born in Danzig (then in Germany, now in Poland), 1923. Emigrated to U.S. with parents, 1934. Naturalized citizen. Jewish faith. Graduated New York University, 1947, BA degree in Business Administration. Convicted grand larceny, fraud, 1954, New York City. Sentenced eight to ten, served three at Attica, New York State Corrections. Released parole, 1960. Employed by T. J. Kidder Construction Company, same year, a Detroit firm, as bookkeeper, with approval of parole officer. No further notations. He must have gone straight."

"I just heard he was in DeHoCo," Mulheisen said.

"If you want to wait a few minutes, I'll check with Prisoner Information for you," the officer said. He was back after a brief wait. "Nope. No Feinschmeckers, no Fines, no Shoes. Any other aliases?"

Mulheisen couldn't think of any. He thanked the officer and hung up. He went back into the other room to ask Brandywine where Lorry hung out, but Brandywine was gone.

Benny shrugged. "He said 'Business calls,' and split."

Mulheisen went back to the telephone and called the 13th Precinct detectives—that was the general area of Lorry's haunts. He got a Sergeant Coleman, who said he knew Lorry quite well.

"Haven't seen him lately," Coleman said. He was fairly certain that if Lorry had been picked up he'd have known about it.

"Do you know where he lives?" Mulheisen asked.

"I'll ask around," Coleman said. A few minutes later he was back. "The Tuttle Hotel," he said.

"How about meeting me there in fifteen minutes?" Mulheisen asked.

"We're kind of short-handed at the moment," Coleman said.

"Yeah, I know. The Great Blind-Pig Raid. This is important," Mulheisen said.

"Fifteen minutes," Coleman said.

The Tuttle Hotel was a ten-story affair just off Woodward Avenue. It was an old hotel, surrounded by liquor stores, bars and small, cheap restaurants that offered soul food or home cooking. It was also the present home of Ol' Earl, but Mulheisen wasn't concerned with that. From the looks of the place the lower floors were reserved for the streetwalker trade. The upper floors would be for the residents, probably most of them welfare recipients or hustlers of one sort or another.

Sergeant Coleman was leaning against the reception desk talking to the night clerk. Coleman was a tall black man of thirty, wearing a business suit and a hat. He shook hands with Mulheisen. With a thumb he gestured at the fat, balding black man who sat behind the desk with an open copy of *Penthouse* under one elbow and a dead cigar in his mouth.

"Buster here sez Lorry's in DeHoCo," Coleman said.

"What for?" Mulheisen asked the clerk.

"I heard he got thirty days for peddling without a license, or some such shit," Buster said.

"Who told you that?" Mulheisen asked.

"His lawyer. He come to pay Lorry's rent. He all paid up till the end of the month."

"Lorry has a lawyer?" Coleman seemed surprised.

"What did the lawyer look like?" Mulheisen asked.

"I didn't see him. Day man saw him."

Coleman nodded. "Let's have the key, Buster."

"I don't know about that," Buster said.

Mulheisen smiled unpleasantly. "The key," he said.

Buster handed the key to Coleman.

The room was small and neat, but chilly. Someone had turned the radiators off. The bed was made. There was a bathroom with a tub. Clothes hung in the closet—not expensive ones but not raggedy, either.

Coleman looked through the dresser. He held up a yarmulke and phylacteries. "What's this?" he said. "I didn't know Lorry was Jewish. Hey, Mul, what do you think?"

Mulheisen was about to stoop and look through a pile of shoe boxes that filled the lower half of the closet. "What is it?" he said.

Coleman indicated the dresser drawer. A clean white towel lined the bottom of the drawer and on it were a safety razor, an expensive shaving brush and a cup of shaving soap. It gave an image of a quiet, clean man—somewhat at odds with Lorry's public image. Mulheisen stared at the fancy aftershave lotion.

"And there's a toothbrush and toothpaste in the bathroom," Coleman said.

Mulheisen got the point. If a man is going away to jail for thirty days, he takes his toilet articles. Especially if he's got a lawyer who is willing to pay his rent for the rest of the month.

"Maybe Lorry didn't go to DeHoCo," Coleman said.

The two detectives stood and looked around the little room. Then Coleman kneeled and peered under the bed. He straightened up with a grunt, then stood up, dusting his knees. "Give me a hand with the bed," he said to Mulheisen.

Carefully they lifted the bed and set it aside. There on the floor was a man-sized package wrapped in a blanket. Mulheisen bent and flipped back the edge of the blanket and Lorry the Shoe gazed up at him. The mouth was slightly open and the eyes were glazed. Mulheisen flipped the blanket back over the face.

"Go make the call," Mulheisen said. He put his hands in his pockets and waited.

When all the photographs had been taken, the medical examiner unwrapped the corpse. More pictures were taken, this time clearly showing the three holes in Lorry the Shoe's chest.

The bed was stripped, and it revealed bloodstains on the sheet and mattress. It seemed likely that if the bullets weren't still in Lorry, they might be in the mattress. The medical examiner rolled the body over, finally, and there were no exit wounds, so that took care of that. He opined that the body had lain there for one to three days, but he wouldn't be able to tell until he did the autopsy. He said the lack of odor was possibly due to the cool temperature of the room.

A man from the Scientific Bureau was carefully removing the shoe boxes from the closet and opening them, wearing plastic gloves. "Hey, hey," he called out. "Look at this, Mul."

There was a .32-caliber revolver in the opened box. "That explains the stains I saw in the other boxes, I bet," the lab man said. "Gun oil." In short order he found two more pistols, a .38 Smith & Wesson automatic and a .38 Colt revolver.

When the body was carted away, they spread the boxes out on the floor. Out of the twenty-odd boxes, only three of them contained guns, but many of them revealed the telltale stain of oil that the lab man had noticed.

Coleman squatted on his heels, looking at the boxes and lids. "What's this?" he asked Mulheisen, pointing to some pencil markings inside several box lids. "Some kind of writing."

Mulheisen examined each one carefully. In some of the lids a name had been scrawled: "Sid," or "Vince." On other boxes there were addresses, usually just partial addresses, but a few complete. "Gratiot and Harper," read one; another, "E. McNichols Ave." Yet another said, "Remington Arms." He assumed that was a reference to a gun, but Coleman pointed out that Remington only made shotguns and rifles and you couldn't get one of them into a shoe box.

"It could be ammunition," the lab man said.

Mulheisen copied down all the notations, anyway, just in case.

The precinct was beginning to jump. The first prisoners of the big raid were there, yelling vigorously, protesting their innocence. Since most of them were drunk, the protests were half-hearted and almost jolly, in a carnival mood. For the most part they were being charged with loitering, but others were found to possess marijuana, cocaine, speed and heroin. Some were carrying illegal knives and unregistered pistols. Because of the overload, anyone who wasn't drunk and had no outstanding warrant on their record, and wasn't holding some illegal substance or weapon, was kicked out of jail. There wasn't room to sleep them all, not even on the floor.

The detectives were in and out, booking people, interrogating them, going back to the street for more. Mulheisen could hear Dennis Noell bellowing at some hapless arrestee. "What the hell you mean it ain't yours? You were carrying it! Speak up! What's that? Louder! You found it? Oh, Lord."

Mulheisen telephoned ATF and told the duty agent about Lorry the Shoe. Phelps was not in, of course; he was out on the Great Raid. In the meantime federal agents were getting closer to the DeJesus flight. They had tracked the airplane as far as Falfurrias, Texas, where it had landed near an abandoned ranch, picked up fuel that had been left there and flown on. Mexican authorities were expected to cooperate.

Mulheisen sat and thought about the flight. Obviously, the Cubans could not have removed the guns from Detroit. Or could they? He had put out an alert for Vanni's missing truck, but that was almost twenty-four hours after the hijacking. A truck could travel a long way in that time. He wondered if highway weigh stations kept a log of every truck that passed over its scales; he wondered how long it would take to collect and review those logs. He decided it wasn't worth it, yet. That was the kind of effort you went to when all other leads had evaporated.

But the fact was, he just had to face it. He didn't have any leads. He felt like a blind man; there seemed to be an awful lot going on around him, but he was damned if he could see a thing.

He was interrupted in his musings by the telephone. It was the state police. A trooper had been to the DenBoer cabin on Duck Lake. It was all shuttered and closed up for the winter, and no sign of any visitors.

After that Mulheisen sat in his cubicle, oblivious of the growing melee around him, ruminating and casting back over his notes. He decided finally that Lorry the Shoe was the closest he had come to an authentic lead. Obviously, Lorry was dealing in guns. Obviously, he had a pipeline through the mob, to keep him supplied. Presumably, he had some kind of relationship with Vanni and DenBoer. But what? Did Vanni supply Lorry with guns, or was it a two-way street?

And what about John Doe? Could he have gotten his gun from Lorry? Mulheisen tried to visualize that. In these days of airport security checks, gunmen didn't travel with a weapon. There were all kinds of arrangements for gun drops, at airports, at hotels, any place that meant that the gunman could be armed as quickly as possible. If Lorry was the armorer, that would probably mean a trip to John Doe's hotel, on Gratiot.

Mulheisen came to his senses and scrabbled through the notes he'd made. On one of the shoe-box lids there was the notation, which he'd copied, of "Gratiot and Harper." As far as he could tell, that was reasonably close to John Doe's hotel. If only, he thought, I'd gotten to Lorry quicker. But he hadn't. That left some of the other addresses to consider. "E. McNichols Ave.," for instance. That wasn't much help. McNichols was a long street, sometimes referred to as Six Mile Road. And then there was "Remington Arms." Just for kicks, Mulheisen reached for the city telephone directory and checked to see if the Remington Arms Company had an office in Detroit. He couldn't find a listing.

So that was that. Perhaps a cryptographer could go over Lorry the Shoe's notations and decipher them, but Mulheisen couldn't see anything there. He was blind again.

Of course—a little thought popped up—"Remington Arms" could be an apartment building. Mulheisen smiled. It was a terrible pun. But builders aren't immune from making puns. Just for fun, he told himself, I'll check the street directory for E. McNichols, see if anything rings a bell.

Ding!

"21000 E. McNichols, Remington Arms, caretaker Lasater, R., apt. A."

Mulheisen stared at the address. There was something familiar about it, but he couldn't say why. Suddenly it came to him. He reached for the telephone directory again and thumbed through it rapidly. Then he found it: "DenBoer, L., 21000 E. McNichols—732-1771."

EIGHTEEN

The manager of the Remington Arms was a thin, ascetic-looking fellow with long hair and a thin beard. He was about thirty. What was going on in his apartment, however, was not ascetic at all. There were about six each of young women and men, the record player was going full blast, and every table and counter top was covered with empty beer cans and overflowing ashtrays. Mulheisen thought he smelled marijuana, but he didn't say anything about it. He cheerfully accepted a can of beer and tried to talk to the amiable manager, R. Lasater, over the din of Z.Z. Top.

Mulheisen finally gave up trying to outshout the record player and flashed his badge, inviting Lasater outside. Lasater didn't seem concerned; he smiled dreamily and came out into the hall. The relative silence was a palpable relief for Mulheisen.

"Don't the other tenants complain? It's four in the morning," Mulheisen said.

"These are the tenants," Lasater explained. "We're just celebrating the release from jail of O. Dzelo."

"Who is O. Dzelo?" Mulheisen asked skeptically.

"He's a great thinker and leader," Lasater said cheerfully. "He was just released from jail in Maracaibo, after three years. He's the leader of a worldwide revolution of the mind."

Mulheisen wondered if he was being put on, but he knew from experience that it didn't pay to react negatively. "Far out," he said, smiling. "Can I help?"

"You are helping." Lasater smiled back.

"I take it this isn't an armed revolution," Mulheisen said.

"Oh, no, man. O. Dzelo isn't into petty arms," Lasater assured him.

Mulheisen assumed that O. Dzelo also eschewed nonpetty arms, from Lasater's tone. "Sounds interesting," he said. "You don't have any literature on the movement, do you?"

"O. Dzelo isn't into books," Lasater said. "He says, 'Don't codify me.' "

"Far out," Mulheisen said. "Say, what about one of your other tenants, Leonard DenBoer? Is he into O. Dzelo, too?"

Lasater shook his head sorrowfully. " 'Fraid not, man. I talked to him about it, and he came to a couple of our meetings. He seemed to enjoy the exercises, but I don't think he really tried to develop the techniques. I think he really just wanted to meet the chicks. In fact, a couple of them said he was hassling them. So he doesn't come around much anymore. Talk about arms, he was always into arms. We call him Generalissimo—all in good fun, of course."

"Of course," Mulheisen said. "Did you ever see any of his friends here—South American types?"

"Oh, yeah," Lasater said. "Nice guys. One of them, Heitor, knows all about O. Dzelo. He said he even saw him once in Valparaiso. Yeah, they used to come by quite often. Haven't seen them lately, though. Haven't seen the Generalissimo, either."

"Unh-hunh," Mulheisen grunted. "Well, the problem is, Mr. Lasater—"

"Just call me Rick."

"Right, Rick. Nobody's seen DenBoer for a couple of days and his family is kind of worried. I rang his doorbell but there was no answer, and he doesn't answer his phone, either."

"Well, I'm pretty sure he isn't home," Rick said. "He hasn't been around for days."

"Maybe we could go up and take a look, eh?" Mulheisen said.

"I don't know, man. Aren't you supposed to have a warrant or something?"

"Not if I have reason to believe that something has happened to the man," Mulheisen said.

"Well, look, man, I've got this party going and everything, and . . . hey, you look like an all-right guy, and uh . . . okay, I guess I better go up with you."

Mulheisen followed him up the stairs to the next floor. It was a modern apartment building, flimsily built out of drywall and almost nothing else. The music from the basement apartment was highly audible throughout the building. At the door Lasater turned and looked Mulheisen right in the eye in a very sincere way. "I just want to know one thing, man," he said. "Are you a narc?"

"No way," Mulheisen said, shaking his head. "I'm just trying to find DenBoer."

Lasater watched Mulheisen's face carefully, then nodded, apparently satisfied. "All right, then." He opened the door.

It was a very ordinary apartment. A living room with drapes drawn across the picture window. A kitchen with a dining area, a bathroom and a bedroom. The furniture was cheap modern and the floors were carpeted with shag, except for the kitchen, which had vinyl tile.

The bedroom was considerably more interesting than the other rooms. For one thing, it was painted a solid, flat black.

"Far out, eh?" Lasater said.

Mulheisen nodded distractedly and went directly to the cluttered desk near the bed.

"Uh, hey, man, the Generalissimo isn't here," Lasater noted. "How about you look around and I'll trip on back downstairs, okay?"

"Sure," Mulheisen said. "I'll stop to see you on my way out."

Lasater said that was fine and left, closing the door behind him. The din of the music was hardly diminished.

In the bedroom there were bookcases full of paperbacks—mostly on war, especially World War II— and more books were stacked on the floor. Among them were *Mein Kampf, The Rise and Fall of the Third Reich,* the *Warren Report* and a pictorial series on great generals of World War II. There were other, more interesting items, to Mulheisen's mind, such as a pamphlet reprinted from an article originally published in *Guns & Ammo: The Stoner 63 Weapons System*.

The bed was rumpled and unmade, and littered with old copies of *Shooter's Bible* and *Military Small Arms of the Twentieth Century*, along with well-thumbed copies of *Guns & Ammo*.

The desk was a mess, awash with jumbled papers and magazine articles, maps and duplicated drawings. The drawers were open and papers spilled out of them. It looked as though it had been hurriedly rifled. Mulheisen squatted down and leafed through the debris. Much of it was duplicated material. It included diagrams of wooden crates containing rifles, with notations on size and weight.

Mulheisen hunched closer. The jumbled mess was a veritable gold mine, he realized. In short order he found duplicated lists of names, including DeJesus, Morazon and Casabianca. Another duplicated list grouped the names into three- and five-man teams, labeled "A," "B," and "C."

Best of all, however, was a little stack of duplicated sections of a Detroit street map. The area included a sizeable portion of the East Side, with the marking "A" superimposed next to the Vernor tower, "B" next to the Cadillac Gage Company and "C" at Gethsemane Cemetery.

Mulheisen stood up, smiling. It was all here. The whole plan. All he needed now was a dispersal diagram. He knelt and rummaged through the debris again, methodically separating the different material into piles. It took at least twenty minutes, and when he was through he had found no escape route. He emptied all the drawers and organized that material into stacks, without finding anything useful.

At last he turned back to the original map and scanned it closely. There were the superimposed letters which corresponded to the team letters, but that was it. And then he saw a small "1," lost in a more or less blank spot on the map, behind the Detroit Terminal Railway lines. At first he had taken it to be an original part of the map. Now he found a tiny "2," near the City Airport, and a "3" on the Edsel Ford Expressway.

Mulheisen felt that the "2" was obvious—it indicated the escape route of the aircraft flown by DeJesus. Evidently, from what the ATF had been able to find out, DeJesus had taken at least two others with him, probably one or more of the other leaders, Morazon and Casabianca. There was a chance, of course, that he had taken Mandy Cecil, or even DenBoer, but Mulheisen couldn't think of any good reason why he would.

As leaders of a movement, it wasn't unreasonable for DeJesus or Morazon or Casabianca to leave the country as soon as their part in the raid was over. But, surely, all of them wouldn't leave, Mulheisen thought. One of them must stay with the guns. The guns were all-important. That made them number "1" on the map, he guessed. And "3" would indicate an escape route for the others, the "soldiers."

Looking at it this way, Mulheisen was fairly certain that the guns, and at least one of the leaders, would be where the "1" was. But the blank area on the map was quite large, a district of several blocks. As far as he could remember, that was just a vast jumble of factories, some of them still operating, but most of them shut down and abandoned. It would be damn near impossible to find anyone in there, he thought.

He noticed, however, that the "1" was located almost on a line with the end of Canfield, the street on which DenBoer had been brought up, and near where Vanni, Mandy and DenBoer had played as children. Mulheisen reached for the telephone.

The duty agent at ATF was excited, but not by Mulheisen's call. Three of the Cuban hijackers, the "soldiers," had been spotted in Chicago and arrested. Phelps was on his way to the airport at the moment, to fly there and interrogate them.

"You better stop him," Mulheisen said. He quickly explained what he'd found. The agent agreed that he had better stop Phelps and hung up.

Mulheisen sat back on his heels and looked about the black bedroom again. There was a pile of *Penthouse* and *Playboy* magazines on the floor to one side of the bed, which was covered with black satin sheets. Mulheisen tried to figure out what it all meant. A womb? Some kind of negation of life? He didn't know. The guy likes black, is all he could come up with. It wasn't necessary to know DenBoer—he had only to know that something was wrong.

Mulheisen walked downstairs. The party was still rocking along in the upper decibels. "This place is going to be crawling with cops in a few minutes," he told Lasater, "including federal agents. If I were you, I'd wind it up. Sorry, Ace, but that's the way it bounces. Oh yeah, I'd flush that pot, too."

He went out to his old Checker and drove off. He knew he should wait for Phelps, but he just couldn't see it. The idea that kept hammering at him was that Mandy Cecil was in trouble; possibly every minute was crucial.

Every city has industrial areas that have been abandoned. At night they have all the gloomy and forbidding ambience of a Victorian London slum, with their myriad lanes and barricades, passageways that end in a pile of fallen brick and plaster, their sudden and empty courtyards echoing with one's footsteps. When the original industry moves out, the successors are invariably poorer, temporary, and they don't maintain the premises. Sometimes demolition is started, then halted. Hippies move in, paint up after a fashion and open obscure enterprises that are soon abandoned.

In this complex all of these things had happened at one time or another, but now it was dark and deserted again. Mulheisen drove along trying to figure out where someone could enter the complex. There were blocks and blocks of buildings, with a tall heavy mesh fence surmounted by barbed wire. All the gates were securely locked. He knew that the neighborhood children must have a dozen "rabbit holes" into the place, but what he was looking for was an access for vehicles.

He drove down several streets that dead-ended against the fence. Then he found a dirt lane that slipped past a corner of the fence and dwindled into a track that skirted an abandoned spur of the Detroit Terminal Railway. It was a kind of service drive, he supposed, now long out of use.

It was very dark back here. No streetlights, just the distant glow of the city. The track ran into an area completely surrounded by hulking shadows of derelict factories. Once, obviously, machines had hummed and crashed and men with lunch pails had hurried along these oil-soaked loading docks. But now it was silent. A habitation for rats and owls.

He stopped the car and got out, taking a large six-celled flashlight with him. The dirt lane was littered with pieces of sodden paper and half overgrown with weeds. By the light of the flash, however, he thought that he could discern recent tracks. Perhaps not. He switched off the light and stood still.

A faint wind caused something to creak, high up in one of the buildings. There was a rustle of trash blown against weeds. Something flapped, a piece of torn tarpaper, perhaps. He could see a little better now. It was an hour before dawn, at least, but the general night glow of the city beyond the silent walls faintly illumined the decayed brick walls. He looked straight up and saw stars, not a common sight in the city.

He took a few steps down the lane and his feet seemed to make an ungodly noise on the gravelly dirt. He paused a moment, then walked on, occasionally flashing the light to see if there were any tire marks.

He wandered into dozens of courtyards, their pavement broken and grass growing in the cracks. He went down narrow and pitch-dark lanes, stumbling over a piece of forgotten machinery or an empty oil can. Occasionally he scared a rat and the rat scared him. He walked on. The courtyards led into more courtyards, more loading docks. There were culs-de-sac littered with bales of wire and scraps of sheet metal. There seemed to be puddles everywhere, but he didn't recall that it had rained in the past week.

Finally, he knew that he was lost. This did not bother him especially. Soon it would be daylight and he would find his way out. But a great and terrible loneliness began to oppress him, wandering in this Stygian maze. He began to feel a little crazy.

Why had he come here? What had he hoped to find? A gang of Cubans standing guard over a pile of guns? The body of Mandy Cecil? He didn't know anymore. He felt an edge of panic and suppressed it. He wanted to shout, but he knew that it was impossible to yell. The sound would merely be lost, as he was, and that would be too horrible to know.

He blundered down another lane and into yet another courtyard. Steel steps went up onto a loading dock. He mounted the steps and walked quietly along one side of a warehouse, next to several sliding doors, some of which were open. And then he stopped. There was some kind of vehicle backed up to the dock.

It was a shiny black hearse, looking not at all out of place here. Mulheisen stood very still. His mind was clear now. No more confusing panic and vague fears, no more craziness. He listened for a long time. He heard an owl flap into some lofty window. The buildings creaked and groaned. But mostly he heard the steady, gentle rush of the city that lay away beyond the walls of the deserted industrial citadel. The sound was quite distant, like a great river far off.

At last he moved slowly and cautiously along the dock toward the hearse. He carried the flashlight in his left hand and slipped the .38 out of its holster with his right. The giant doors to the warehouse were pulled wide open, but it was so dark that he could not distinguish between the outside and the inside. At the edge of the door he waited and listened, holding his breath.

Not a sound, but for the creaking of the building. He strained his eyes, peering inside, but all he got was a sensation of space and emptiness, as of a great hall. He took a deep breath and switched on the flashlight.

He was blinded by the light at first, but quickly adjusted. What he was faced with was a great hall, a stockroom with twenty-foot ceilings. That was not what caught his eye, however. What did were the bodies. The minute he saw them he smelled them, as if the one sense had triggered the other.

There were three of them, lying in a tangle in the middle of the floor. By the flashlight he could see that they had been dead a day or more. They had been shot, and shot a lot. There was a lake of dried blood, and in it the footprints of small animals—rats. On closer examination, it appeared that parts of the fingers had been gnawed, and even parts of faces.

It looked to Mulheisen as if the three men had run into a sudden hailstorm of bullets. He supposed that someone had shot them with a Stoner rifle. Thinking of that, he flashed the light around. There was no sign of the stolen guns.

The three men were Cubans. He recognized them from the night at Brandywine's. Young ones, the laughing soldiers.

There was a metal stairway up one side of the room. He clambered up that and found the loft where they had all stayed. It was nicely provisioned: cots, a CB radio, a Coleman camp stove, Army-surplus mess kits, boxes of canned goods, even a case of Stroh's beer. There was also a table with benches, and sprawled on the floor next to it was Francisco Morazon, with a bayonet in his back.

Mulheisen went back out onto the loading dock. It was getting light now. Pretty soon he could start picking his way out of the labyrinth. He felt as if he should have a ball of yarn, to tie one end to the door-nail and roll it out so as to find his way back again.

He jumped down to the cracked paving of the courtyard and looked the hearse over. Mud had splashed and dried on the shiny finish, he noticed. And then he noticed something else: someone had traced a name in the dried dirt on the side of the hearse. The name was "MUL."

NINETEEN

Carl Lofgren was a tall, sandy-haired man with a ruddy complexion that came from working out of doors. He was yelling at the kid who worked for him in the boatyard.

"Nick! You got it?"

The kid did not answer. Carl waited patiently for several seconds, then yelled again. This time there was a muffled reply from the other side of the boat, a small cabin cruiser.

"Okay, I got it!" the kid yelled.

" 'Bout time," Lofgren said under his breath. He started the power hoist. The boat rose slowly out of the water. It was completely out and on a dolly rolling toward the yard before Lofgren noticed the short, dark man who stood watching.

"Hi," the man said, smiling.

"Hello," Carl said noncommittally. "Help you?"

"I'm looking for Jerry Vanni's boat," the man said.

Carl stopped the motorized dolly. "You a friend of Jerry's?"

"Not really. He said he was thinking about selling it, so I thought I'd take a look."

"News to me," Lofgren said. He shook out a Camel and lit it, without offering one to the stranger.

"Say, you're an old hand around boats," the man said. "What do you think she's worth?"

"The *Seabitch?* Well . . ." Lofgren paused warily. "I better not say. What's Jerry asking?"

"He wouldn't put a price on her," the man said. "He wants me to make an offer. I figure if I like her I'll have to get a marine appraiser in, anyway. Is she down this way, or did you pull her out already?"

Lofgren gestured down the wooden dock. About two-thirds of the boat wells were empty. "Number eighteen," he told the man.

"Thanks." The man walked off whistling with his hands in his windbreaker pockets.

A few minutes later the man was back. He waited while Lofgren and Nick lowered the cabin cruiser onto wooden trestles. "She's gone," he said, when Lofgren looked up questioningly.

"Gone?" Lofgren said. Then he shrugged his shoulders. "Well, I guess Jerry or Lenny's taken her out. I didn't see her leave, though."

"Was she here yesterday?" the man asked.

Lofgren's eyes narrowed. "I guess so," he said. "Why?"

"No reason," the man said. He smiled and walked away, then turned and came back. "Could I use your phone?" he asked.

Lofgren pointed to a pay booth near the office. "You can use that," he said.

"I'm glad you called," Fatman wheezed. "You didn't find anything, did you? I knew you didn't. The reason I know is, I just got a call from the kid."

"Ah," Joe said, "the romance is back on."

Fatman chuckled. "You aren't doing too well, are you, Joey boy? What did he do, give you the slip?"

"Oh, I suppose I'd have found him in time," Service replied. "So what's the deal?"

"The details are kind of sketchy," Fatman said, "but it looks like we're back in business. The kid wants to meet, work out a deal."

"I thought you had a deal, once," Joe said.

"We did, but since they weren't able to follow through like they were supposed to, a new deal is in order."

"Is this your idea, or the kid's?" Joe asked. He stood in the telephone booth watching some gulls drift slowly along the docks. It was a sunny, brisk morning.

"His," Fatman said. "But we have no objections. I think we're in a better position now. I notice in the *Free Press* this morning, they collared the Cubans in Chicago."

"Not all of them," Joe said.

"True. Well, I'll leave the details to you, Joe. Carmine says you haven't earned your fee yet. The kid is going to call back in a half-hour. What he wants is two hundred and fifty grand. He says the guns are in a safe place, and he'll let us know where as soon as the money is paid. He said he'd be happy to meet with you, Joe."

"All right," Joe said. "Where?"

"They'll call in half an hour," Fatman said. "So you call me in forty minutes. I know I don't have to explain things, Joe, but just so you don't get confused, we must know if they really got the guns, what the whole deal was—"

"Just exactly how fucked up it is, eh?" Joe said. "I know, Fat. Don't worry. Do I make an offer if it sounds like they can deliver?"

"Yeah, but no quarter of a million. Their ass is in a sling. Offer a hundred big ones. Be firm. If he bitches too much, go to one-twenty-five, but that's tops. After that, tell him he can shove the guns some comfortable place. We don't need the hassle. The heat in this town is something terrific."

"You're telling me," Joe said. "If I didn't know better, I'd think I was in Miami. I've been dodging that cop, Mulheisen, all night."

Two hours later Joe Service ambled along the Civic Center waterfront, between Cobo Hall and the Henry and Edsel Ford Auditorium. The huge new towers of the Renaissance Center loomed to the east. It was late morning and a chilly wind ruffled his hair. Only a few cars were parked on the drive and a handful of citizens were staring into the Detroit River. When he reached Cobo Hall, he turned and walked back upriver. Out in the channel, an ore boat was downbound and an ocean freighter was upbound. There were a few barges, but no pleasure boats that he could see. It wasn't the weather for pleasure-boating.

He was nearing the end of the promenade when a thirty-foot cabin cruiser slipped out from behind the ore boat and came alongside rapidly. Joe stopped and smiled. It was a pretty clever maneuver, the cruiser coming downstream in the shelter of the ore boat.

A stout man of thirty, badly in need of a shave, stepped out of the bridge area and waved Joe aboard. Joe jumped down into the boat. The man had one hand in his windbreaker pocket and he withdrew it slightly, to show Joe that he held a small automatic pistol.

"In here," the man said, gesturing with his free hand toward the bridge. When they were inside, the man said, "Unzip your jacket."

Joe unzipped his jacket. "What for?" he asked.

"I want to see if you're packing a rod," the man said.

"You mean this?" Joe said. Suddenly he had a snub-nosed .38 Smith & Wesson in his hand, almost in the guy's face.

The man paled. He had never seen anything so fast. His own pistol was still in his pocket.

"Now what?" the man said.

"We going to talk here?" Joe said. He smiled and slipped the .38 back into the pancake holster over his right kidney.

The man relaxed and managed a faint smile. "No," he said. He stepped to the wheel and gunned the engine. The boat swung out and away, headed upstream. They came up to Belle Isle and ran along the Detroit shore without talking. The man cut the engine to idle as they passed under the MacArthur Bridge and came out into the old Gold Cup unlimited powerboat race course, between the island and Detroit. Joe could see the Detroit Boat Club and the deserted municipal beach.

"You must be DenBoer," he said.

"That's right, and you're Service. I see you didn't bring the money," DenBoer said.

"All in good time, my man," Joe said. "We need to get a few things straightened out first."

"Like what?"

"Like, where's the guns?" Joe said.

DenBoer was a jowly man, somewhat taller than Joe, but out of shape. He had lank black hair and brown eyes. He was a nondescript-looking man at first glance, but he had a firm jaw and an intelligent alertness. "The guns are in a good place," he said. "You bring the money and I'll call Fatman. He can send someone to look at the guns if he wants. The guy calls me, you give me the money. Safe enough?"

"Not bad," Joe said. "Fatman is worried about heat. We want to know how it all worked out. For all we know, the guns aren't yours to sell."

"They're mine," DenBoer said. "You don't have to worry about that."

"What about the Cubans?" Joe said. "We don't want a bunch of crazy revolutionaries screwing up the works."

"The Cubans are all taken care of," DenBoer said with a grim smile.

"I don't think you've even got the guns," Joe said.

"Look behind you."

There was a long boxlike thing on the deck with a couple of yellow slickers draped over it. Joe lifted the slickers and saw a wooden box stamped with the

words "Cadillac Gage Company." He stooped and
lifted the lid. Inside were the Stoner rifles, resting in
racks.

"Well, you've got one box, anyway," Joe said,
letting the lid drop and rearranging the slickers.
"How much do you want for it?"

"I've got all the boxes," DenBoer said.

"What happened to the Cubans?" Joe asked.

DenBoer laughed—a rough, almost hysterical
bark. "Those boobs! They're all over the place by
now."

"How are you going to work it out with them?"
Joe persisted.

"I'm not. What do you care?"

Joe shook his head. "No good. I don't think we
can deal with you. It's too fucked up."

"You don't have to worry about the Cubans,"
DenBoer repeated.

"I don't understand," Joe said. "Tell me about it.
I take it they weren't in for the money; they wanted
the guns."

"That's it," DenBoer said. "They had some
cockamamie plan to smuggle them out of the country. I went along with it. They were going to pay me
for my help, but I don't think they planned to pay me
with money. Only, I paid them first."

"What was their plan?"

"Oh, just bullshit," DenBoer said impatiently.
"Like, they're going to take the guns out to a
freighter in the middle of Lake St. Clair at night!
They had a deal all set up, they said. I mean, imagine!
All those guns in a boat! What boat? You couldn't
load that many guns in this boat. It'd take a week to
transport them. Well, they had a contingency plan,

too, they said. They were going to set up a kind of pipe line, with cars, to drive the guns, a box at a time, down south. I didn't believe any of that shit.

"The fact is, they weren't too clear on what they were going to do with guns, once we got them. I don't think they figured on me and Jerry being around, then. So they just told us any kind of crap."

They were coming up to the Roostertail Restaurant. DenBoer gave the throttle a shove and headed away, back toward the channel, then cut to idle again.

"What about the girl?" Joe said.

DenBoer looked at him sharply. "What girl?"

"The ATF agent. Where is she?"

DenBoer shrugged. "Search me," he said.

"I intend to," Joe said. He flicked the .38 out again, grinning at DenBoer's amazement. He gestured toward the cabin door. There was a padlock on it. "Open up," he said.

DenBoer glowered, then fished a key out of his pants pocket. He unlocked the master lock and stepped back at Joe's gesture.

Joe opened the door and peered in. Mandy Cecil was lying on the large forward bunk. She was completely naked and her wrists and ankles were bound with surgical tape. Another strip of tape covered her mouth. Her hair was wild and her eyes were pleading. Apparently, a blanket had been thrown over her but it had slipped to the deck. Joe looked at her for a moment, then winked. He closed the door and DenBoer snapped the lock back on the hasp.

Joe put the .38 away. "What happened to her clothes?"

"I ripped them off her," DenBoer said. "They

were in the way. Besides, it keeps her from thinking about escape."

"Very smart," Joe said.

"Thanks, I thought of it myself."

Joe nodded toward the cabin and grinned conspiratorially. "How was it?"

DenBoer caught his meaning. He grinned back. "Not bad. I had better. Had worse."

"What happens to her now?" Joe asked.

"None of your business," DenBoer said.

"Oh yes, it is. We want to know what your plans are. She knows a lot about this whole deal."

"I'll take care of her," DenBoer said.

Joe was persistent. "Does that mean you're going to kill her?"

DenBoer did not respond. He tended the wheel. They turned idly in the Scott Middle Ground, between Belle Isle and the mainland.

"Are you going to shoot her?" Joe asked. "Then what? Dump the body?"

DenBoer was clearly annoyed. "I haven't thought about it. I didn't think of shooting her."

"Maybe you'll chop her up," Joe suggested, "or weigh her down with cement blocks and toss her in the lake. Remember, you have to use at least as much as her own weight. Decaying bodies are very buoyant, from the gas caused by the bacteria. You should use a couple hundred pounds of weight, probably, say three or four cement blocks, and tie it with wire."

"That's enough of that!" DenBoer snapped.

"What's the matter?" Joe raised his eyebrows in surprise.

"I know what I'll do, and it won't be that," DenBoer said.

"You just don't like to think about it," Joe said. "I can understand that. But somebody has to think about it. Anyway, what are you going to do after you get the money? You've blown your life here. You see that, don't you?"

"Nobody has anything on me," DenBoer said.

"I do," Joe said. "And Vanni does. And the Cubans do. Of course, Vanni might come out of it, all right. He seems to have played his cards pretty neatly. He might have to weather a lot of suspicion, and maybe even an indictment, but it'll come to nothing, I suspect. Funny how that worked out. He'll have this boat, too, won't he? I know it belongs to both of you, but you won't be here to use it. You'll be on the run."

"All right, knock it off," DenBoer snarled.

"It was a pretty snazzy operation, though. I really had to admire it. Who planned it? DeJesus?"

"DeJesus!" DenBoer snorted derisively. He yanked on the wheel again and turned them back toward the head of Belle Isle.

"You?" Joe seemed surprised. "Just you? Vanni didn't mastermind this?"

"It was mostly my plan, and my organization of things," DenBoer said in a travesty of modesty.

"Well, I'm impressed," Joe said. "I thought maybe Morazon, at least . . ."

"He helped," DenBoer said.

"And where is he now?" Joe said.

"Read the papers," DenBoer said.

"I don't have to," Joe said, but DenBoer didn't seem to hear him. They were crossing toward the channel now, at the head of Belle Isle. Before them lay a low, partially wooded island.

"This is Peche Island," DenBoer shouted over the roar of the engine. "It's Canadian. I was thinking we might meet here this evening. Lots of lagoons and inlets on the other side. I'll show you." They swung at full speed around the head of the island.

"Looks lonely," Joe shouted. "Good place to bury someone, eh?" He winked and pointed to the cabin door with his thumb. DenBoer's face darkened and he looked away.

"Right around here," DenBoer said a few minutes later, cutting the engine. "I'll come around nightfall, maybe a little later. You get yourself a boat and a bundle of money and wait for me."

"We're offering a hundred thousand. Period," Joe said.

"What!" DenBoer's face turned red. An enormous argument began. DenBoer raged about how he had risked his life, how his future depended on this— "You said yourself, I'm blown in this town!" he exclaimed.

"I didn't steal any guns," Joe said. It was just hard economics, he went on: the guns were almost too hot to handle; it would be a long time before the mob could realize their investment; they would have to invest even more in distribution and bribes, and in transporting the guns. "Fatman told me that he was ready to counsel Carmine against the whole deal," Joe said.

The argument raged on. In the end DenBoer agreed to settle for $125,000, plus assistance in traveling out of the country. Joe was very agreeable and said he thought that Fatman might see his way to finding DenBoer a place in, say, Brazil, where he might be able to invest in a casino or some other mob-run enterprise. It was a deal.

"One more thing," Joe said as they ran back across the channel toward Detroit. "We get the girl."

That just about blew the deal. DenBoer was adamant. He shook his head stubbornly and refused to discuss it. They came straight back for Detroit, near Windmill Point. There was a canal there and DenBoer throttled down as he entered, going past the old Marine Hospital.

"No," said Joe, "I've been thinking about it, and the girl has to go with the deal. You're going to have your hands full as it is. You'd have to dump her this afternoon, no later, and I can see you're not up to it. We just can't trust you, DenBoer. Besides, she'll be useful to us for a while. No telling what she knows about mob operations in Detroit, and around the country. And then we'll get rid of her quietly and effectively."

DenBoer wouldn't hear of it. "No way. Mandy goes with me."

"Ah hah! That's it," Joe crowed, delighted. "You had some notion of taking her with you. No, DenBoer, it doesn't work that way." He lowered his voice as DenBoer brought the *Seabitch* alongside a little dock. "It's light now, or I'd take her with me, but I can wait until tonight."

DenBoer shook his head again stubbornly.

"Well, if you feel that strongly about it," Joe said, "you can keep her. But there's no deal. I speak for Fatman, and for Carmine. No girl, no deal."

"What are you going to do with her?" DenBoer asked.

Joe smiled. "Don't worry, it won't be bad. We

just want to talk to her. If she plays ball, who knows? Maybe she can work a deal with Carmine."

DenBoer looked uneasy. Joe stepped out on the little wooden dock.

"See you tonight," Joe said. "Remember, we want the girl. Alive."

"You just be there," DenBoer growled. He began to back the *Seabitch*.

TWENTY

The car wasn't as far as Mulheisen had anticipated. He drove to a pay telephone and called the Communications Center. They would automatically notify all the bureaus and offices necessary to respond. Then he called ATF. The duty agent said that Phelps was at DenBoer's apartment. Mulheisen asked the agent to notify Phelps. Then he went back to wait on a side street so that he could lead everybody to the scene.

A half-hour later the place was alive with men and vehicles. When he had finished examining the bodies of the three Cubans downstairs, and Morazon upstairs, the medical examiner turned to Mulheisen.

"Now, let's have a look at you," Dr. Brennan said, stripping off his plastic gloves.

Mulheisen protested that he was all right.

"Stick out your tongue," Brennan insisted. He checked Mulheisen's pulse, peeled back his eyelids and generally prodded and peered. Finally he said,

"Not bad, considering. Go home, take an aspirin and a shot of whiskey, and go to bed."

Mulheisen looked at him with exasperation. "I'm all right, Doc. Let me be."

"When's the last time you slept, Mul?"

Mulheisen thought. It was at least a couple of nights ago, but he wasn't sure. At any rate, except for a little tension and irritableness, he didn't feel too bad. "I slept yesterday," he lied.

"Bullshit," Brennan said. "You're not a kid anymore, Mul. You can't go all day and all night without serious consequences. If you collapse, you won't be any good to anybody. And even if you don't collapse, your judgment is impaired. You're probably functioning about two-thirds normal right now."

"I've got a couple things to do first," Mulheisen said, walking away.

Phelps intercepted him before he got too far. He seemed cheerful. At last he had something to report on the case. Besides the four dead Cubans, three others had been apprehended in Chicago, and the trail into Mexico was still warm. He felt confident now that he would roll up the whole gang.

"What do you think happened here?" Mulheisen asked him.

"It's obvious," Phelps said. "The Cubans came here to hole up with the guns, some sort of dispute broke out—possibly over the girl—and the survivors split with the guns. One good thing, Cecil must still be alive, or she'd be one of the victims here."

They walked on a little ways in the bright morning sun, away from the decaying buildings. Mulheisen lit a cigar. When they reached his car, he said, "And how do you figure DenBoer?"

"I don't figure DenBoer," Phelps replied. "You do." He glanced at his watch, a fancy digital type. "I have to be downtown in twenty minutes for a conference with the U.S. attorney and the county prosecutor. Care to come along? I'm sure they have lots of questions you could answer. And then at noon I'm flying to Chicago. What I'm saying is, it's up to you to pursue the DenBoer angle; I'm banking on the Cubans we've already arrested to lead us to the guns."

Mulheisen begged off on the conference; he knew only too well what a waste of time and emotion it would be. The federal and county prosecutors would both be clamoring for information, demanding to be brought up to date on a case that, in Mulheisen's eyes, at least, was still a jigsaw puzzle with only half of the border pieces assembled. At the same time, the feds would want to take control of the most sensational part of the case and throw the difficult part to the county. The county, naturally, would want to do the same to the feds.

"Well, if you're not going with me," Phelps said, "at least give me an idea of how you see the situation."

"In two easy minutes?" Mulheisen said acidly.

Phelps unbent a little. "All right, I understand. Believe me, I do. But I have to have something to throw them."

Mulheisen sighed and took a drag on his cigar. He leaned against the old Checker and savored the warmth of the sun. "Let's face it, Phelps, we don't have much. You've got no case against Vanni; your undercover agent is missing, and you have no idea whether she is alive or where she could possibly be;

Vanni's partner and buddy, DenBoer, is missing and definitely part of the hijack team, maybe even a leader, but we don't know where he is. Vanni has an alibi for the whole period—I checked. Maybe one of the two women are lying, but I don't think so. It's quite possible that Vanni isn't involved at all.''

"Do you believe that?" Phelps asked.

"I don't know," Mulheisen said truthfully. "The question I ask myself is how much of Vanni is flash, and how much is smoke."

"And where's the real fire?" Phelps put in.

"Exactly. I've been so blinded by Vanni's flash that I couldn't see DenBoer. That was a big mistake and I take full blame for it. But there's another complication: the mob. I didn't say anything back there, but I'm fairly sure that someone was in DenBoer's apartment ahead of me. I've got an idea who it was, but I'm not going to say right now, because it doesn't mean that much and I'm not sure it's important. But it's clear that the mob is interested in this operation —they have to be. This is their turf; nobody does anything without their tacit approval, or without knowing that they're going up against the mob."

Phelps nodded. "That's where the gunman in the garage comes in, eh? And the shoot-up at the Town Pump?"

"Yes," Mulheisen said. "I naturally assumed that the gunman was there to hit Vanni, but he wasn't. He was there to hit Mandy. Someone knew she was an agent."

Phelps nodded. "I didn't see it myself," he admitted.

"As for the shoot-up"—Mulheisen shrugged— "who knows? It may not even have been the same faction of the mob involved. It might be something to do with Vanni's vending business, like I thought at first."

"How about this?" Phelps suggested. "The mob agrees to take out Cecil, to help Vanni, or DenBoer, or the Cubans. Who knows? The attempt fails, because of the fortuitous appearance of the patrolmen. Another attempt is laid on, for the Town Pump—the point is, the mob has to do it in the presence of Vanni, to make it look like he's the real target."

Mulheisen made a face. "I don't know about that last part. Maybe you're right. Chances are we'll never know. The point is, I feel I have to get after DenBoer. I can't help thinking that where he is, Cecil will be found. As for the guns, frankly I couldn't care less right now. I hope they're found, if only to keep them out of the hands of the nuts roaming these streets."

Phelps clapped him on the shoulder. "Go to it, Mul." He glanced at his watch again. "I've got to run." And he actually ran.

Mulheisen didn't even have a chance to ask him how the Great Blind-Pig Raid had turned out.

Most of the fish caught in the nets of the raid had been set free or sent to court by the time Mulheisen arrived at the precinct. As usual, there was a great pile of memos waiting for him, demanding that he call several different people immediately. The one on top was from Andy Deane, so he called him first.

"I been trying to get hold of you for days, Mul," Deane complained. "What have you been doing, goofing off?"

"Something like that," Mulheisen said. "In the last twenty-four hours I've found five corpses."

"I heard about that," Deane said. "That fellow at the Tuttle is an old acquaintance of mine. I took my pictures of Maio and Panella over there this morning and showed them to the day man. Guess what? The guy who was supposed to be the Shoe's lawyer? It was Maio. Positive identification."

"Odd that they'd show their hand like that, isn't it?" Mulheisen asked.

"Not so very," Andy Deane said. "These guys are enforcers. They want it known that they bumped the Shoe. It keeps everybody on the Street loose. They're so arrogant, Mul! Apparently, Lorry had been shooting off his mouth—something about a big gun deal."

"But that's kind of Lorry's trademark, isn't it? He talks big, everybody discounts what he says, but when they want a gun they remember and go back to him, just in case he isn't all talk. Isn't that the way it works?"

"Exactly, Mul. It was a regular routine with Lorry. But there's times when the big boys don't want anybody flapping their jaws about anything. I'm afraid Lorry didn't realize how big a deal he was gassing about."

"There's another angle," Mulheisen said. "Lorry was the connection between the mob and the hijackers. He armed them. If the mob brought Maio and Panella into town for Vanni's sake, they might have figured to make good use of them as insurance, and eliminate a useful but expendable guy like Lorry."

Deane said that sounded likely. "Do you think they could have done that shooting over at the warehouse?" he asked.

Mulheisen didn't think so. "That bayonet in

Morazon's neck doesn't sound like a couple of mob soldiers to me."

Deane agreed. He was intensifying his search for the two killers, he said, and he'd let Mulheisen know what developed.

The next memo on the pile was from Leonard DenBoer's mother. Mulheisen dialed the number, and it was answered before it completed its first ring.

"I talked to my husband last night, Mr. Mulheisen, about what you said yesterday. He's very worried. But he reminded me of one other place that Junior might be. Junior and Jerry bought a boat together, you know, and they both spend an awful lot of time on it. Last summer there were several nights when he didn't come home and he told me that he and Jerry had slept on the boat."

"Where do they keep the boat, Mrs. DenBoer?"

"Lofgren's. It's just at the foot of Fairview."

Thirty seconds later Mulheisen had Carl Lofgren on the phone.

"That's funny, Sergeant," Lofgren said, "there was a fellow in here asking about the *Seabitch*, just a half-hour ago. Like I told him, Lenny or Jerry took it out yesterday and they haven't been back in."

"Was he alone?" Mulheisen asked.

"The guy who was asking? Yeah," Lofgren said.

"No, Lenny."

"I didn't see her leave," Lofgren said.

"What did the guy look like?" Mulheisen asked.

"A little guy, dark hair. Nice-looking fella," Lofgren said.

"Damn!" Mulheisen threw down the telephone.

Twenty minutes later he was down at the marina. Lofgren showed him the empty boatwell. But what interested Mulheisen more was a gray late-model Ford parked in the lot. He was pretty sure it was Mandy Cecil's car.

Mulheisen called the precinct and asked for Jensen and Field. Then he called the harbormaster and asked for a boat to pick him up at the Lofgren marina. The harbor master wanted some kind of authorization; Mulheisen referred them to McClain at Homicide. Apparently, that worked, for the police launch arrived shortly after Jensen and Field did.

Mulheisen explained the situation to the two inseparable detectives, told them to get statements from Lofgren and his helper, notify the various bureaus, especially the Scientific Bureau, and otherwise comb the car for evidence. He didn't mention that he had already been through the vehicle, without success.

The launch commander was a Lieutenant Morigeau, a twenty-year veteran who had spent half of his years in the Mounted Bureau, on Belle Isle. His transfer to the harbor master had been simple, since that bureau was on Belle Isle, too. Mulheisen explained that he was looking for a private pleasure craft. Lofgren had provided an excellent description of the boat. He also explained that DenBoer should be considered extremely dangerous.

"I have a feeling he's still in the area," Mulheisen said. "He can't have taken the guns with him and I just can't believe that he used the boat merely to flee the country."

Morigeau ordered the boat under way. He lit a pipe and shouted to Mulheisen over the roar of the engine, "Not many pleasure boats out this time of year! I saw one on my way up, sort of like the one you describe, but it's gone now!" He and Mulheisen scanned the river. There was plenty of heavy ship traffic, but, as Morigeau had said, almost no pleasure craft on the busy waterway.

They swung out into the Fleming Channel and coasted down between Belle Isle and the Canada shore. Whenever they saw a power boat even remotely resembling the *Seabitch*, they put on the power and ran it down. But they had no luck. Of the many bars and restaurants that catered to river traffic, only a few of them were still open, and none of those had the *Seabitch* moored in their wells. They ran all the way down to the Fighting Island Channel and beyond, to the Livingstone Channel, but the task began to seem more and more futile.

"There's just too many places he could moor," Lieutenant Morigeau said. "Hell, he could be out in Lake Erie, just sitting and fishing behind some little island." Morigeau saw the momentary gleam in Mulheisen's eye and hastened to dampen any hopes: "It would be a season-long job, Mul."

They turned north again, around the southern tip of Grosse Ile and running up the Trenton Channel, spot-checking in the many little marinas there. At the Humbug Marina they saw a boat identical with the *Seabitch*, but a couple of diehard sailors setting out in a 24-foot Sea Ray were hailed and they vouched for the craft.

Disconsolate, Mulheisen urged the lieutenant to run back upstream. He felt that it was more likely that DenBoer would stay in the upriver area, where he was probably more familiar with the islands and harbors. Even running at high speed it was a long trek. It was getting toward nightfall as they approached Belle Isle again.

"Let's try some of those bars on the Canadian side," Mulheisen suggested.

Morigeau made a face. "Out of our jurisdiction," he said.

"I'm just making inquiries," Mulheisen pointed out.

"You may be in civvies," Morigeau said, "but this boat isn't."

But Mulheisen persisted, and just as darkness fell, Morigeau pulled into a pier near Peche Island, where the welcoming neon sign of a bar blinked like a beacon.

The bar man looked at Mulheisen skeptically. It wasn't often that someone in a sports jacket and a tie, with a dirty collar and two days' growth of beard, got off a police launch there. Mulheisen's hair was unruly from the wind and his face felt burned and chapped. He ordered a double Black Jack Ditch and had to explain to the bartender what it was.

There was hardly anyone in the bar, and the bartender came and talked to him, complaining about business. Mulheisen asked about DenBoer and gave a description.

"Yeah, he's been in here a couple of times lately," the man said. "Just about the only customer I had. He used the phone a couple of times."

"How long ago did he leave?" Mulheisen demanded excitedly.

"About a half-hour ago, soon as he got off the phone."

"Did he have anybody with him? A girl, maybe?"

"Nope."

"Did he say where he was going?"

"Nope. He just pulled out of here in a big Chris-Craft and headed straight out toward Peche."

Mulheisen bolted the rest of his whiskey, choked a bit, and ran from the bar.

TWENTY-ONE

Joe Service wasn't sure if he was in the right cove. He sat in a small runabout that had a huge Mercury outboard motor on the stern. He'd chugged slowly around the southern shore of Peche Island trying to find DenBoer, without success. Beside him was a black plastic briefcase containing $100,000 in cash and a letter that would introduce DenBoer to some people in Toronto. Joe wasn't positive, but he had a feeling that DenBoer would be stupid to use the letter. It was very likely that the people in Toronto had instructions to relieve DenBoer of the cash, half of which they could probably keep for "burial expenses."

The payoff was $25,000 short because that's the way Carmine wanted it. Fatman had explained it to Joe: "One, he ain't going to count it all; and two, so what? You just tell him that we're supplying extra 'services.' A guy with a hundred big boys in his hand won't argue too much, not with the heat he must be feeling on his fanny right now." Joe thought Fatman was probably right.

It was getting dark. Joe cut the engine in the most likely-looking cove and decided to let DenBoer find him. It proved to be the proper tactic. Within ten minutes the *Seabitch* rumbled out of the gathering darkness and came alongside.

DenBoer looked down over the side of the cruiser into Joe's boat. "You got the money?" he demanded.

Joe held up the heavy briefcase.

DenBoer reached down for the briefcase, but Joe pulled it back. "No, no. I want to see the girl and I want to know where the guns are. Then we go make our phone call. Then we wait. If the guns are there and if the girl's all right, then you get the dough."

DenBoer stood there, as if undecided, then he said, "All right. Wait a sec." He turned away toward the cabin and was lost from Joe's sight. A moment later, however, he reappeared, and he cradled a Stoner rifle in his arms.

Joe didn't hesitate. He dove for cover, frantically scrambling for protection against the side of the small runabout.

DenBoer leaned over the side of the *Seabitch* and pulled the trigger. The bullets sluiced out in a red torrent, so fast they seemed to have been fired simultaneously.

It was a miracle that Joe wasn't hit. Perhaps it was the rocking of the boats. Joe considered leaping overboard, but then he heard the metallic click that meant that DenBoer was ejecting an empty magazine clip and fumbling to insert a fresh one.

Joe rolled away from the gunwale and went into a crouch with the .38 out and cocked. "Hold it!" he screamed at DenBoer.

But DenBoer was again leaning over the side and raising the Stoner. Joe shot him twice in the chest, and the rifle went flying as DenBoer was knocked flat and out of Joe's sight.

The boats were five feet apart now, and Joe had to crouch on the stern of the runabout and lean far out to grasp for the side of the *Seabitch*. He still held the .38 in his right hand, and when he did snag onto the larger boat, it was only a left-handed grab at the chrome rail and he lost his balance. For a few seconds he stretched between the two boats, his feet still hooked onto the gunwale of the runabout like some ridiculous cartoon character, but slowly he drew the two boats together and hoisted himself up, peering over the railing, pistol at the ready.

DenBoer was sprawled on his back, arms wide, under the wheel on the bridge. Joe clambered aboard and went to him. There was a lot of blood and the man was barely breathing, his eyes half open.

Joe slipped the .38 back into the hip grip and ripped DenBoer's shirt open. There were two neat holes above the sternum. If the bullets had not hit the heart, they had come damn close. From the rapid loss of heat and respiration, Joe judged that he'd shot away part of the main artery, and the man was rapidly bleeding to death.

"Don't die, you bastard!" he snarled. "Where's those goddamn guns?" There was no answer, of course, and Joe turned away. There was blood all over the place, making the deck slippery. He saw that the padlock was still in place on the door to the cabin. He went back to DenBoer and emptied his pants pockets until he found the key.

It was dark inside the cabin and he switched on a light. Mandy Cecil cowered as best she could against the far bulkhead, her mouth still taped and her eyes wide with fear. She was still naked and her hands and feet were still taped. Joe dug out a pocket knife and sliced through the tape on her wrists. Then he gingerly peeled away the broad tape that covered her mouth.

"Take it easy," he told her gently. "I'm not going to hurt you." His hand was on her bare shoulder and he realized that she was shivering. He wrapped a blanket around her.

Mandy poked her desiccated tongue through bruised lips. She made a husky, inarticulate sound.

"Water?" Joe said. "You need water. Jesus, the bastard didn't even give you water." He searched the cabin and found a small refrigerator and inside it a water jug. He poured some into a paper cup and gave it to her, helping her to sit upright and holding the cup. She sucked greedily at it, then gagged, and some of the water spilled onto her breasts, which had become uncovered when the blanket slipped away. Joe tugged the blanket around her again and got another cup of water.

It took five cups before she could talk.

"More water," she rasped.

He fetched the water jug then, and watched her glug away at it for several seconds before he took it from her. "That's enough," he said. "Okay, now there's some things I have to know."

She looked at him blankly, her arms drooping weakly on her lap. The blanket had fallen open again.

"You're in shock," Joe said. "But here's the deal. Can you understand me?"

She nodded.

"You've been through a rough time, but you aren't out of the woods yet. I'm not going to hurt you, if you tell me what I want to know. You got that?"

"Yes," she said faintly.

"Where are the guns?"

"I don't know."

"You don't know? You were with him. What did he do with the guns?"

"He locked me in the trunk of my car," she said hoarsely. "Then he drove the truck away."

"What truck?" Joe demanded.

"The dump truck," she said.

"When was this?"

"I don't know. Yesterday, the day before. After he shot Paco and the others."

"In the warehouse?" Joe said. She nodded and the blanket slipped to her hips. Neither she nor Joe made a move to replace it.

"Where'd he take the guns?" Joe asked.

"I don't know," she said.

"How long was he gone?"

"I'm not sure. It seemed like hours. Then he came back and let me out and made me drive to the marina and we got on the boat, and then he made me strip."

She didn't go on and Joe didn't ask her to. He sat back and considered what she'd said for a minute. Then he said, "He never mentioned what he'd done with the guns?"

Mandy shook her head.

"I guess it was pretty rough, eh?" Joe said.

"He was crazy," Mandy said softly. "I thought he was going to rape me. It was unbelievable."

"He didn't rape you?"

"He said he wanted to be my boyfriend. We would go away together and live together and it would be like old times. I couldn't understand what he meant. I laughed at him and he got angry. He said I'd never see Jerry again. Then he slapped me several times and used the tape."

Joe didn't know what to make of this. But it was obvious that the girl was no help. He stood up, hardly stooping in the cabin. "You're going to have to stay here for the time being," he told her. "But you're all right, now." He went out and closed the door, slipping the lock onto the hasp but not locking it.

It was full night now. The motorboat had drifted several yards away. Joe looked over the controls of the *Seabitch.* The engine still idled. He found reverse and backed the big cruiser until he was alongside the runabout. He threw it into idle, then jumped down into the smaller boat to retrieve the payoff money. The bottom of the boat was awash; DenBoer's full clip of thirty .223-caliber bullets had ripped right through the bottom of the hull. Joe scrambled back onto the *Seabitch,* clutching the briefcase. A minute later he was under way.

As he chugged out of the cove he could see a bright light flickering not far away. It seemed to be a spotlight of some kind. He searched the control panel until he found a switch that cut his own running lights, then he turned on the power and moved out into the channel. A freighter was upbound, and he ran ahead of it around the lighted buoy near the head of the island, then turned north toward the Michigan shore.

He had forgotten that the lights were still on in the cabin. He was halfway across the downbound channel when a brilliant spotlight caught the *Seabitch* from the rear. Joe didn't hesitate. He pushed the throttle wide open and flew. The boat surged under him, then seemed to get up and run. The wind whipped around the bridge and she hammered into several large bow waves before Joe realized that he was dead on toward an immense ore boat. He'd been looking back at the spotlight and not noticing what was going on. It was a 400-footer and he was approaching at nearly midships. He turned downstream and ran as fast as the *Seabitch* could make it. The police launch came after him.

It was a mistake by Morigeau. Recklessly Joe cranked the wheel and skittered past the bow of the ore boat. The *Seabitch* lurched in the bow wave on the other side, rocking dangerously, then the screws dug in and the boat found its way again.

Joe shouted with delight. "That'll slow the bastards!" he shouted. He was just a few hundred yards from shore now, and he saw the place he needed. DenBoer had taken him into the canal off Windmill Point, but downstream from that was a park, a place for high school kids to park and pet. Already, even this early, there were cars parked there. Joe drove the *Seabitch* directly at the rocky shore by the park. At the last minute he saw the rocks loom up and he braced himself.

There was a horrible crunching, splintering noise and the boat shivered violently, then caught on the beach.

Joe flopped into the partially diluted blood on the deck, then scrambled to his feet, found the brief-case and vaulted over the side onto dry ground. He fell to his knees on some rocks and scraped them badly.

He looked back and saw the police launch coming on at full speed, the spotlight fixed on the *Seabitch.* They wouldn't see him, he knew. He sprinted away into the darkness of the park.

He ran until he found a car that still had its motor running. The windows were fogged. He snatched the door open. The interior light revealed a large, handsome lad of eighteen with his hand inside the blouse of a pretty, dark-haired girl.

Joe had the .38 out. "Get out!" he screamed. "Out, out! The other door! Out!"

The couple, dazed and frightened out of their wits, leaped out of the car. Joe threw the briefcase into the back seat and slipped behind the wheel. He backed, tires spitting gravel, and whirled out of the parking lot, the passenger door slamming shut by it-self.

Once out of the park he drove sedately. He dumped the car a few blocks away, on Jefferson Avenue, just ahead of a bus headed downtown. He boarded the bus with his knee bleeding and the trousers torn, carrying the briefcase. Nobody paid any attention to him. He got off near a bar and went in to settle his nerves and think.

After a while, he came to a decision. There was only one thing left to do. He had accomplished what Fatman's Toronto affiliates would have done, so Joe felt that he could, in all conscience, keep $50,000 out of the amount in the briefcase at his feet. Carmine

had promised a bonus if he actually discovered the
location of the guns. Joe figured $50,000 was proba-
bly what Carmine had planned to pay. Therefore, all
he had to do was find the guns. He didn't think that
would be much of a problem; it just needed to be
checked out.

That, and one more little errand that he had
promised himself, and he could get the hell out of
this damn town. If he never heard the name Mulheisen again in his life, it would be just fine with Joe.

"Call me a cab," he said to the bartender.

A half-hour later, he was in a small café on Eight
Mile Road. From the pay telephone in front of the
café, Joe could just see the gates of the Vanni Trucking Company.

"Hello, Fat? Yeah. Bingo. But you better hurry. I
have a feeling that time is running out." Joe listened
to Fatman for a moment, then broke in. "I can't
move them myself, Fat. It's up to you now." He explained where the guns were.

"That's great, Joe. Just great. I knew we could
count on you. Carmine says you'll get a bonus out of
this."

"Thanks, Fat, but I'm happy with what I've got,"
Joe said. "Don't call me any more, Fat. The cops in
this town are too much." And he hung up.

TWENTY-TWO

The *Seabitch* settled slowly onto the rocks at the verge of Riverfront Park. It was too shallow for the water to reach the body of Leonard DenBoer, but the deck canted and the body slid down until it rolled against the gunwale. Mulheisen slipped the padlock off the hasp and peered into the cabin, which was still lighted.

Mandy Cecil flung herself into his arms. A few minutes later they both issued forth, with a blanket securely wrapped around her. Morigeau had already radioed for assistance. While they waited, Mulheisen found a bottle of brandy on the *Seabitch*. Mandy wasn't the only one to taste the brandy.

"Mul, take me home," she said, after the brandy. Morigeau turned away and busied himself with his men about the *Seabitch*. "I don't want to go to a hospital," she said. "I'm going to be all right."

Mulheisen protested, but ended up promising

her. When the squad car arrived, driving across the lawn of the park, it turned out to be Marshall and Stanos.

"Hey, Sarge, what the hell's going on?" Stanos bellowed. "There's a couple out in the parking lot, says their car was stolen."

"I don't know anything about that," Mulheisen said. "Forget it." He bundled Mandy into the back of the patrol car. "Let's go."

"What hospital?" Marshall asked from the driver's seat.

"No hospital. St. Clair Shores."

Marshall started to object, then shut his mouth and drove. They passed another squad car in the parking lot, where an officer was talking to a tall kid and his girlfriend.

On the way to Mandy's apartment, Mulheisen got the whole story.

"First I heard the shooting," she said. "It was just like at the warehouse. I knew it was the Stoner. Then there were just two shots. After that the guy came in. I was hoping it was you, but then I saw it was the guy who came aboard earlier."

"Did he hurt you?" Mulheisen asked.

"No. I was frightened at first, but he was very calm. I told him everything he wanted to know."

"Damn," Mulheisen said.

"Who was he, Mul?"

"I've run into him before," Mulheisen said. "Oh, well. Tell me about the hijack again."

She went over it again, how she had followed DenBoer into the cemetery, unsuspecting but puzzled. Then she'd been crammed into her trunk for the first time. Later they'd arrived at the warehouse and she'd been let out. A huge argument had followed, but it died down as they settled in to wait. The next day, when they received the message over the CB to move, the three Cubans had been downstairs and Lenny had suddenly attacked Francisco with the bayonet. She had watched the whole thing.

Motioning her to be quiet, Lenny had gone downstairs with the Stoner rifle. A few seconds later she heard that awful racket of the magazine being emptied. Then it was back in the trunk for her, for a while.

Mulheisen took her up to her apartment. He hung around for a bit, with the squad car waiting, until he was sure she was all right, then he left.

When he came out of the apartment building, Mulheisen made a rotating gesture with his hands to the two policeman lounging against the car, smoking cigarettes. "Let's go," he said.

First they went to Vanni's house, but it was dark. Mulheisen hadn't dared telephone. Next, they tried the Town Pump, since it was nearby, but Dick hadn't seen Vanni. Finally, they drove out to Eight Mile Road.

All the yard lights were still on at the Vanni Trucking Company and the gate was open. The yard was filled with row after row of large yellow dump trucks. Another dump truck, with its attached trailer, was still parked next to the excavation site to one side of the office. Vanni's car was parked in front of the office.

"Pull up directly behind his car," Mulheisen said. The three policemen got out of the car. "Stanos, you stay outside; Jimmy and I will go in," Mulheisen said. Stanos made a face but didn't complain. He lounged against the side of the squad car, arms folded. Mulheisen and Marshall went up to the door of the small wooden building and disappeared inside without knocking. Stanos settled down for a long wait.

A few minutes later the Big 4 cruised past the Vanni Trucking Company. Dennis the Menace sat in the front passenger seat, always looking. "Stop," he told the driver. "Back up to the gate." He got out and strolled over to Stanos.

"You're Stanos, aren't you?" he said. He shook hands with the young patrolman.

"I liked the work you did in the alley over on Collins," Dennis said. "What's going on here?"

"Sergeant Mulheisen's inside, sir," Stanos said. "He's talking to the owner."

"What's it all about?" Dennis asked.

"I'm not sure, sir, but I think that Mul—Mulheisen—thinks the guy had something to do with that Stoner rifle hijack."

"No shit?" the Menace said. "That was some slick deal. I'd like to have one of them rifles myself."

"I thought you had one, sir," Stanos said. "In the Flyer, I mean."

"Yeah, but I meant for me. You want to see it?"

Stanos said he would and, with a backward look, walked over to the Big 4 Flyer. "Gimme the keys," Dennis shouted to the driver. The driver unlocked the trunk and Stanos was able to feast his eyes on the Stoner. "Little beauty, ain't it?" the Menace said.

The two men stood there, handling the light but lethal weapons system and their conversation turned to esoteric subjects like rounds per minute, feet per second and free recoil energy.

They didn't notice a large U-Haul truck that cruised slowly past the Vanni Trucking Company. The driver of the U-Haul peered suspiciously at the two police cars barring the gate of the trucking company and did not hesitate. He drove on.

"Oh, it's you," Jerry Vanni said, as Mulheisen and Marshall entered. "I thought I heard someone out in the yard a little while ago. I went out but I didn't see anyone." He sat behind the large wooden desk that filled one end of the small office. "What can I do for you, Sergeant?"

Mulheisen stepped inside the railing and turned a chair around to straddle it, his arms folded on the top. Jimmy Marshall leaned against a filing cabinet, one hand resting lightly on his service revolver.

"I've got some bad news for you, Jerry," Mulheisen said. "Your partner is dead."

"Mandy's dead? I can't believe . . ." He half rose, then sank back into his chair.

"Not Mandy," Mulheisen said. "Why did you think I meant Mandy? Were you expecting her to be dead?"

Two red spots appeared in the otherwise white skin of Vanni's face. "No, of course not," he said. "I don't know why . . . then, it's Lenny? Lenny's dead? How did it happen?"

"He was shot to death," Mulheisen said. "On board the *Seabitch.*"

Vanni didn't say anything. He just stared at Mulheisen.

"Mandy's all right," Mulheisen said. "The boat's kind of a mess. She's on the rocks at Riverfront Park."

"Good God," Vanni said. "What happened?" He leaned forward with his hands in his lap, hidden below the top of the desk. "It was Lenny, wasn't it? I knew it! That stupid ass! Well, Sergeant, say something. How did it all happen?"

Mulheisen smiled a long, slow smile that showed all his teeth. It was a sad smile. "I'm not sure yet," he said. "The details don't really matter, I guess. It started a long time ago, with three kids playing in a field. I guess if you get three kids playing together for a long time one of them comes out on top. But that doesn't mean the other kids give up trying to be on top, even if they act like it for years at a time. The top dog goes on acting like the top dog and the bottom dog goes on acting like the bottom dog. But the bottom dog doesn't necessarily think of himself as the bottom dog. Do you know what I mean?" He bared his teeth in another smile, but Vanni didn't react.

"Well, the kid who is the top dog comes to think of himself as a top dog, always encouraged by his pals. One day, when he's older, he finds himself with a little money and he goes into a small business. Like landscaping, say. He does all right. He buys a couple trucks, hires a couple drivers, even hires his old bottom dog. And he keeps doing all right.

"By now, he is somebody. Everybody loves him. He plays poker down at the corner saloon and one night he finds himself a better game at a blind pig. He wins a lot. Everybody's hero. One night one of the players at the blind pig invites him to an even bigger game and he wins, at first. Pretty soon, one of his new poker pals tells him that for a small piece of change he can make sure that our hero gets a lucrative road-hauling contract. The deal works out."

Mulheisen took out a cigar and clipped it and lit it. "I don't know if this is exactly the ways things went," he confessed, "but I wouldn't doubt it. The point is, all the way along, our hero pulls his old playmate with him, because he needs the encouragement he gets from the bottom dog."

Vanni continued to sit behind the desk, hunched with his hands in his lap. His face was white and drawn.

"Our hero is rolling in dough," Mulheisen went on. "He's got a good business, twenty or thirty trucks, making money hand over fist. He's even branching out into other things, like jukeboxes and vending machines. And then he meets a guy—let's call him Lorry—who tells him he knows an easy way our hero can pick up a few bucks if he'll only haul some guns off an air base."

Mulheisen looked up through the cigar smoke. Vanni didn't bat an eyelash.

"By this time, the other playmate came back. She was a big complication. She didn't look like she used to look. Our hero probably knew better, but he couldn't resist bringing her into the game. I'd say that was a mistake." Mulheisen took another drag on the cigar. It was very quiet in the room.

"I could go on with this little story, but I guess I don't have to," Mulheisen said finally. He gazed placidly at Vanni. "You're sitting there quietly enough, but you're scared, aren't you? You don't know whether Lenny spilled his guts before he died, or how much Mandy can tell us. Hell, you don't know anything, do you?" Mulheisen grinned maliciously.

"I'll let you in on a little secret, Vanni," Mulheisen said. "I don't know everything. Oh, I know most of it, but not everything. I—"

"Let's see your cards, Sergeant," Vanni interrupted.

Mulheisen laughed—a short and humorless bark. "I like that, Vanni. That's the old poker player talking. You're tired of my bluffing, aren't you? Well, here's my hole card, then, and I'm damned if it isn't an ace: I know where the guns are, Jerry. And they're not in a place that's convenient for you at the moment."

Mulheisen turned and looked pointedly out the window, toward the yellow truck parked by the excavation site.

Vanni stared at him wildly.

"You bastard!" Vanni shouted. He kicked the desk forward, away from himself. It was this that saved Mulheisen's life. The desk slammed into Mulheisen's chair, tipping it backward and spilling Mulheisen onto the floor. Two roaring shots from Vanni's .45 automatic blasted across the desk top and smashed the top of the chair to kindling. But Mulheisen wasn't there.

Mulheisen lay in a tangle on the floor, fighting with his raincoat to get at his .38. Marshall had dived behind a filing cabinet. Vanni leaped to the top of the desk, then vaulted across the tiny room. He kicked viciously at Marshall's gun hand, sending the service revolver flying. Then he smashed a broad shoulder into the rear door of the office and ran out into the floodlit yard.

Dennis the Menace had just locked the Stoner rifle away in the trunk of the Flyer when he heard the shots. He immediately fumbled with the keys to un-lock it again.

Stanos set off across the yard on a run, pistol out. He saw Vanni racing for the truck parked near the excavation and yelled "Halt!"

Vanni stopped, pivoted and aimed the .45 at arm's length. A single shot took Stanos's right leg out from under him. Stanos rolled to the cover of the squad car as Vanni ran on.

Vanni leaped into the big International and turned on the key. The engine roared to life. Several bullets smacked into the sides of the box and the cab. Vanni could see a figure running to one side and he blasted a couple of shots in that direction, then threw the truck into gear. It was pointed toward the rear of the lot and that was the direction he wanted to go—the Big 4 Flyer was blocking the front gate.

The truck moved slowly at first, but began to pick up speed as it lumbered past the ranks of parked trucks, down the side lane.

Beyond the yard, on the other side of the tall cyclone fence that surrounded it, lay an open field. Vanni saw it was his only chance.

Through the side mirror, Vanni saw Marshall running after him. He laughed excitedly and pushed the gas pedal to the floor. The truck was going forty-five miles per hour when it hit the fence. The fence bowed and sagged outward. The huge truck's front tires mounted halfway up the fence with a mighty clanging of the box and the trailer. Sand and guns flew in all directions. Then the inertia of the truck pushed it onward and the fence slammed flat. The truck lumbered on in the clear.

Vanni cranked the wheel hard to the left and

made his run, still standing on the gas pedal. He had several hundred feet to go to the first of several dark side streets that beckoned to him as a hole would to a fox. In the mirror, he could see Mulheisen and Marshall firing at the fleeing truck, but their bullets whacked harmlessly into the thick steel sides and he was leaving them behind.

"By God!" he exulted. "I did it!" He shifted to a higher gear.

Then he saw the Flyer. It came flashing up the side street and slewed to a stop, sideways, blocking the street. The Big 4 piled out on all sides.

Vanni headed the powerful rig directly at the Chrysler. A shotgun burst from one of the Big 4 took out the windshield of the truck, momentarily blinding Vanni, but then he thrust the .45 through the jagged opening, and with blood streaming down his face where fragments of glass had struck, he emptied the magazine.

Dennis the Menace stood to one side of the Flyer with the Stoner rifle at his shoulder. He pulled the trigger and a spew of flame swept the cab of the oncoming truck. The truck smashed into the Chrysler and slammed it to one side, nearly hitting one of the Big 4, who was firing the Sten gun. The juggernaut ran on across the street and smacked into the brick wall of a paint factory, crumpling in the wall. Then the truck's engine died and everything was silent.

Stoner rifles lay everywhere, pitched from their ruptured crates. Mulheisen panted up to the sand-strewn scene and yanked the cab door open. Jerry Vanni toppled sideways out of the cab in a torrent of blood, his head a pulpy, shattered mess.

Noell looked around him, taking stock. His men

were all safe. They still stood in defensive postures, Sten gun and Tommy gun raised and aimed. Then they let the gun barrels drop slowly. Noell reversed the clip on the Stoner and jammed it home. He stepped up to Mulheisen, who stood looking down at the ruined face of Jerry Vanni.

Mulheisen turned away. "Call for a wagon," he said to Dennis. "Possible fatal."

Andy Deane was explaining on the telephone how he'd nabbed Maio and Panella. He'd picked them up at a riverfront bar, preparing to leave Detroit in a boat. "I got the idea from you, Mul," he said. "DenBoer had the right idea. I wouldn't be surprised if the mob got the idea from DenBoer, too." He went on to say that the two thugs were very uncooperative, but he had the night clerk from the Tuttle for a witness, he had the slugs from Lorry the Shoe, and the gunmen had been stupid enough not to get rid of their weapons. "I guess they figured, since they weren't going through an airport check, or across the regular border area, they might as well take the guns along."

"Maybe they planned to dump them in the river," Mulheisen suggested. He thanked Deane for his help and hung up.

Then he had to go in and see Buchanan. Stanos was up for a medal and a promotion, but not Marshall. Mulheisen pointed out that just because Marshall hadn't been shot, that wasn't a reason not to give him a citation for bravery. Buchanan hemmed and hawed, muttering something about blacks having to make their own way, but finally he gave in.

Mulheisen broke the good news to Marshall in his cubicle a few minutes later.

"There's so many loose ends," Marshall said, talking about the case. "I never knew it was like this."

"Well, we try to clean up as many of them as we can," Mulheisen said, "but it's generally like this. You just have to face the fact that you never know everything about a case. There's a lot we'll never know, but at least we got the guns back. For instance, we'll never know if DenBoer meant to split with the money or not. Of course, Vanni would still have the guns and he might be able to work some kind of deal with the mob, since he's going to still be around. Maybe they'd be willing to play ball with him because he'd still be useful to them. But he was in way over his head and he didn't realize it. Those guys are just too slick for him. Like DenBoer, he had his head in the clouds, dreaming about fancy capers and wheeling and dealing with the big shots. As it stands, you notice, except for the two gunsels, we don't have anything on the mob."

Marshall listened avidly, nodding in admiration at Mulheisen's explanations. "How did you know the guns were in the truck, though, Sarge?" he asked.

Mulheisen smiled ruefully. "I should have known long before. When I stopped to see Vanni the other morning he was loading sand into the truck. The sand was piled way over the top of the trailer and the truck box. But there wasn't all that much gone from the excavation pile. I didn't pay much attention to it, unfortunately. But later I realized that the perfect place to hide a truck is among a bunch of other trucks."

He took a long, comfortable drag on his cigar and contemplated the smoke. "And now we're back to our original mystery," he said.

"What's that?" Marshall asked.

"Who was the dead man in the alley?"

They sat and thought about that for a minute, and the telephone rang. It was the medical examiner's office, Dr. Brennan. Before Brennan could say anything, Mulheisen said, "You can let that John Doe go, now, Doc. The case is wrapped. Go ahead and chop him up, or whatever you do."

"I'm glad to hear that, Mul," Brennan said. "I was just calling to say that I'm afraid we kind of screwed up. One of the assistants here signed the body out first thing this morning."

"Oh? Who to?"

"Friend of the deceased. He came in early and claimed the body. Identified him and everything, all proper and orderly. I didn't see the papers on it until after lunch. Sorry."

"What did this 'friend' look like?" Mulheisen asked. He listened attentively to Brennan, nodding thoughtfully to himself. When Brennan finished, Mulheisen hung up and said to Jimmy Marshall, "You can tell your buddy Stanos, when you visit him in the hospital, that we now know who he blasted. His name was Sidney Carton."

"Sidney Carton?" Marshall repeated. "That sounds kind of familiar. Who was Sidney Carton?"

Mulheisen got up and put on his coat. "Think about it for a minute," he said. "He was a man who had a good friend. In this case, the friend was named Joe Service." He walked out.

Maki stopped him in the hall and asked if he wanted to stop for a beer.

"No," Mulheisen told him. "I've got to see a witness."